THE DEEDS OF POUNCE

by Benjamin Wachs

Published 2016 by Beating Windward Press LLC

For contact information, please visit:
http://www.BeatingWindward.com

Text Copyright © Benjamin Wachs, 2017
All Rights Reserved
Book Design: Copyright © KP Creative, 2017
Cover Design by Jayde Reid, 2017
Cover Illustration by Sean Bieri, 2017

First Edition
ISBN: 978-1-940761-27-5

To Laura Phillips Bence,
who was in the room when two goblins
first crawled out of my subconscious and into the world.
Your unwavering enthusiasm, support,
and all those wonderful rides home,
have made a difference in my art.

Chapter 1

Most rabbits can't play poker. They get spooked too easily by a good bluff. But the O'Shaughnessy brothers were tough—some said they were tough as rats. Not only did they play poker, but they ran the game in Golden Gate Park, inside the Japanese Tea Garden. If you were an animal in San Francisco who liked playing for high stakes, then Willie, Gerardo, Jake, Aaron, Sean, and Bevan O'Shaughnessy had the only game that mattered.

Willie was shuffling the cards tonight, and everyone knew he cheated. Gerardo and Jake were watching the door, whiskers aquiver, ears turned up, holding long metal spoons as billy clubs, just in case. Sean was running the bar, he mixed a mean sake martini, and Aaron was counting the money. Aaron always counted the money. He was the brains of the group. Only Bevan was out: tonight was his monthly meeting for politically active gay rabbits. There was a rumor Bevan was going to get into politics, that he wanted to be mayor of the San Francisco underworld. With Willie's smile and Aaron's bankroll and Jake's muscle behind him, it could happen. Some folks, especially the pigeons, thought that the O'Shaughnessys saw themselves as a dynasty in waiting.

They had a rich crowd that night; the duck with the dueling scar and the duke of the rats were there, and so was Spindlethrift the calico cat—big, big money, on top of the four other players. It had promised to be a good night and Jake was smiling, but Gerardo was chewing nervously because he said he could smell trouble on the wind. Gerardo was always smarter than Jake.

They heard the footsteps approaching about 1:00 a.m. Heavy feet, like big dogs but with much longer claws, working their way around the koi pond and up to the souvenir shop . . . then skittering, fast like cats or spiders, around the side of the walls and down under the stairs to the Buddha garden, where the game was played.

Jake and Gerardo raised their spoons, then looked at each other. Gerardo nodded, and they took out Swiss army knives too. Everyone looked up to see the two pairs of glowing red eyes staring at them from each end of the stone Buddha's pedestal. The duck pulled out his pistol.

Aaron locked the steel box with a picture of the Golden Gate Bridge on it, where he kept the money. The lock clicked tight. The wind rustled the leaves, and carried the scent of some South American plants up from the botanical garden a half mile away.

They could hear the two things with the red eyes breathing.

"This is a private game, ya' know," said Jake. He was fearless because he wasn't so smart.

"You can deal in," said Gerardo, "if you've brought the minimum stakes, and we like the look of you."

From the darkness, one of the red-eyed things laughed. So did the other one. Every animal in the world knows this sound: the laugh of a predator.

"If like look of us," chuckled one of the red-eyed things.

"Rabbits," said the other one. You could hear him licking his lips. "Ducks."

Cards scattered on the table. With a great flapping and cry, the duck with the dueling scar flew away.

"Chase?" asked one of the things.

"No chase," said the other one. "Not yet."

The duke of rats twitched his whiskers at the empty space beside him where the duck had been. "I'd always thought he was courageous," he muttered.

"Oh, he is, your Grace," Willie O'Shaughnessy said. He was known to be close with the duck. "It's just that he also has wings."

"Smart rabbit," said one of the things.

"Smart rabbit," agreed the other, sadly. "Brains no taste good."

"Let's see," said the first, "if like our looks." Their claws dug into the dirt as they stepped into the light.

The animals gasped.

They were scaly and furry at the same time, with teeth like a shark's and claws like a lion's. Their ears were concave and pointed, like a cat's, and their noses flat like leaves. As tall as human children, they walked upright, like men.

"Monsters!" hissed Spindlethrift the calico cat.

Jake and Gerardo held up their spoons and Swiss army knives but didn't fool anyone.

"Goblins," said the duke of rats. Distastefully. "My kind remembers yours."

Goblins. The word spread around the rabbits and across the card table.

The O'Shaughnessys all looked at Aaron, who shook his head: no one could remember the last time there had been goblins in San Francisco.

"Gherin," said one, pointing at the other.

"Leptin," said the other, pointing at the one. "Maybe heard of him? Yah? Yah? Yes? No?"

"No," said Leptin. "No famous. Not here."

"Oh." Gherin's bushy eyebrows fell over his scaly eyes. "Hmmmm."

"Do you fine gentlemen want to play cards?" Willie asked.

Gherin laughed his predator's laugh.

"We looking," said Leptin, "for animal. Maybe you know."

"Help us find," said Gherin, "and we not have time be hungry."

"No time at all," said Leptin. "Much too busy. But if not busy, maybe stay. Play games."

"Not know how play cards," said Gherin.

Leptin smiled.

Aaron and Willie looked at each other, their whiskers twitching. The two oldest, they were as different as brothers could be, but they'd bonded over one thing in their childhoods: the knowledge that if you speak a language no one else understands, you can put one over on the rest of the world.

"Well, you gentlemen are in luck," said Willie. "I know almost everyone." He hopped over to the bar, and nodded to Sean to pour a few martinis. "You tell me who you want to find, and I'll tell you how hard that is."

The goblins darted their eyes back and forth, looking at each other. They also spoke a language no one else could understand.

From behind the bar, Sean poured carrot juice and gin into shot glasses.

Leptin and Gherin stepped closer to the card table, their talons digging up dirt. Gherin reached a clawed finger into his mouth and pulled an old piece of meat out from between his teeth. He flicked it at the direction of the bar.

"His name," said Leptin, " . . . Pitter Patter Pounce."

Sean dropped a glass behind the bar. No one else made a sound.

Aaron and Willie twitched their whiskers at each other so quickly they slurred their words.

"You say know everyone," Leptin said to Willie.

"Want drink when tell us?" Gherin asked.

"Drinking better than playing games," said Leptin.

"Much better," Gherin agreed. "Dancing good too."

"Not know how dance," said Leptin.

"Maybe," said Gherin, "smart rabbit teach us."

Willie was known for having a comeback to everything. "Well. . . well," he said. "Well . . . ," he said again, staring at their fangs, "I know of him, of course. I know he's in town. Everyone does. But that's not the . . . not the same as . . . that's a hard one," he finished.

Leptin tapped a finger on the table, spearing an ace of spades with his claw.

The duke of the rats sighed. "He doesn't want to be found, and he wouldn't share our company for all the garbage in Chinatown" he said, imperiously. "Do any of us look like mice?"

Leptin looked at the rat and twisted his lips. "Yah, little," he said.

The duke of rats wrinkled his nose and his tail thrashed against the ground. "I am afraid, gentlemen," he said, "that you've got the wrong game."

"Gentlemen," chuckled Leptin.

"Funny," said Gherin.

"Me think," said Leptin, slowly, "they telling us gentlemen they no help."

"Less funny," said Gherin.

Willie gestured to Sean, who started mixing drinks again. "I'm not saying that at all," he said. "I'm saying I can't tell you where he is . . . right now. But I could find him for you, if I get some time."

The goblins looked at each other.

"Ohhhhhhhh," said Gherin. "Understand now. Rabbit think us stupid."

Leptin nodded. "Rabbit want us come back later. Lotsa time get away." He stroked his chin. "Maybe got better idea. Kill rabbit, find mouse, then come back park anyway. Very pretty. Take real time learn nature."

"Never been tea garden," Gherin said. "Like pond. But not really understand cultural heritage." He considered. "Maybe is Japanese rabbit we kill. Study insides. Learn culture."

Willie grabbed two carrot juice martinis from Sean and held them out to the goblins. "Come on now," he said, gesturing for Sean to make more. "You're treating this like a hostage situation. I'm offering you a business proposition. I think gentlemen like you have a lot to offer. Put the right offer on the table, and I'll have you a location for Pitter Patter Pounce by Sunday." He smiled his famous smile. "Everything's negotiable."

Leptin's jaw hung open.

Gherin shook his head in disbelief. "Bribe . . . rabbit?" he asked.

The two goblins looked at each other in obvious disgust.

The wind picked up. Aaron nodded his head, just a little bit. Jake and Gerardo sprung forward, their Swiss army knives open.

Willie tossed the drinks in the goblins' faces, then jumped back over the counter. Sean pulled a BB gun from underneath the bar, and fired.

Wet from the drinks, the goblins didn't turn in time to face Jake and Gerardo, both experienced knife fighters. The blades hit, but goblin skin is thick and tough, and even at full speed the blades didn't penetrate far. Leptin shoved, and Gerardo went flying into the koi pond. Gherin whirled, and Jake staggered back, thick red gashes appearing on his gentle white underbelly.

Sean's BB hit the back of Gherin's head and bounced off, landing at the feet of the large Buddha.

The goblins howled, sounding happy. Gherin skittered after Willie while Leptin snatched the BB gun out of Sean's trembling grasp. Aaron grabbed a metal pipe and the duke of rats smashed a bottle of vodka on the table to give it a jagged edge. Spindlethrift yowled and extended his claws. They advanced.

The wind changed again, and this time it came with an almost roar, an almost din of thunder that wouldn't go away—a sound too big to be ignored.

The goblins, towering over their prey, looked up. A moment later they saw forty ducks flying over the trees, blocking out the moon, quacking a war quack.

Each duck, carrying a rotting orange or apple in between its feet, aimed and released, sending a cascade of fruit from high altitude down on Gherin and Leptin, splattering and smashing.

Sopping wet Gerardo crawled out of the pond. Sean and Willie ran to Jake and hoisted him up on their shoulders.

"Run!" Aaron shouted, holding the cash box, while Willie gestured to the Duke of Rats and pointed upward. The duck with the dueling scar soared near the flock, directing it for a second barrage.

"I told you he was brave, your Grace," Willie said. "It's just that he's got wings."

Fast as rabbits they scattered their separate ways. The O'Shaughnessys deeper into the park, to their secret safe house; the duke of the rats to his manorial estate in the sewer pipes beneath the DeYoung museum, where he would sound the alarm to his legions; Spindlethrift into the Richmond neighborhood as fast as his legs would carry him, where he could hide in the corner of a Burmese restaurant and drink coconut milk. Their mission accomplished, the ducks flew east to the bay.

By the time Gherin and Leptin unburied themselves and wiped the fruit from their eyes, the garden was empty of every animal but fish.

"Bah," said Gherin.

"Bah," said Leptin. "Hate fruit."

"Hate ducks," said Gherin. He walked over to a spot near a lotus flower, and ran his claws into the ground. "Blood," he said. "Track?"

"Nah," said Leptin. "Not know nothing."

"Know us here now," said Gherin. "And me hungry."

Leptin shook his head. "Rat knows us here too," he said. "Can't kill all rats. Bad night."

"Yah. Hungry."

"Bad night."

They both walked over to the koi pond and began splashing water on themselves to get the fruit off.

"Go home," said Leptin. "Think next move."

"Thai restaurant near park?" asked Gherin. "Maybe eat rabbit in sweet basil sauce?"

"Feh," Leptin snarled. "Food is food."

"Zagat mentioned."

"Fine," Leptin said. "Break into Thai restaurant, maybe eat noodles. Then go home. Daylight soon." He shook himself, like a dog, to get the water off. "Hate fruit."

"Kiwi?" asked Gherin.

"Yah. Hate it."

"Sorry. Not know."

"Okay."

A moment later, they too were gone.

Chapter 2

The cat, nine years old with fur the color of moonlight on Russian snow, had been hissing and yowling all day.

"Yes! I hear you!" James yelled back, putting the last plate on the drying rack. James always ended up doing the dishes. Their arrangement was to share the chores fifty-fifty, but Mari let the dishes stack until the plates got precarious. With a sigh he'd grab a sponge, turn the hot water tap, and start rinsing.

Mari had complained that he shouldn't be using so much hot water; Mari had complained that he used too much soap. Eventually, James had snapped that if she wanted the dishes done her way she could take her turn like she was supposed to. Mari had closed up, then, like a flower in winter, and said that she was always the one who ended up cleaning the bathtub. And the toilet.

The argument was becoming routine, and each time sharpened its edge just a bit. Some nights they both hated themselves for tripping over the little things.

Their apartment was a small one-bedroom—and they were both used to having their own space before trying to live together. There was never any place to go to cool off, no place to feel safe from intrusion.

Now they had to recover. It was late. There wasn't much time. And they were distracted by the cat.

Yowl!

"What's gotten into Caramel?" Mari asked.

"I have no idea," said James, dangling a toy on a string where Caramel was sure to see it. "She doesn't . . . ," he bounced the toy up and down a few times ". . . well, she doesn't want to play. She didn't want to be brushed, and she's tried to hide in the bedroom a lot. I've had to kick her out three or four times."

Mari scowled. "She knows she's not allowed in there."

James sighed. "Yeah." They disagreed on that rule. When James asked, why not let the cat on the bed, Mari responded that it was her cat, and her bed. It was another small argument that was becoming routine. "Yeah," James said again.

"Do you think she feels sick?" Mari asked. "Could this be her way of telling us she needs attention?"

"When she's sick she usually wants to be petted," James said, putting the toy and string down on the coffee table. "Now she just wants to hiss and scratch."

"I don't know," Mari said, yawning.

"Maybe sometimes hissing and scratching is its own goal," said James.

"Maybe if I were a cat that's what I'd want to do," Mari agreed. "Do you know that San Francisco has a law that you can't declaw cats?"

"I did, in fact." James rubbed his eyes and looked over at his laptop.

"Are you going to play games all night?"

James' eyes snapped back. "No."

"Okay."

"The thing about that law," said James . . .

"I think it's a good law."

"Absolutely! Declawing cats is cruel. It's inhumane."

"It's like cutting off your fingers at the knuckles."

"Right, but . . ." James took a deep breath. "If someone wants to get their cat declawed, they can just drive over to Daly City or Oakland to do it."

"So?"

"So I'm saying . . . it's a pretty ineffective law."

She sat up straight on the futon. "I'm glad they passed it."

"Sure. Me too." James' stomach growled. They were trying a reduced-calorie meal plan for the month. She didn't need it, he did. "I just wish they'd spend their time doing more . . . effective . . . things."

"I'm going to bed."

"Yeah, it's time."

They looked at each other, for a moment, unsure whether he would join her in their bedroom or spend the night on the futon, the way he had more often lately. She threw a throw pillow at him, and that decided it. He put his arm around her waist, hoisted her up, and they walked into the bedroom together, closing the door behind them, leaving the cat hissing at the kitchen cabinet where the pots were kept.

Hisssss! Caramel slowly stepped back and sat in the corner as far away from the kitchen as she could get.

A few minutes later, the cabinet doors opened from the inside and Leptin crept out, landing softly on the floor. Caramel dashed under the futon, yowling. From underneath, she saw Gherin leap out too.

Yowl! Yowl!

She'd been trying to tell them all day.

From inside the bedroom, Mari called out "Caramel, stop it!"

Gherin looked over at the trembling Caramel, and put his fingers to his lips. "Shhhhhhh," he hissed softly. He then displayed his claws, to show her that his were longer.

Caramel scowled, but got the message.

The goblins had selected this apartment, in a building a few blocks up a hill from Golden Gate Park, because there was absolutely no reason they would stay here. They assumed that the rats and the ducks and the rabbits would sound an alarm, and that by afternoon every wild animal in San Francisco would be looking for them. The duke of rats might even offer a reward. Everyone would have a theory about where two goblins would go to hide in San Francisco. The graveyards and the piers and Coit tower had probably been under constant scrutiny.

But not here, not in a small domestic apartment, chosen for its proximity to a Thai restaurant, with only a couple too distracted by an impending break-up to pay attention, and a house cat who never got to go outside.

Perfect.

Except that these humans . . . they were . . .

"Ahhhhh," said Leptin, shaking his head. "She should not argue. Bad bad idea. Get big big trouble."

Gherin was staring at the bedroom door. "She soooooo beautiful," he said softly.

Leptin blinked. "What?"

"She soooooo beautiful," Gherin said again, looking at the door but seeing only Mari's red hair.

"You . . . ," Leptin hesitated. "Her? Human girl?"

"Ohhhhhhhh," said Gherin. "Most beautiful girl in world."

"Kkkkkkcccccckkkkkkhs," Leptin mutterd. "You crush so easy."

"No," said Gherin. "Is beautiful. Red, red, hair. Pale white skin. Beautiful blue eyes . . . like painting. Like Picasso."

"Not like Picasso," said Leptin.

"Oh. Not like Picasso," Gherin corrected. "Most beautiful girl in the world. Like Warhol."

Leptin scratched his scaly chin. "You not know art so good."

Gherin shook his head. "Lover, not critic," he agreed. He clicked his claws together. "Got idea."

"Yah?"

"Yah. Go in bedroom, kill man. Make beautiful woman happy. Good?"

Leptin's eyes widened in terror. "No!" he hissed. His hands flew through the air and covered Gherin's mouth. "Shhhh! You crazy! Get us killed!"

"Mwmphf!"

"Shhhh! Quiet! Get killed!"

Yowl!

"Mwmphf!"

"Caramel, STOP IT!" Mari shouted. "Don't make me put you in the bathroom!"

Gherin grabbed Leptin's wrists and cast his arms away. "Look what you do!" he hissed. "Beautiful girl upset! Put nice cat in bathroom!"

Leptin leaned his face into Gherin's, their flat animal noses almost touching. "Cat NOT nice," he whispered.

Gherin thought about it. "No, cat not nice. Maybe kill."

"No! Get us killed! Big killed! Not small killed!"

Gherin snorted. Derisively. "Why? Why killed?" he asked. "His eyes narrowed. "You think . . . maybe . . . wizard is still around?"

Leptin shook his head. "No. No. Wizard dead. Long dead. Wizard must be long dead. Wizard . . . got to be . . . long dead. Not wizard. Can't be."

Gherin tilted his head. "Wizard sneaky, though."

"Yah," Leptin agreed. "Sneaky. But dead."

"Got to be," Gherin agreed. "So what? Why not kill man? And cat? Or maybe just man? Make girl happy?"

Leptin slapped Gherin across the face.

Gherin's eyes narrowed to slits. He spoke very slowly. "What?"

Leptin leaned back in close. "You not know man?"

"Know man?" Gherin tried to understand. "Recognize? It . . . it man." He tried to explain to his friend. "Like rabbit, but bigger."

"Not just man!" Leptin insisted.

Gherin wasn't finished. "Less fur," he explained.

"Is not just man!" Leptin insisted. "Is . . . ," he hesitated. He took a deep breath. "Is Excior, Dark General of Skaris Cragg."

The world held its breath as that name passed through it.

Gherin blinked. Looked at the bedroom door. Blinked again. "Him?"

"Not see?"

Gherin rubbed his eyes.

Under the couch, Caramel squinted in disbelief.

"Him?"

"Yah!" Leptin said. "Is him. If touch his woman, him kill us with great fiery sword!"

Gherin scratched his head. "Seems . . . fat."

"Put on weight, yah," Leptin agreed.

Gherin stroked his chin. "Seems . . . ," he stroked more. "Dark General wash dishes?"

Leptin sighed. "Listen," he said.

"Seems fat," Gherin offered.

"Saw him once," said Leptin, as though describing a dream. "Long time ago."

"Would have be," Gherin agreed.

"Just after Battle of Goren Vaj . . . ,"

"Oooooooooo. Bad."

"Yah. Bad. A thousand trolls herded off cliff into fiery ravine. Boulders fall from moon. Tentacles from ground pull Seelie prince into giant maw of demon. Big demon. Big . . . red . . . demon. Yes, bad. Through it rides Dark General, on bronze chariot, flaming sword in hand, leaves only death behind. Everything die. Even moon."

Gherin bared his fangs. "That not—"

Leptin put his hands on Gherin's shounders. "Even moon die that day."

Gherin nodded.

"Me hiding. Hide good. Inside corpse. See through dead eyes. See Dark General chariot come to stop. See dark armor. See flaming sword. See Dark General look around. Survey grim work. See Dark General remove helmet. See face Excior of Skaris Cragg."

For a time even the wind stopped rustling.

"Is him," said Leptin. "Excior vanish, not know where. You know where?"

"Lots me not know."

"No one know where. Is here. This his apartment."

Gherin scowled. "Why not two bedroom?"

Leptin considered. "San Francisco market inflated."

Gherin took a deep breath. Scratched his armpit. Considered his words carefully. "Leptin, this. . . unlikely . . . ."

"Saw what saw."

"Improbable."

"It him."

Gherin looked to Caramel for support. She shook her head.

"Leptin, this just you. Not him."

Leptin's lips pulled back, his fangs extended, his eyes grew red. "Battle!" he snarled. "You respect scars! Respect blood!"

Gherin put up his hands, palms out. "Respect scars," he said. "Respect scars. Yah, respect blood. But this—"

"We go now," said Leptin. "Run far. Find other place. Live."

"Leptin . . . this you. Him fat, sad man. Do dishes. Get scratched by cat. Snore. Lose beautiful girl soon." He sighed. "Like rabbit," he explained. "But less happy."

"We go. No come back."

"Less tasty."

They stared at each other. Eyes wide.

"Beautiful woman," Gherin said. "Most beautiful girl in world. Live for beauty."

Leptin hissed in disgust.

"Red, red, hair," said Gherin.

They stared at one another. Neither blinked.

Gherin pursed his lips. Leptin scratched his wrist.

"Find mouse?" said Leptin.

"Stop mouse?" said Gherin.

As one, they nodded. Settle later. Their claws skittered across the wooden floor, leaving marks that would be blamed on Caramel. A window opened, a window closed. The moon rose higher. James and Mari slept fitfully. Caramel didn't sleep at all.

Chapter 3

The moon glistened on the ripples underneath the Third Street bridge, but the light wasn't bright enough that MacDuff could see his face in the water. He tried, on bright nights, when he thought there was no one else around. During the day when he walked up Mission Street and down Valencia, when he passed small storefronts with windows or when he went to a church bathroom, he never looked at the reflection. He wanted to see himself at night, and only at night.

He knew his body had decayed over the years, and he thought his cracked skin and wild hair would look better at night. He imagined he looked like a spirit out of Africa. He imagined there was something royal about the way he looked, something uncompromising and fierce. That would be the reason so many eyes stared at him; that would be the reason so many eyes turned away.

He called himself MacDuff, and that was the only name he gave, because he knew it was royal.

He never asked for money, he never begged for change, but he knew a guy who knew a guy whose cousin slept with a girl who worked at an organic pie shop in the Mission, and on good composting days MacDuff got the call. Tonight, his breath smelled like pluots and strawberries.

"Come on, come on," he said, crouching over the shoreline, staring into the water, a little blinded by the moon. It was late enough that no more trains ran over the bridge, but sometimes a car did. People on their way from events they didn't really want to attend to homes that were like prisons. Not a goddamn one of them knew real freedom. He balanced on the balls of his feet, careful not to get his pants and coat wet. "Come on, come on." His eyes were in there somewhere.

Above the moon, a pair of red eyes glistened on the water. And then another. MacDuff reached up to feel his eyes, just in case. Just to be sure.

"Did you know moon dead?" asked Leptin. "Very sad."

"Me just learn," said Gherin. "This explain why it never call back."

MacDuff turned around. He'd never seen goblins before, but he'd seen worse. He looked them over. Compared to what he'd seen, they didn't seem so tough. He opened his mouth. Bared his rotting teeth. "Ahhhhhhhh!" he shouted at them, lurching forward.

Gherin and Leptin looked at each other, then back at him.

MacDuff opened his heavy long coat and pulled out a golf club he kept inside, fastened by some loops made of duct tape. He waved it in front of him the way a hero would a shining sword. "Ahhhhhhhh!" he shouted. " Aarrrraaaaaaah!"

"Huh," said Gherin, considering. "Maybe you try more like this: Aaauuuuuuuuuuuuuuuh! See? From back of throat, with hissing sound. Work better."

MacDuff paused, for a moment. He was a big man, and most of the time this scared people off. He hadn't had to get violent with anybody in . . . he wasn't sure how long, actually. He couldn't really tell the seasons in San Francisco, so he wasn't sure how much time had passed since he'd taken the greyhound up from Houston and decided this was home. He didn't really like violence, hitting things sometimes had consequences. Well, he decided, too bad—this was a bad scene.

"Right on," he whispered, hefting the golf club. Feeling his body get tense and excited. "Right on." He swung hard at Gherin's head.

Gherin ducked gracefully. MacDuff's swing went wild. Leptin caught the club in one hand, and ripped it out of MacDuff's grasp. Gherin pushed against MacDuff's chest, and slammed him to the ground. Leptin put the golf club across the prone man's neck, and applied just a little pressure.

"You listen Gherin," Leptin said. "Him right: from back of throat. Aauuuuuuuuuuuuuuuh!"

"What name?" asked Gherin.

MacDuff struggled, so Leptin pushed down harder.

"What you name?" Gherin asked again.

MacDuff reached up and punched Gherin's shoulder. His face began to turn red as he gasped for air.

Leptin considered. "If me crush you throat, you no talk. So me no do that. But if you pass out before answer question, wake up with no eyes."

"No eyes," agreed Gherin, showing his claws.

MacDuff put his hands on the ground. Didn't move. Leptin let the pressure up.

He coughed, then gasped. "MacDuff," the big man said, staring at the moon.

Leptin smiled. "MacDuff," he said.

Gherin grinned. "MacDuff. Right name."

"That right name," Leptin agreed. He looked back down at MacDuff. "Funny, you no look Scottish."

"You right," Gherin said thoughtfully, and ran a single claw along MacDuff's cheek. He picked a bead of sweat up on his claw and put it to his lips. "No taste Scottish." He looked up at Leptin. "Maybe wrong MacDuff?"

Leptin tilted his head. "You think?"

"Maybe."

"Hmmmmmm." Leptin lifted one hand up to scratch his head, keeping an eye on MacDuff to make sure he didn't try to escape from under the golf club. "Ask possum."

Gherin raised a finger in the air. "Yes!" He stepped a few paces back, into the darkness, under the bridge, and returned holding a large leather pouch in one hand.

He opened up the pouch, reached his hand in, and lifted a small possum out between his claws, its grey fur streaked with blood and littered with scars. "Possum possum," Gherin said merrily.

The possum twisted and turned. Gherin's claws were like hooks digging into his flesh.

Gherin held the possum over the prone man. "This him?" he asked.

The possum twisted again, and stopped when he realized it hurt more to move. "You'll let me go?" he asked, meekly.

"Yes."

The possum sobbed a little. "You promise?"

"Oh yes."

The possum whimpered. He didn't know what else to do. He only had one really good trick, playing dead, and they'd seen through that. "You promise on something important?" he asked.

Gherin's claws dug in a little deeper. "Like what?" the goblin asked.

The possum's mind raced, wincing, hurting, grasping for the most important thing he could think of. "Apples!" he shrieked. "Apples!"

Gherin smiled. "Oh yah," he said. "Swear on lots of—"

"Wait!" said Leptin.

Gherin and the possum looked over.

"What kind apples?" Leptin asked.

"Um . . . ," said the possum.

"They got kinds?" asked Gherin.

"Fuji," said the possum softly. "Tart, juicy, Fuji, from Japan."

Leptin considered. "Acceptable."

Gherin nodded. "Okay. Swear on Fuji apples, we let you go you tell us truth."

The possum looked at the man below him, held to the ground. "It's him," he said. "That's the guy. I've seen 'em together. I'm . . . I'm so sorry, MacDuff."

MacDuff's chest sank. "Aw . . . Henry"

"I'm sorry! They've got big claws! I'm so . . . sorry!"

"You sold me out."

"I couldn't hold on!"

"You were my friend!" MacDuff looked up at the moon. "We were in this together!"

"Soooooo," said Leptin, leaning down over the prone MacDuff's head. "You the human who—"

"Let me go!" shrieked Henry. "Let me go! You promised! On apples! On apples!"

Leptin turned and smiled sweetly. "You noisy. Got no more tell us."

The possum's tail thrashed. "Let me go! You promised!"

"Okay Gherin," said Leptin. "You know what do."

Gherin chuckled and licked the claws on his free hand. "Ohhhhhhhh, yah. Time now?"

"Time now," said Leptin.

Gherin nodded, reached his arm out, kneeled down to the ground, and set the possum on it. He reached into the pouch, and pulled out a small yellow block. "Have cheese," he said. "You probably hungry. Take with."

Henry grabbed the cheese and darted onto the street and across the road. "I'm sorry!" he shrieked as he ran.

Eventually they only heard the sound of the water against the shore.

Leptin blinked. "Uh, Gherin?"

Gherin turned. "Yah?"

"What you just do?"

Gherin blinked. "Let possum go. Like said."

"What?"

"You said okay to promise on Fuji apples, so I promise. You say let possum go."

"No. I say you know what do."

"Yah. So I keep promise. Let go."

Leptin rubbed his temples. "Okay. This my fault."

"What?"

"Me explain clearer next time. We make plan advance."

"What wrong?"

"It . . . ," Leptin shook his head. "We talk later." He turned back to the man on the ground. "So . . . you the human who . . ."

"Leptin?"

Leptin scowled and turned around again. "Yah?"

"What kind apples you not want make swear on?"

"I was . . . I was kind of wondering the same thing," said MacDuff. The man used Leptin's distraction to prop himself up by his elbows.

Leptin's eyes darted over to MacDuff, and then back to his friend. "Golden delicious."

"Ohhhhh."

A thought struck. "Hey," said MacDuff, suddenly. "Aren't you not supposed to be allowed to hurt me . . . or something?" Leptin turned back to stare at him, his eyes gleaming, and MacDuff stammered. "That's . . . that's what I heard."

Gherin chuckled. "You? You think you protected by treaty?"

Leptin laughed too, a little, although he was mostly just impatient. "You not protected by treaty. We can kill you."

A momentary hope in MacDuff refused to be extinguished once and for all. "Why not me?"

Gherin laughed again. "You man who talk to animals!"

"This is persecution! Racism!" MacDuff tried to sit up, but Leptin's hand blocked him. "They talked to me first!"

Gherin, walked over, putting a small piece of cheese in his mouth. "Ever notice animals that pets no talk?"

MacDuff's face twisted as he considered. "That . . . yeah, yeah. I seen that.'"

Gherin nodded. "Animals spend lots time around humans lose their talk. Only wild animals talk. If animal talks you, it means you wild human. Then no treaty."

Leptin picked his teeth with a claw. "Wizard no care wild humans."

"Wizard care cities and towers and agriculture," said Gherin.

"Of course, we sure can kill you anyway," said Leptin. "Wizard long dead."

"Long dead," agreed Gherin.

"Very dead," said Leptin. "Like moon."

Gherin stroked his chin. "Sneaky though."

"Very sneaky," agreed Leptin. "Sneaky wizard. But you wild human. Is no problem." Leptin stared at MacDuff, then back at Gherin. "We do this now?"

"Want cheese first?" asked Gherin.

Leptin glared at him, and Gherin closed the pouch and tossed it over his shoulder. He walked over to Leptin, and they looked down at MacDuff.

"So," said Leptin. "We hear you know mouse."

"We hear you friend of mouse," said Gherin.

"We hear maybe you tell us where find mouse," said Leptin.

"M . . . mouse?" asked MacDuff, unconvincingly.

Gherin leaned in and ran a single claw around MacDuff's left eye. "Oh, MacDuff who not Scottish, you know better."

"Yah," said Leptin.

"I . . . I can't." MacDuff could see the moonlight glinting off that claw.

"Sure you can. Keep eyes."

"He . . . he saved my life."

Gherin put a claw alongside each eye. "We save life."

"You don't understand! It was horrible!"

Gherin paused, and the goblins looked at each other.

Leptin leaned down. Gherin moved his claws away. "Tell more," Leptin said.

MacDuff took a deep breath and dug his hands into the dirt beneath him. "I won't do it."

"No no," said Leptin. "Not where mouse, not how find mouse. Tell us how mouse save you."

MacDuff's eyes darted back and forth between the two of them. Together, they were almost blocking out the moon. "You . . . you wanna know . . . how he saved me?"

The goblins looked at each other again.

"Think so," said Gherin. "Tell us story."

MacDuff waited a long time. He realized his throat was dry. He swallowed—it hurt—and looked at his captors. "Can I . . . can I sit up?"

Leptin scowled, but Gherin nodded. "Yah, okay."

Slowly, not making any sudden moves, MacDuff lifted himself up until he was sitting, a position that made him about as tall as the goblins. It never once crossed his mind that he could fight his way out of this. Not after they took him down so quickly. MacDuff had played some football in college, he knew what it was like to be up against strong and fast. He tried to imagine death, which he was sure was coming for him tonight, whatever happened. But he understood, now, that he didn't have it in himself to go down heroically. If they were going to give him a thread to cling to, he'd grab it with all his might. In his heart, he forgave Henry.

"Okay," he said. "I'll tell you."

"Good," said Leptin.

"Want cheese?" asked Gherin.

Leptin scowled. "Him fine."

"I do," MacDuff hadn't turned down food in years.

"Him fine," said Leptin. He turned back to MacDuff. "You tell."

"Good cheese," muttered Gherin.

MacDuff took a deep breath. "In the BART train tunnels. There's all kinds of work tunnels down there, and they close everything off at midnight, so if you can get in and hide just before they lock the doors, you got the whole system to yourself. Sometimes there's rats who'll be my lookout, help me stay out of sight. It's dark, but it's shelter, you know? No fog, no rain, no dew, nice and dry. Even turn the power off, so you won't kill yourself on the third rail. I can take most nights outside, but those really rainy ones kill me. I get soaked, and my lungs start to fill up and I can't breathe. I have to get out of the rain. So you go in, and you find a place that's out of sight, because you want to be out of sight. Because if someone else is in there, someone you don't know, you're locked in for the night and your only way out is through miles of tunnel, you know? BART don't go above ground in San Francisco. So sometimes, if you think somebody else is creeping around, you go deep. And sometimes, you go really deep. That's what I did. I went deep."

He took another deep breath, closed his eyes, and shuddered. "I found a place, way down, a pretty big room like, I don't know what it was for, the floor wasn't even, maybe they started digging there and then decided to go another way. I don't know the history, but—"

"What station?" Leptin interrupted.

"What?"

"What station you in?" Leptin demanded.

"Oh. Under . . . I was under Balboa Park station," MacDuff stammered.

Leptin eyed him closely, looking for lies, looking for the way they crawled under the skin. Finally he nodded. "Go on story."

MacDuff nodded. "I'm used to rough ground, and I can use my coat as a pillow, and I was going to go to sleep . . . and I couldn't close my eyes because something was wrong. I didn't know what, you know? I didn't know what. And then it sounded like hissing. Like a snake hissing, from everywhere. Every tunnel. The way I came, the ways I could go, hissing everywhere, getting louder. And it crept into my brain and I couldn't close my eyes and I just stood there and I don't even know where I could have run but I couldn't move anyway. I tried to turn my head, to look at things, I could feel the sweat running down my face, but I couldn't wipe it off. And then . . . ."

MacDuff closed his eyes. "And then the snake. . . unwound . . . and it was everywhere, like it had been wrapped around the room all the time, and somehow it came from the tunnels behind me and the tunnels in front of me at once, and there it was, in the room, filling it up, longer than a BART train, looking at me with its snake eyes and hissing, and man I could see poison dripping from its fangs."

Gherin and Leptin looked at each other. Gherin scowled, while Leptin growled a soft, deep, growl.

"And I knew I was dead," said MacDuff. "Even more dead than I am now."

"Yah," agreed Gherin. "Big dead. We just little dead."

"Then?" asked Leptin.

"Then?" asked MacDuff. "Then . . . then there was the mouse. He also came out of nowhere, I don't know how he got in the room, and he laughed and he sang this catchy war song . . . I can still hear it in my head. And he waved around this tiny little sword, it was shining like a light saber . . . and it was one of the craziest things I've ever seen. And he fought the snake. And he won. It was . . . it was impossible. Damn. Impossible. But he led me out of there, and I left the station and saw the dawn a living man."

"Him . . . kill serpent?"

"Yeah. Drove his tiny sword into its heart."

This time it was Leptin who scowled and Gherin who growled.

"Bad," said Gherin.

"Bad bad," Leptin agreed. He drummed his fingers against his leg. "Not like. No good."

"When this?" asked Gherin.

"What?"

"When mouse save you life from serpent?"

MacDuff considered. He had trouble tracking time. "Maybe a month?"

"Ohhhhh. Bad."

"Yah. Bad."

They stared at each other for a time, communing in their private language, developing a strategy. Leptin put his hand on MacDuff's shoulder to make sure he knew that he was still under the ground, surrounded by death.

Suddenly his claws dug in. MacDuff screamed as blood soaked into his coat. "Where we find mouse?" Leptin asked.

"I don't know!"

A moment's pause. "That really too bad."

"He didn't tell me where he lives!" MacDuff shouted. "He keeps to himself! I don't know! I don't know!"

"Soooo sad." Leptin's other hand wrapped around MacDuff's other shoulder.

"BUT I KNOW HOW TO REACH HIM!" It was a primal scream, something primitive, a survival instinct that his brain still hadn't caught up with.

Leptin drummed his talons along MacDuff's shoulder while Gherin stood in front of him and ran his claws gently down his cheeks. "Yah?"

The words came out before he even understood them. "He said if I ever needed him, I could leave a message under the holy water basin besides the labyrinth in Grace Cathedral! He said he'd find me! He promised!"

"Ohhhhhhhh," said Leptin.

"Ohhhhhhhh," said Gherin.

MacDuff wept.

"Yah."

"Yah."

They waited until his heaving stopped and his eyes were dry. Then Gherin knelt down in front of him. "Guess what?"

MacDuff didn't respond. His eyes reflected the moon. Gherin went on. "Mouse save life twice."

"You go cathedral," said Leptin, pulling his claws out of MacDuff's shoulder. That made him move. "You send mouse message. You tell him meet us."

"Why . . . why would he do that?" MacDuff asked, trying to move his shoulder and finding he couldn't. Not without agony.

Leptin smiled. "Because if he no find us, we find more his friends. Not ask nice anymore."

MacDuff nodded. "How . . . does he find you?"

Gherin chuckled. "If Pitter Patter Pounce really want find us, him know how."

Gherin looked at Leptin, and Leptin nodded. "You go now," Gherin said.

MacDuff tried to stand up, but his legs wouldn't hold him. He tried to prop himself up, but his right arm was useless. The idea that he would survive was unreal, and he couldn't keep it together. He fell on the ground, his head just touching the water. He gasped, and wept. He was alone.

In the morning, a homeless outreach team came to ask if he wanted any help. They sent him to San Francisco General Hospital. He took their bandages, took their antibiotics, but refused to stay for observation—even when they promised to feed him. He asked for a pen and paper before he left. He reached Grace Cathedral late that afternoon.

He wrote his note, ending it with the words "I'm sorry." Then he went out to the street and hustled for change. In the early dusk, he took his handful of change, went to a market in the Mission, and bought an apple. He put it in his pocket and went looking for Henry.

Chapter 4

James slammed his hands down on the sink. "What do you mean you're going to bed now?"

Mari shrunk back into the futon. "I'm tired."

"But you wanted to stay in so we could spend time together!"

She looked away. "Now I'm tired."

James threw up his hands. "It's not even nine o'clock!"

"I enjoyed dinner," she said.

"If you'd told me you were going to go to bed before nine I would have gone to the party in Oakland!"

"By yourself," she said.

He stared at her. She still wouldn't look at him. "Yes, by myself, if you won't come. I stayed home to spend time with you, but if you're just going to go to bed, and we're not going to screw, what's the point?"

She didn't answer for a long time. "You can still go. By yourself."

He threw a dishrag against a wall. "It'll be 10:30 by the time I get there! The last train back leaves around midnight! What's the point?"

"I don't know," she said softly.

"Then why would you ask me to stay home if you just want to go to bed right after dinner!"

She got up. She still wouldn't look at him. "I can't talk to you when you're like this."

He stepped forward. Right behind her. "You're the one who's not talking to me! You're the one who's shutting me out!"

"Please don't shout."

"It's not my shouting that's the problem!"

"No, it's not you, it's always me, isn't it. It's always my fault."

"That's not what I'm . . . I gave up my place to live with you!"

"Yes," she said. "Yes you did. I never asked you to."

"Oh come on!"

"I'm going to bed," she said softly. She moved quickly. A moment later the bedroom door slammed.

He walked over to the door. For a moment, he held his hand over the knob. He shook his head. He turned around. He picked up the dish towel and threw it against another wall. He went to his computer and called up a war game. He led the forces of darkness to victory after victory until 1:30 a.m., right about the time he might have gotten home from the party. His eyes drooped. He lay down on the futon, next to Caramel, and covered himself with a blanket that they kept near the futon for this kind of thing. Half an hour later, he was snoring.

The linen closet opened, and the goblins hopped to the ground. They stared at the prone human, his feet sticking out from under the blanket.

"Don't understand," said Leptin.

"Leptin," his friend said gently.

"No make sense."

"Leptin . . . him no Dark General."

Leptin nodded, acknowledging the obvious. "When see him . . . all come flashing back. The war, terrible war. Flaming sword. All. No understand."

"Leptin, him drooling."

Leptin spit on the ground.

Gherin pat Leptin's shoulder. "Make feel better, him very good leader in game. Build bone castles quick. Kill lots elves."

"Bah."

"Soon," said Gherin, "beautiful woman leave him. Never return."

Leptin scowled. "Her not so beautiful."

Gherin smiled dreamily. "Most beautiful girl in world."

"You deluded," said Leptin. "See what want see in humans. Like me."

They looked at each other, then shrugged. A moment later, they were out the window. Caramel shuddered and burrowed deeply under James' arm.

Chapter 5

To them, the Balboa Park BART station looked like a fortress: big stone walls, large doors—easy to defend from a siege. They liked it, even if inside it was drab and grey, with little more than a line of ticket kiosks and a long escalator going far down under the ground. As MacDuff had told them, no trains ran this late at night, no one was working—no one was supposed to be there.

"Need better locks," Gherin complained. "Fortress like this, need better locks. Keep Vikings out."

"Not fort," said Leptin. "No Vikings."

"Not fort?" Gherin scratched his head.

"Not fort. More foyer for trains."

"No Vikings?"

"No Vikings. Wrong part world, wrong time."

"Hmmmmmm." Gherin considered. "Still need better locks. Keep Canadians out."

They were standing on a large concrete island in between two underground train tracks. So far, they had seen no vagrants tonight.

"One track go here," Leptin said, pointing "back into city. One track go here, out of city. And Scotsman go . . . ."

"*Not* Scotsman," said Gherin.

"Not Scotsman go . . . ," Leptin considered carefully, searched for signs: not of MacDuff, but of the thing that had attacked him. "That way." He pointed. The two skittered across the concrete island and hopped into the tunnel, running on their claws.

There is no skill among goblin travelers more valued than tracking.

They did not expect Pitter Patter Pounce to meet their demand. They were long past such trust. But sending him this message, threatening his friends, could let them see who made sudden moves. That would be one more footstep they could follow, one more scent they could hunt.

In the meantime, they knew their prey had fought a tremendous battle down beneath the underground trains, and warriors often leave clues behind after a battle.

They went carefully. It was pitch-black, except for the occasional safety light, but darkness did not bother them. They feared no humans, but something terrible had been nesting down below. They knew of this creature, and, even if it was dead, they were afraid.

They came to a side tunnel. They scoured the ground. "Burns," said Leptin. "From venom."

"Yah," said Gherin. They turned to the side. The tunnel sloped. They crawled along the walls and the ceiling. There were no rats here, no insects. Even the earthworms had died.

"Which come first?" Gherin asked. "Train or nest?"

Leptin shrugged. "Don't know. Guess train."

Gherin considered. "Strange," he pronounced. Then he stopped. He pointed a talon at the tunnel wall. "Skin," he said. "Shed."

Leptin looked closer. The tunnel wall was covered by a fine filament that glittered even in the darkness.

"Come here, shed skin," Gherin said. "Eat nearby."

"Good," said Leptin. "Good."

Gherin held up a pouch and put some filament inside.

"What for?" asked Leptin.

"Eldritch," said Gherin. "Rare rare. Ingredient potions and powders."

Leptin raised an eyebrow. "You make potions?"

"Nah. Got cousin. Alchemist."

"Fancy," said Leptin, and it was a word mixed with admiration and disdain.

Gherin gave him a puzzled look, but said nothing. He scooped as much of the snake skin filament into the pouch as he could, then placed it with the other pouches, in the secret spot on his person where no one ever looked.

"Ready?" asked Leptin.

"Yah."

"Sure?"

"Yah. Want cheese?"

Leptin scowled.

"Sheep's milk," said Gherin. "From little shop round corner apartment. Shop get mentioned in Moody's Guide San Francisco. Got everything. This Spanish. Got mushroom in it."

Leptin scowled harder.

"Taste earthy," Gherin finished.

Leptin's breathing was heavy. "Ready?"

"Yah."

"Okay." Leptin took a step down the tunnel.

"It just, got no more room for cheese in pouch. Filled with eldritch."

Slowly, Leptin turned around.

Gherin held it forward. "So, we eat. No waste. Too good waste. Be shame."

Leptin took a deep breath. His hands twitched, showing his claws. He pursed his lips. "Give cheese," he said at last.

Smiling, Gherin handed the small white block over. Leptin's mouth slid over it, and ripped half off at once. He chewed savagely, until it was mince and paste, then swallowed.

He considered, looked at it carefully, and then ate the rest just as quickly. "Good cheese," he said at last.

"Yah," said Gherin.

"Earthy."

"Got mushrooms," Gherin agreed. "San Francisco good town for cheese."

Leptin scowled. "You used to finer things, Gherin."

"Yah," said Gherin. Then, "What?"

Leptin said nothing.

"Oh," said Gherin. He considered. "You want talk."

"Let's go."

"Okay."

They nodded to each other and skittered down the tunnel.

Soon the smooth tunnel walls became increasingly rough. There was a turnoff. They stopped, for a moment, and examined the tunnel floor. Leptin pointed at the tunnel they were following. "Slants up," he said. "Rejoin main tracks."

Gherin pointed at the turn off. "Slant down after fifty feet," he said. "We go down."

Leptin nodded, and they crawled, carefully, deeper under the earth.

By the time the tunnel expanded into a cavern, they knew they had found it. There was a noise that wasn't a noise, the echo of screams and hissing that had stopped but would never really be over. Time was just one more jungle to track through, and it often ran a circuitous path.

"Ugly," said Gherin.

Leptin shrugged. "Seen worse," he said. But he, too, shivered.

To the casual glance there was nothing on the floor except small piles of rubble, and nothing on the walls but cold stone. The serpent's body had gone the way of all ancient things, leaving not even bones behind. But they crept into the room, eyes looking closely over every surface, disturbing as little as they could, reading the stone and the rubble like the pages of a novel they had opened to the middle. And trying to reconstruct the opening scene.

"See footwork?" asked Gherin.

"Yah."

"Mouse good."

"Mouse very good," corrected Leptin.

"Don't know how he kill serpent, though," said Gherin. "Very not sure."

Leptin's eyes narrowed. "Ohhhhh," he said, bending at the knees, reaching down carefully to pull a small scrap of fabric up in his claws. "What this?"

"What what?"

Leptin examined it closely. "Piece felt."

"Huh," said Gherin.

"Yah, it . . . ," Leptin looked up at Gherin and his eyes went wide. "Stop!"

Gherin froze in place. His eyes darted back and forth.

"No move!" said Leptin, walking . . . very . . . carefully . . . over to him.

"Yah," whispered Gherin.

Standing behind Gherin, Leptin put his arms on his shoulders. "Go limp," he said.

Gherin leaned back and let his weight go into Leptin's arm. Slowly, carefully, Leptin began to pull Gherin back.

It wasn't enough. The top of the claw on Gherin's big toe pulled a small trip wire spread between two rocks. Leptin yanked Gherin back as the line went taut and an explosion from under the rocks blasted into the cavern.

The two goblins flew across the room.

The dust began to settle.

A few moments later, from the northeast corner, Leptin's voice came out. "Gherin okay?"

"Ohhhhh," came the reply from the northwest. "Bruised. Broke claw." Then, "Leptin okay?"

"Yah," said Leptin. Then, a moment later, "Yah."

Slowly, they began to stand up.

"What that?" asked Gherin.

Leptin began to dust himself off. "Trap."

"Yah?"

"Yah." Leptin checked himself over for cuts. "Good trap. Hand grenades on tripwire. Hard to see. Sneaky. Set by good trapper."

"Ohhhhhhhh." A moment later, "Why?"

Leptin nodded. "Good question. Why fight ancient serpent, kill ancient serpent, then set trap?"

Gherin shook his head, then pounded it with the flat of his hand, trying to shake the ringing out of his ears. "Maybe think more ancient serpent?"

Leptin's hand brushed that aside. "Nah. Explosion no kill ancient serpent."

"Baby serpent?" asked Gherin.

"Nah."

"Hmmmmmm." Of the two, Gherin's skin was more scratched and bruised, but he was determined not to show weakness. He tilted his head. "Kill goblins?"

Leptin nodded. "Maybe."

"Ohhhhhhhh," said Gherin.

"Ohhhhhhhh," said Leptin.

"Hmmmmmm," said Gherin. "Somebody very unkind us."

"Think so."

"Mouse?"

They were silent for a moment.

Gherin answered his own question. "Nah. Mouse got chivalry."

"Yah," Leptin admitted. "Not mouse."

"Hmmmmmm. Someone else."

They scratched their chins. Then Leptin shrugged. "Got felt?" he asked.

"Yah," said Gherin. Leptin considered asking where he was keeping it, then changed his mind. If Gherin said he had it, that was enough.

Carefully scanning the floor for traps, a care they had not taken just minutes ago, the two skittered back down the tunnel and up toward the train tracks.

It was nearly dawn by the time they emerged out of the tunnel system, over a mile away at the Glen Park BART station, and their habitual spot was too distant to reach before morning. They dashed across the streets until Gherin spotted a yoga studio next to a Korean barbecue, which he said he'd always wanted to try. They ate beef in spicy sauce out of the refrigerator, then Gherin picked the studio's locks and they hid away inside a supply closet just as the sun rose over the bay.

Chapter 6

"Sean!" Rosie shouted from the studio floor. "There's a light bulb out by the waterfall! Can you fix it before class starts!"

"That's like ten minutes!"

"Yeah!"

Sean sighed. He knew "The green bud was too good last night—you're lucky I'm here at all" wasn't an excuse, and he couldn't think of a better excuse because the green bud had been too good last night. His life was full of these intricate little traps.

"Sean!" she shouted. She always did an uninterrupted pre-class workout. Without fail. For a spiritually enlightened being, Rosie was really high maintenance. It was also, he thought, a really stupid idea to have a waterfall in the yoga studio. It looked cheesy and had this really mechanical hum, which was totally not spiritual.

"Yeah, okay," he called back. Then, "where are the light bulbs?"

"I don't know!"

"Well . . . ," things were starting to look up.

"Check the supply closet!"

Dammit.

He walked to the back of the studio, staring at Rosie as he passed her workout because she looked like a movie star, and stopped in front of the supply closet. Did it lock? No. He opened it up. Pitch-black inside: Without the ambient light from the waterfall, it was like a cave back here.

He scratched his head. Wasn't there a light in the closet? Of course there was. The switch was on the right side of the door.

He reached his hand in and stroked it along the wall.

Okay, the left side of the door. Right? Right? Yep. There it was. God this city sucked. He couldn't wait until Burning Man. He flipped the switch. Nothing happened.

Huh. He flipped it again, up and down, a couple of times. Nothing.

"Rosie!"

"Yeah?"

"Where . . . where in the closet are the light bulbs?" He stared into the darkness, and felt that old primeval fear of man—that when you stare into the darkness, something is staring back.

"I don't know! Look for them!"

Sean hadn't had it this bad since . . . since he was a kid and his big sister had locked him in the boiler room of their apartment building. It was the first time he'd ever been down there, and everything looked like it was going to kill him. Now it was all coming back. Now it was like something in the darkness, sharpening its talons, was waiting for him to take a foolish step forward or reach his hands where he didn't belong.

"I'm getting too old to party," he whispered to himself, his instincts screaming "RUN!"

"Well, you see," he shouted back, "the light bulb's out in the closet too, so I can't really see where they are—"

"Well, root around!"

"There might not even be any light bulbs in there."

"Use your cell phone as a flashlight!"

He stared deeper into the supply closet. For a moment, he thought he heard something breathing. He stepped back. "It's . . . my cell phone's not very good at that."

"There's an app you can download!"

"Is it for iPhone or Android?"

"Oh for . . . ."

He slammed the closet door shut. "There aren't . . . I don't think there are any light bulbs in there," he said. He couldn't believe he was doing this—he was a gutless wonder. "I'll run to Walgreens and get some." But the brain is all chemicals, right? And if you introduce new chemicals, stuff happens, right? Of course. We're all just chemicals. Really spiritual chemicals. That's all. He just had too much fear in his system, and it was just a side effect.

"Sean . . . ."

"I'm telling you," he said, walking briskly across the studio, "there's no light bulbs in there. I'll be back in five."

Rosie pushed herself up from downward dog just in time to give him the finger as he raced out the door.

It took Sean fifteen minutes to get back, and he had to install the light bulb by the water fountain during warm-up. He never got around to going back to the supply closet. By the time she left at 7:00, Rosie had convinced herself she needed a new assistant. Fucking stoners.

Chapter 7

The facade of the Regal Hatters building, in the upper Haight, was a mural painted by a former gang member who had been convinced he could do something more with his life. He'd painted an urban *Inferno* with four sides, showing an innocent child getting jumped into a gang and becoming more and more demonic in each scene as he embraced gang life, until there was little human left. He'd planned to paint a second mural on the building next door—he'd gotten permission—showing the path to redemption, but after finishing just one side had been arrested for dealing pot to pay for art supplies. He'd been sent away for twenty-five to life. A few community activist groups and a black church said the evidence had been planted.

The owner of the second building had eventually sold it and the redemption mural had been painted over. But Regal Hatters was a family business and the Gordon family said their *Inferno* was never coming down.

Inside, Craig was gradually closing up for the night. It had been a slow day and he was thinking about pizza—about whether it was worth paying $4.75 for a slice across the street or waiting an hour after he got home to order a whole pizza for $20. He didn't like to think of himself as the kind of person who cared so much about money but, come on, almost $5 for a slice? "There's no justice in the world," he muttered to himself as he closed out the register.

"Hey," said a voice stuck between a scrape and a hiss, "maybe you help us settle bet."

He looked up.

"Is Hillary Clinton real person?" asked Gherin. "Or one them fake TV lawyers you people always make up?"

Leptin shook his head. "So hard tell."

"Shit," said Craig. He ducked under the register. He came up with a loaded shotgun. He pointed it where the goblins had been . . . and didn't see them.

He began to step back . . . get his back against a wall . . . when he felt their hands around his legs. Damn they were fast! His feet went out from under him and his back slammed against a display of men's hats in the styles of the 1920s. The gun was pulled from his hands. His body pushed against the floor.

The next thing he saw clearly was Leptin, nodding his approval. "You got good reflexes," Leptin said. "Quick. Bet you good shot too."

"Cowboys?" said Gherin. "Them exciting. Kings? Classic. Good drama. Artists? Sure. Got lotsa passion." He scratched his head. "What so good 'bout lawyers, always make new ones put on TV?"

Hats tumbled over and landed around them.

"Never watch TV," Gherin admitted. "So, maybe miss something. Want try sometime. Hear good things."

"What the . . . ," Craig looked back and forth between them. "What ARE YOU?"

The goblins looked at each other.

"Ohhhhhhhh," said Leptin. "No play stupid."

Gherin wagged his finger. "Tsk tsk."

"Go straight for gun," Leptin said.

"Not say 'who is you guys'," said Gherin. "No say 'Is this joke?' or 'Aaak!' or 'Welcome hat shop. You got heads?' Noooo. Not even talk 'bout lawyers when me ask good question. Nope." He narrowed his eyes. "Bad customer service. What if want hat?"

"Go straight for gun," Leptin said again. "Move fast."

"Ready shoot goblins walk in shop," said Gherin. "Now play dumb."

"We got eyes," said Leptin, putting his taloned foot on Craig's chest. "We watch. We know you part of network."

Gherin walked over to a row of soft hats. "And," he said, holding up a small piece of fabric. "We got felt." He fingered it. "Quality. Nice stitching." He held it up, moving it from hat to hat on the wall, comparing, until he stopped at a men's 8 ½ fedora.

"Got match," he said.

"Thought so," said Leptin. "You friend of mouse."

Craig looked up at Leptin from under his foot, his eyes wide, the goblin's claws just barely poking into his ribcage. He considered his options.

He spit on Leptin's knee.

"Ooooooooooo," said Gherin, his eyes wide.

The claws in Leptin's foot tightened their grip. Craig winced and his face turned red, but he bit his lip so that he wouldn't scream.

Leptin looked down at him and nodded, noticing the effort. He held the shotgun in his hands. Felt its weight. "Could shoot," he said. "But you die quick. Not talk." He flipped the weapon over in his hands. "Could beat you with handle. But clumsy. No craftsmanship. Good weapon made by hand, by craftsman. Beautiful. Not flashy, beautiful. Difference." He put this shotgun on the sales counter. "Not beautiful."

He held up his hands and let his talons shine as his fingers swerved in the light. "This beautiful," he said. "Good weapon want be this."

His arms flashed down and the front of Craig's shirt was in tatters. Leptin raised his hands up again and held eight strips of fabric up, four caught on the claws of each hand, and waved them like streamers. "Do that flesh next," he said. "No kill, very hurt. Make puppet show from body. You watch."

Gherin chuckled. "Him make appendix talk. Big funny. Good bit. Like Edger Bergen, Charlie McCarthy, 'cept audience beg 'make it stop!'"

"Only reason not to," said Leptin, looking back down. "Is take time. Rather you talk now. Be quick. Time get food, nice place for night. So hard find good apartment in city. So if you—"

He stopped and looked more closely. Across Craig's chest was a tattoo of a soaring eagle over an American flag, clutching rifles in each of its talons. And words, in black script: "405—Semper Fi—Never Say Die."

Leptin whispered. "You got ink,"

"What?" Gherin turned from looking at the hats. "Oh. Pretty. Well, kinda pretty."

Leptin stroked his chin with his talons. Considering. For a long time. Finally he took a deep breath. "You serve?"

Craig blinked. "What?"

"Ink." Leptin pointed. "You serve?"

Craig blinked again. "Yeah."

Leptin's claws tightened, just a little. "Who."

Craig winced. "Who, what, did I serve with?"

"Yah." He bared his teeth. "Who."

Craig tried to push his chest out, but the claws were in too deep. "U.S. Marines, 405."

"Yah," Leptin muttered. "Semper Fi."

Gherin peered closer. "Leptin? What me not get?"

"When?" Leptin asked Craig.

"You make fun with appendix now?"

"A tour in Desert Storm," said Craig. "Then two tours in Afghanistan, and half a tour in Iraq."

Gherin shrugged and went back to looking at the hats.

"Half tour?" asked Leptin. "Wounded?"

Craig didn't say anything, for a moment. Then "I'm missing two toes on my left foot." He winced as he said it.

Leptin nodded slowly. "Okay," he said. "Okay." He thought for a moment more. Craig tried to breathe.

"Gherin," said Leptin. "Do favor."

"Yah?"

"Get whiskey."

Gherin blinked and turned away from the row of fedoras. "Whiskey?"

"Yah."

"Um . . . ," Gherin considered. "Maybe after torture?"

"Gherin—"

"Want watch."

"Gherin, what you not know: American soldiers—two thousand years greatest non-magic fighting force in history."

Gherin fidgeted with a hat. "Yah?"

"No doubt. Better Rome. Better Khan. Better Her Majesty's Navy. Better Rommel tanks. Better Han Alliance. Way better New Federatsii."

Gherin nodded, trying to keep up. "Better than Yankees?"

"Baseball team!" Leptin corrected, his teeth bared.

"Win lotsa pennants."

"Gherin! You do favor. Get whiskey. Good whiskey! Take time. We have soldier talk. Talk like men."

Gherin threw up his arms. "Yah? Why?" He tossed the hat over his shoulder. "Why?"

Leptin pointed one hand at Craig, and the other, talon exposed, at Gherin. "RESPECT SCARS! GHERIN RESPECT SCARS! GHERIN RESPECT BLOOD!"

Slowly Gherin raised his hands in front of his chest. "Okay. Okay, Leptin. Get scotch. Single malt. Maybe Macallan, or Bunnahabhain. Maybe Talisker, if find."

Slowly, Leptin lowered his hands. "Talisker too floral."

"But . . . yah, yah. Okay." Gherin slowly crept around toward the back of the store where the entrance to the alley was. Then he stopped. "Get snacks? Maybe German sausages? Book says is place—"

"Yah. Go, Gherin. Go. Come back whiskey . . . and sausages okay."

"Yah."

A moment later, Gherin was gone.

Leptin took a deep breath—his whole body shook—and slowly he lifted his foot off Craig's chest, pulling the talons out one at a time. He lowered himself down so that he was sitting with his back against the sales counter. "Sit," he instructed Craig. "No stand. Sit."

Slowly, wincing, breathing deeply, Craig sat up opposite the goblin.

Leptin pointed to the top of the counter, where the shotgun lay. "No stupid," he said. "You marine. Yah? Me marine." Leptin thought hard, running through terms he recalled being appropriate. "Me special forces. Me navy seals. Me black ops. Yah?"

Slowly, Craig nodded.

"You be stupid, just make me sad. Me torture slower when sad. Take twice long."

Craig didn't blink.

Leptin smiled. Then snickered. "Two toes on foot? Seen little girls hurt worse, go back fight."

After a long moment, Craig nodded. "I didn't ask to be discharged," he said. "I wasn't . . . I didn't want to be there, but I didn't want to leave that way. I tried to stay."

Leptin nodded again. "Good."

They sat in silence.

"You know," Craig said, not sure what to do, "that sausage place he's talking about is really good. Really . . . good."

Leptin blew air through his lips and waved his hand. "Yah. Sure. Gherin know. Gherin good that stuff. Gherin fancy boy, from big family. Important family. Political family. Yah?"

Craig nodded.

"Family like that, get know all finer things from world. Forbidden things. No rules mean 'no' for family. Leptin got big important mission, go human world, find mouse, make right. Gherin think big chance, see human world, fine things." He sighed. "Nothing me to do. Me just soldier. Gherin . . . political. So Gherin come. Gherin talented, yah. Good kid. Yah. But . . . rules are scars. Gherin no scars!"

Leptin shook his head, growling, and stared at the ground.

Craig clotted the neat puncture wounds Leptin's talons had left in his chest with what remained of his shirt. There would be a scar on the flag. "Yeah," he said. "I knew two lieutenants in Storm like that. Rich ROTC kids who joined because they wanted a line on their résumé and never thought there would be another war."

"Yah." Leptin didn't look up.

"They spent the whole war acting like it was a personal inconvenience, like all the killing we did was keeping them from their office in Goldman Sachs."

"Yah."

"Didn't know anybody like that in Afghanistan, though. Lot of stupid kids, but, nobody on my side I wanted to frag. At least not for a good reason. I wonder if any of the lieutenants from Storm got called back to Iraq. I bet they did. Not in the 405 anymore, though."

Something occurred to Craig. "You're a long way from home, man." He felt his chest, and winced. Was this what Stockholm syndrome felt like?

"Yah."

Craig started to speak, then stopped. Realized that anything important he said would lead him one step quicker to treachery or torture. Nothing to do but sit here. Nothing to do but sit here and breathe. Unless, they had another kind of conversation.

"Hey," he said.

Leptin seemed deep in thought. Eventually he raised his eyebrows.

"The things you said . . . about the U.S. military . . . there were a couple of names I didn't . . . I didn't recognize. Were those . . . from the future?"

"Yah."

"You can travel through time?"

Leptin sighed. "Time . . . complicated. Like river. Like many rivers. Some go one way, some go other way. Some just circle around. Time . . . flexible. But tough. Like thick mud."

"Many rivers of thick mud," Craig said.

"No—forest of thick mud, with water rivers going one way, going other way, some crossing. Some over big rocks. Some waterfalls. You get in river, you follow current. You get off river, you get stuck in mud. It . . . complicated. Not easy. All time is one time, but all time moving around each other . . . ," Leptin waved it away. "Don't got words. Can't travel easy most places, some places easier others."

"Okay, I get that I can't understand it, but you can answer this question?" He said. "Can you go back in time and change the past? Can you do that? Or if you go back in time, has everything you do there already happened?"

Leptin blinked. "Stupid question."

"What do you mean?"

"Everything changing all the time. Always changing. Only way it is."

"Oh." He thought about it. Then he got a chill. "What happens to America?"

"What?"

"You said my corps is as good as it ever gets. What happens to America in fifty years? One hundred years? Are we going downhill?"

Leptin scowled. "Hard say. Next one hundred years here very muddy. Try to cross through, get stuck. Don't know well. World not same, though. Maybe Gherin know."

"Okay," Craig nodded. "What about—"

Leptin's eyes opened wide. Leptin's claws dug into the wooden floor. "Stop talking," he said.

Craig stopped.

"Listen now. Me know you not want betray mouse. Mouse good general. Me understand. Respect. But you listen, because you no understand. Mouse good man, but mouse not good guy. Mouse do terrible thing, very dangerous thing. Mouse has you do very bad thing, maybe destroy world."

Craig didn't say anything.

"How many things you kill?" Leptin asked.

Craig waited an extra moment, to make sure the question wasn't rhetorical. "How many men?"

"No men! Things. Creatures. Scary like never scared in life. How many?"

"I don't—"

"You there when mouse kill big snake?"

Craig shuddered, and that was all Leptin needed to see. "Like that! How many?"

"Three!" Craig said, without thinking.

Leptin nodded. "Good soldier. Snake and what else?"

Craig closed his eyes. "There was . . . it was like a green ogre, with puss bleeding out of its skin and a golden crown."

Leptin shook his head and groaned. "Bad."

"The other one was . . . like a giant squid that swam through stone. It would reach its tentacles out of rock—and each one had a hundred eyes and mouths—and pull you down into the sidewalk, or the foundation of a building." His hands began shaking.

"You survive," said Leptin. "Good. Good man. Terrible battles. Me know. But you survive. Big important."

"I didn't kill them," Craig whispered. "I want to be clear on that. I had guns, and explosives, but it was the mouse who killed them. Every time."

"Believe you."

Craig looked up, his eyes almost bulging out of his head. "I've seen action. You know that. But I've never seen anything like that. You're telling me the mouse is doing wrong? No. No, those things had to die."

Leptin sighed. "Terrible things, yah," he said. "Monsters. Monstrosities. But you not know what are. Not just monsters."

"No?"

"No," Leptin said, his teeth bared, his voice almost reverent. "They symbols."

"What?"

"Yah. Symbols. Things that mean other things. Things not really what they are. Symbols."

Craig shook his head. "I'm not . . . ."

"Long time ago, world filled with symbols. Everywhere. Big. Juicy. Ripe like poison fruit. World very different. Wizard want change world for humans. Say life better, fewer symbols. Teach man how kill them. Carve man-world out of wild-world. Okay. Now you here. Got symphonies and chocolatiers and big buildings. Yah?"

Leptin looked at Craig, reached out, and punched his arm with the back of his hand. "Yah?"

Craig flinched, although it didn't hurt. "No," he said. "No, I don't . . . is this like Middle Earth?"

Leptin leaned his head back against the counter. "Nah. Middle Earth fiction book, yah? Fiction book high culture. High culture wizard's trick, what you got 'stead of symbols. Yah?"

"What?" Craig's chest really hurt. Hurt almost as bad as his foot. "But I thought art was symbolic."

"Not art! Leptin growled. "High culture! Got art in cave, got art in museum, but cave not museum! It different! It . . . ," he stopped, and shook his head. "Me not scholar. No mind. This what important: now there lot less symbols. That okay, because ones left very big. Big enough. Big and old and dark and powerful, yah? Scare even high-culture man in dark. Lurk in dream. World keep turning this way. Stay on track. But mouse . . . mouse want kill off, make world even safer. World can't get too safe. Big danger. Kill last big symbols, world go off track."

"But . . . how?"

"What mean, how?"

"How? I mean . . . how? Symbols aren't real!"

Leptin grimaced. "You makin' this hard, Craig."

Craig's eyes were wide, his breathing shallow. Leptin stared at him closely. He had seen this before: a soldier who was even more lost than he was afraid. He sighed and leaned his back against the counter.

"Not got answer. Me not good explain big things. Not got words. Maybe Gherin. Gherin got lots words. But me know what mouse not tell you. Mouse should tell you many things. Maybe mouse not know—but mouse should know. Kill last big symbols, world get safe, then stop spinning. Maybe go off axis. Maybe crash sun and end in fire, maybe go dance into darkness forever. Maybe stay in place, half burn half freeze. Hard tell. But mouse not understand. Mouse think he killing last of monsters. Mouse think that we protect them because we monster too. You look us, you think we like them, yah? Yah? But monsters no friend other monsters. World better without deep buried monsters. But they symbols. Got to live. Dare not run out symbols."

The back door creaked open. Gherin announcing his presence clearly, just in case.

"Good," said Leptin. "Whiskey." He reached out to grip Craig's shoulder. "We here tell mouse what mouse need know.

"Whiskey," muttered Craig. "Good."

Gherin crept into the room bearing a sack over his back. "Got treats," he said.

"What got?" said Leptin. "Hurry, pour."

"Want smoky? Sweet?"

"Smoky," said Leptin.

"Sweet," said Craig.

Leptin looked at his captive, whose eyes were closed, and then waved it away. "Sweet," he said.

Gherin looked at Leptin carefully, and when the older goblin nodded, he pulled a bottle out of the sack. "Start Dalwhinnie," he said. "Central highlands."

Leptin nodded. "Good choice. Got smoky aftertaste."

Gherin pulled out three shot glasses, bit the top of the bottle off with his teeth, spit the shards out, and poured each glass full.

Craig worked to steady his hands as he picked his glass up. "You guys . . . really know your whiskey."

Gherin and Leptin chuckled.

"Come from us," said Gherin. "Goblins invented."

"Taught it you," said Leptin. "Long, long time ago."

Craig nodded. "Makes . . . sense?"

Leptin growled something guttural . . . a signal . . . a toast . . . and the goblins tilted the whiskey back. A moment later, Craig followed.

"Yah," said Leptin.

"Yeah," said Craig.

Gherin poured again.

Craig had never been a whiskey man, but he drank now, the vision of the crowned ogre and tentacles emerging from stone impossible to shove back down. They were dead now. Dead.

"Do you really have food?" he asked by the third round. "I'm . . . hungry."

Gherin reached back in the sack and pulled out small cardboard boxes. "This," he said, "Hungarian smoked pork sausage." He pointed to the second box. "This wild boar sausage with apple and spice. And this beer smoked sausage, pork and beef." He scowled. "Almost got potato salad, but, too risky."

Craig reached over. Opened the wild boar. "Love this place. You steal it?" He didn't wait for the obvious answer. "No buns?" he asked.

"Not miracle worker."

"It's okay, this is . . . ," he picked a sausage, still lukewarm, up in his hands and ate, in between sips of whiskey. He'd been hungry before this had started.

"Gherin," Leptin said, eating his own meal. "Soldier help kill three ancients for mouse."

"Yah?"

"Yah. Snake, ogre, and Mersechquestun."

"Ohhhhh. Mersechquestun bad. Very bad."

"Yah. He thinks did good thing."

"Oh." Gherin licked his fingers of Hungarian pork. "Take short view."

"Yah." Leptin tapped Craig on the shoulder, and Craig flinched. "But him good soldier. Survive. Kill. Got scars. Not him job take long view. Me want him be good. Live long. Live happy."

He turned to look at the human. "You want that, soldier?"

His mouth full, Craig nodded.

Leptin smiled. There was meat in his teeth. "You got do three things me. First you tell mouse what me tell you. Tell him, and tell him meet us."

Slowly, his head spinning from whiskey and his stomach filling with lukewarm gourmet sausages, Craig nodded again.

"Next: you got tell me where you fought Mersechquestun."

Craig swallowed "The what?"

"Tentacles in stone."

Craig hesitated.

"Not betray mouse, tell me where it die. Need know."

Craig finished another sausage. "The sack," he said.

The goblins gave him a puzzled look.

"The sack that you carried all the scotch and the meat in," Craig said to Gherin. "You weren't carrying that when you . . . came in. Where did you get it?"

Gherin opened his mouth but Leptin cut him off. "Don't ask. Decide not want know."

"But . . . ."

Leptin's gaze was stern. "Where fight?"

Craig held out his glass and Gherin filled it.

"Under City Hall."

Gherin chuckled. Leptin nodded.

"What?"

Leptin shook his head. "Not joke for you. You go home soon. Sleep in bed."

Craig took another drink, then coughed. The goblins watched, unblinking.

"What's the third thing?" he asked.

Leptin nodded. "Good explosives?" he asked.

"What?"

"You good explosives?" he asked.

"Um . . . yeah. Yeah, I've used 'em."

Leptin nodded. "You set trap, in tunnel, after fight?"

"What?"

"Tell truth. Just want know. You set explosion trap in tunnel?"

"But . . . why?"

Gherin smirked. "Blow goblins up."

Leptin scowled at him, and then looked back at Craig. Studied him closely. Craig didn't blink.

"Okay," Leptin said. He turned to Gherin. "We go."

Gherin stared, wide-eyed. "But . . . sausages!"

"We go."

"Whiskey!"

"Time now."

Gherin's voice was a low snarl. "Whiskey, Leptin."

Leptin growled. "Take one bottle. Leave rest."

"Leptin—"

Leptin turned and bared his fangs. "Leave whiskey for wounded soldier!"

Slowly, slowly, Gherin backed away. He grabbed a bottle then stepped into the back room, out of sight.

"Go home," Leptin told Craig. "Go home, try not dream hard."

Chapter 8

The view from the top of the Golden Gate Bridge at night is of a river of light driving far below. Cars flood across the banks at all hours, and the city of San Francisco can be seen naked in one easy turn. On the other side of the bridge are oceans and mountains swaddled in darkness. Their natural splendor will take anyone's breath during the day, but at night there's no turning away from the city. The closer you stare, the closer you seem to come to anything happening all at once.

Gherin and Leptin sat on the railing high at the top of the bridge, their legs gripping against the wind, passing a bottle of scotch back and forth. Sometimes they stared at the city, sometimes out at the darkness . . . which looked like home.

They did not look at each other.

"No kill," Gherin said at last.

Leptin ignored him.

"No human," Gherin said.

Leptin held his hand out for the bottle.

Gherin passed it.

Leptin swirled it around and stared out at the ocean.

"You great soldier," said Gherin. "Get big honors. But no kill tonight. No kill last night. No kill night before."

Leptin poured the whiskey down his throat.

"Seen you kill," said Gherin. "You kill easy. Kill good. Big fun. Why not now? Why you take excuse . . . him soldier, respect scars? Soldiers die, Leptin. Killed by other soldiers. Is job."

Leptin took another swig, swirled it around his tongue, let it burn down his throat.

"No kill culture humans, yah," Gherin said. "Protect by treaty. Wizard dead . . . long dead . . . but, good honor treaty. Good thing. Wild humans no got treaty. What problem?" He held his hand out for the bottle.

Eventually, Leptin passed it back.

"Why no kill?" Gherin asked again, holding the bottle close.

"You like cheese," Leptin said.

"Yah."

"Killing not like cheese."

Gherin considered this as he downed a gulp of whiskey.

"Okay," he said.

"Yah."

"Really like cheese."

"Me know."

Gherin took another swig from the bottle. "Leptin?"

"Yah."

"Like dogs."

Leptin considered. "Yah. Dogs okay."

Gherin passed him the bottle. "Like wyverins too."

Leptin smiled as he drank. "Got good teeth."

"Leptin?"

"Yah?"

"Think bad us not got high culture?"

Leptin blinked.

Gherin looked away.

Leptin stared at the back of his head. "You got taste for finer things, Gherin."

"So?" Gherin still didn't look at him.

Leptin shook his head sadly. "High culture big trouble, Gherin. Kills symbols. Kills magic. Tames minds. Domesticates wild. You know. You got wise tutors, tell you this."

Gherin turned to face him now. "Maybe me want hear symphony. See what that like."

"So? Hear symphony. Humans got lotsa symphony."

"Maybe," Gherin said slowly, "me want write symphony."

Leptin shuddered. "Gherin . . . ."

Gherin grabbed the bottle. "Maybe me want write book. About whiskey. Maybe me want write whole book about how me love whiskey."

"Howl poem instead," Leptin said sensibly.

"Me love whiskey more can howl. Want write book."

Leptin shook his head. He pointed his talon into Gherin's chest. "No. No you not want write book." He stabbed Gherin with his finger again. "You not want write symphony. You not poet. You not musician. You make up. You make all up for argument. High culture got nothing you love. You love hunting prey across iron desert. You love dancing round fire. You love sex. You melancholy? Okay. First time away. Away home, away family, no guards, no servants. Okay. You sad. But high culture got nothing but toys."

Gherin considered his next words carefully. "Like cheese."

"Goblins got cheese."

"Humans got better cheese."

Leptin threw up his hands. "Cheese, Gherin! Cheese! You want do forbidden thing for *cheese*?"

"Don't know."

"Never go home! Never find path back wearing high culture on head! No potions! No howling! No Hunt! No deathwatch! Moon always out of reach! All for *cheese*?"

Gherin turned to look back at San Francisco, at the river of light running across the bridge and through the city. He drank heavily from the bottle. He took a long time swallowing.

"Yah," he said.

Leptin waited.

"Yah," Gherin said again. "You right. Want go home. Stop mouse, go home."

He passed the bottle back to Leptin. They sat on the bridge, staring in opposite directions, all night.

Chapter 9

"Suitable," said Mari, putting the tiles down. "That's an eight letter word, and a triple word score."

"Wow, nice," said James, writing down the score.

"That's probably my best word of the night!" She grinned at him.

"Yeah."

"Your turn!"

"Yeah." He put the pencil down. "Okay, let's see . . . ."

"Take your time."

"Yeah." He picked up a tile from his hand and put it down again, studying them closely. He looked over at the board. Then back at his hand. "You know," he said absently, "I went to the neighborhood community meeting tonight."

"Oh good! I'm sorry I had to work."

"Yeah. Supervisor Chiu was there, talking about neighborhood development and taking questions and I just . . . ." He stopped and looked back at his hand.

"What?"

Yowl! Yowl!

"Caramel!" She looked over at the cat, who was sitting under a standing lamp in the corner. "What has gotten into you lately!"

Yowl!

"Do you want to be brushed?"

Yowl!

"Stop it!"

"Leave her alone," said James. "She just wants attention."

"I don't know, . . . maybe I should take her to the vet."

"Maybe."

"You were going to say something?"

He sighed. "Just . . . he spent the whole night congratulating us on everything we did, even the most stupid thing, and giving us platitudes about what he's going to do, and I kept thinking, what a hollow, superficial man."

"That's disappointing."

"And when you get a hollow, superficial man who's as ambitious as he is, that's a dangerous man."

"Is he ambitious?"

"Obviously. He . . . he got three degrees at Harvard. He's worked for Democrats and Republicans—whoever will get him the next step. He's running for mayor . . . he's never stood for anything . . . there's not a single principle that's lasted more than an election cycle . . . and I'm listening to him blowing smoke up our asses, with really obvious platitudes and I—it offends me that I'm supposed to look up to someone like this. But they're all like this. And it just . . . ."

She waited quietly.

"It makes me angry," he said. "They're all hollow, superficial men, and it makes me want to raise the black flag and . . . ," he shook his head.

"What?" she asked.

"Flag," he said, and put the tiles down. "It's not a great word, but . . . ."

"No, it's a good word."

He gave her a look. "Don't you start humoring me too."

"I'm sorry he made you mad."

"I wanted to go ballistic, right there."

She raised her eyebrows. "But you didn't, did you?"

"No. Because . . . because . . . you can't really, can you."

"No."

"You have to play along to get along."

"Hedonist!" she said

"What?"

She started putting tiles down. "Eight letter word!"

"Wow."

"I'm really impressed with myself!"

"Yeah."

She looked back up at him. "Your turn."

"Thanks."

He stared down at his tiles. He looked over at the board.

She cleared her throat. "This . . . this isn't really about your job, is it?"

He shook his head. "No . . . no . . . it's not. Although that doesn't help."

"No," she agreed.

"Sometimes I think I've made a terrible mistake. Sometimes I want to change everything about my life."

She didn't say anything.

"Goblin!" he said.

Yowl! Yowl!

A pot fell in the kitchen.

"Great word!" said Mari. "Really great!" She turned toward the kitchen. "Caramel! Stop . . . ," she paused and looked over to the other side of the apartment, where Caramel was still crouched under the lamp. "That's weird."

"Yeah," James said. "Odd." He started writing down the score.

"Maybe I'll put her in the bathroom tonight."

James looked at the ceiling. "Actually, you know, the board's kind of full now, maybe we should call it a game."

She looked at him. "Really? But . . . you just got a good word. If we quit now you won't be able to catch up."

"That's okay."

"Are you sure?"

"Congratulations."

She shrunk into herself a bit. "You never really like this game."

"I enjoyed playing it with you."

"Thank you," she said, but she didn't come out.

He looked at her. She didn't look back. He sighed. She got up. She walked into the bedroom and closed the door behind her. He walked over to the kitchen and washed the heaviest dishes—the pots and pans. He picked up the pot that had fallen and put it in the sink. He walked over to the futon and picked up his laptop. He played war games until his eyes dropped, and he fell asleep. Leaderless, his troops begged for mercy from the slaughter until his computer went to sleep too.

Only then did Leptin and Gherin crawl out of the kitchen's shadows.

Yowl!

They both turned to stare at her, their eyes gleaming. Caramel ran into the bathroom.

They turned their eyes to the sleeping James.

"Is strange," Leptin said, hanging from the ceiling. "See man. Memories come. Like flood. Over head. Breathe air of many years ago. See old battles. Look man again? Nothing. Just man. Memory strange. Humans strange."

"Yah," Gherin said. "Kill man. Make woman happy."

"Kkkkkkccccckkkkkkhs!" Leptin said sternly. "Culture human! Wizard make treaty!"

"Pffff," said Gherin. "Him not want be culture human. Listen him. He want be wild. Want so much." Gherin smiled and flashed his claws.

Leptin shook his head sadly. "Him no wild."

"No," said Gherin. "But girl want wild."

"Maybe."

"Give what want."

"Kkkkkkcccccckkkkkkhs!"

"But—"

"Gherin! Me admit wrong! See for real! Why you not same?"

"But—"

"She drool in sleep too, Gherin."

Gherin sighed. "Yah."

"Come. Got work." Leptin skittered over to the window. From the ceiling he unfastened the latch and slipped out.

From the ground Gherin followed, slipping over to the window. "But beautiful," he muttered. "Most beautiful girl in world." He stepped through to meet Leptin on the first escape, and they closed it behind them, then scampered out into the night.

Chapter 10

"Floor shiny," said Gherin.

The dome of San Francisco's city hall is the fifth largest in the world. Built nine years after the great 1906 earthquake, it looks like a classical triumph of white marble and towers … unless you look closely. To the careful observer, the patterns in the floors and the walls, the sconces on the ceilings, the details in the rotunda, are far more complicated than anything ever found in ancient Rome or Greece. Some of the patterns are distinct. Different. Perhaps unprecedented.

They were the product of architect Arthur Brown Jr., a respected and sociable fellow who was said to have grown strangely cold and obsessive during the construction, screaming at workers over the smallest of details – the doorknobs chosen, the font put on the signs. He was, history suggests, on the verge of a nervous collapse when his wife implored the City Fathers to pay his final commission and send him home.

Brown went into seclusion for several months following the celebrated opening, then sprang back to his life, denying that there had ever been a strain. He went on to build other monuments in San Francisco – the Opera House, Coit Tower – and even government buildings in Washington D.C.. But by then he was known as a minimalist who strove to keep excess complexity from ruining the power of simple lines and forms. He spoke little of his earlier triumphs. He died in 1957, delirious, murmuring that it all had to be torn down.

"Big shiny," Gherin added.

The goblins looked around the darkened basement level below city hall. Down here the ceilings were far lower than they were in the vast stories above. The basement was sturdy and cavernous, with pillars: the way Imperial Rome might have designed a basement. Leptin nodded his approval.

"Yah." Leptin said.

"How they get shiny floor?"

"Not know."

"Maybe got shiny rocks."

It was dark now: only the occasional maintenance light showed the shape of the hallways underground. They approved.

They crouched through the hallways looking for a scent, a sign, an echo of a trail. When they were finished they went around it all again.

"No good," said Gherin.

"No good," said Leptin. He stroked his chin. "Must get deeper."

"Deeper?"

"Yah."

Gherin stomped his foot on the ground. "Knew not trust shiny floor."

"Yah. Evil floor," Leptin agreed. "Go under. Where?"

"Hmmmmmm." Gherin looked around. "Soldier man fight Mersechquestun, so hole be man-big."

"Yah," Leptin said thoughtfully. "Door. Stairway. Secret place." They looked at each other, then scampered down the corridors a third time.

There were many doors in the basement: doors to the Department of Elections and the lockers for the security guards and the janitorial staff. All of them contained closets to look in and suspicious mounds of carpeting to get under. Leptin muttered under his breath: this was not good hunting. Worse, every office had a portrait of a past city official, and Gherin insisted on reading the names on each frame and checking to see if they were mentioned in his city guidebook. "Ooooo," he said once. "Him first Chinese commissioner public works. Big step forward oppressed minority."

At times like those, Leptin just stared.

The door to the offices of the city's Ethics Commission had two extra locks.

Leptin raised his eyebrows as he sprung them with his talons. The wooden double doors creaked and distant echoes came back, as though a hundred far away doors had been pried open. Gherin shrugged.

The office carpet reeked of ancient blood. They were amazed they hadn't smelled it before. "Liked shiny floor better," Gherin said and Leptin nodded.

"Floor new," he said. "Someone put in, hide old things."

Gherin growled.

Once inside it took them two minutes to find the trap door in the supply closet in the back of the executive director's office. When its padlock was sprung, it creaked open with the same sound the double doors had made. It was the sound, they realized, of a much bigger door opening long, long ago, echoing through these smaller repetitions.

"Sounds like door of Montrose castle cell when Skvag walk to get head cut off," Gherin said as he looked down the hole below. Once, he could tell, a ladder had stood there. Now it was gone.

"Nah," said Leptin. "Sounds like doors of last Khan's palace opening to assassins."

"You say so."

"There, twelve assassins, from mountain, come kill Khan. Terrible day. Big knives," Leptin said.

"Whose side you?"

"Khan."

Gherin looked up to stare at him.

"Leptin . . . ," Gherin said cautiously. "Was thirteen assassins."

Leptin turned to look at him sharply. "Twelve."

Gherin shook his head.

"You there?" Leptin asked.

"Nah," said Gherin. "But hear story. Old lore-teller say thirteen. Always."

Leptin growled. "Was there. Big knives."

Gherin grinned. "You old. Memory old."

Leptin swatted Gherin on the head. Gherin flinched, then chuckled.

"Remember face every enemy," Leptin said.

Gherin was still laughing as he jumped down the hole.

Leptin snarled and muttered. "Hate you whole family," then scampered after.

The tunnel went twenty feet down. They landed gracefully and stood back-to-back, looking around the pitch black cavern. Once the walls had been square and carved into blocks. Once, the floor had been smooth and even. Once, the room had been full of pillars. Now everything was cracked and disjoined—half of the pillars lay in pieces around them.

"Huh," said Gherin.

"Earthquakes," said Leptin. "Old room. Big quakes. Ground shift. Room crack. Go boom."

"Ooooo," said Gherin. "Boom."

"Yah."

Gherin scratched his head. "No repair?"

Leptin shrugged. "Lazy."

Gherin shook his head. "Nah. Humans got lotsa buildings. Fall down, build again. Real nice building on top this hole. Big dome. Pretty. Somebody know this here. Got ladder. Got locks. Why no repair?"

Leptin scowled. "Secret room?"

Gherin nodded. "Yah. Think so. Somebody got secret. This room part."

Leptin's scowl deepened. "Think who?"

Gherin's ears twitched in thought. "City parks commissioner."

Leptin blinked.

"Saw portrait in office. Look suspicious," Gherin explained.

Leptin shook his head and turned back to the room.

"Got sloping forehead," said Gherin. "Like gnome."

Leptin pointed. "Used be hallway there, but collapse long time."

"Want eat gnome."

"Yah, tasty." Leptin bent down and put his hand to the floor. "Mersechquestun hunt here," he said.

Gherin kneeled down too. Put his ear to the floor. "Yah. Stone still scream."

Leptin sighed. "Hard believe dead."

Gherin nodded, his ear still to the ground. "How mouse kill?"

"Not know. Not know how kill Mersechquestun." Leptin considered. "Maybe poke in eye."

"Mouse got big legend," said Gherin.

"Yah."

"You meet mouse?"

"Yah."

"When?"

"Blood Oasis War."

"What like?"

Leptin turned his head. "Ask now?"

Gherin lifted his head up from the ground. "Stone go away? Scream long time."

Leptin sighed. "Mouse . . . mouse hero. Always want do right. Always want save world. Always think big victory close. Just over hill. Just past forest. Just in cave. So good make speech, so good make fight, you think too."

Gherin nodded thoughtfully.

"Better killer you?"

The cavern was silent.

"Different," Leptin said at last.

"Yah?"

Leptin took a deep breath. "Mouse . . . better killer. Leptin better survivor."

Gherin scratched his head. "Yah?"

Leptin pursed his lips and licked his fangs. "Yah. Mouse kill Mersechquestun. Leptin never try kill Mersechquestun. Never think: got kill Mersechquestun today. So mouse get kill Leptin not. Get good kill like that. Yah?"

Gherin nodded. "Yah."

"Leptin survive battle Goren Vaj. Mouse never fight Goren Vaj. Leptin hide in corpse. Mouse never think hide in corpse. Mouse never learn survive fight no win, just fight harder. Mouse fight Goren Vaj, mouse die. Someday, Mouse fight harder, die. Leptin survive. Yah?"

Gherin turned this over and over in his mind. "Yah."

"Okay."

"Okay."

"Track now."

Gherin put his ear back on the stone floor. He listened for a few moments, and pointed. "Louder."

Cautiously they crept toward the northwest side of the cavern. Gherin put his ear back on the ground and nodded, pointing. They were getting closer to the place where the ancient beast had eaten its victims . . . and the epicenter of the fight that killed it.

There had once been a hallway here, but it had been filled in with rubble from an earthquake more than a hundred years ago. That same earthquake, however, had opened a jagged and narrow passageway through a wall and around to the other side of the blockage.

They looked around the rest of the room first, before going near this new tunnel. In the far corner, Gherin lifted something up between his fingers, hidden in the deepest shadows.

"What got?"

Gherin held it up, careful not to let it slip through his fingers. "Dander. Little fur."

"Ohhhhh," said Leptin.

"Yah," said Gherin. "Not belong here."

"Fuzzy?" asked Leptin.

"Yah."

"White?"

"Yah."

Leptin nodded. "Good."

Gherin considered asking, but instead put it, very carefully, in a pouch.

The room cleared, they looked ahead toward the cracks in the wall that could get them around the blocked tunnel. Gherin moved forward, but Leptin held his hand out, stopping him.

"Wait."

Gherin looked up. "Yah?"

Leptin hesitated. He sniffed the air. He blinked his eyes. He did not speak until he was sure. "Big problem."

Gherin's eyes darted back and forth. "Yah?"

Leptin nodded. "Missing. All missing."

"What?"

"Should seen sooner. Last monster. No think good."

Gherin looked around again. "What?"

Leptin pursed his lips. "We fight. Goblins fight. Fight claws. Fight swords. Fight daggers. Fight iron rods. Fight potions and powders. Yah?"

"Yah," Gherin agreed.

"Mouse too," said Leptin.

Gherin thought for a moment. "Yah."

Leptin shook his head. "But humans fight . . . marine say brought guns. We no bring guns. Explosives. Modern war."

"Okay . . . ," Gherin said, hesitantly.

"So . . . ," Leptin looked around. "Where shell casings? Where holes in stone? Where blast marks? Where bones? Flesh bits?"

Gherin blinked. "Gone?"

"Yah. Gone. Why?"

Gherin stroked his chin. "Mouse . . . clean up?"

Leptin shook his head. "Why?"

Gherin grimaced. "Dunno."

"Last site clean too," Leptin said. "Have bomb. Trap for goblins. Not like mouse clean up, and marine say no leave trap. So not mouse."

Gherin nodded. "Not mouse. So who?"

"White fur. Dander. Mouse?"

Gherin considered. He pulled it out again. Sniffed it. "Not mouse."

"Got guess. But this know: this site clean. So . . . ."

"Got bomb?"

Leptin nodded slowly. Pointed to the crack in the wall. "Narrow tunnel good spot put bomb."

Gherin considered. "What do?"

Leptin motioned and they stepped back. He looked around and picked a rock up off the floor. He eyed the rough tunnel carefully, then hurled it inside, skipping it off the tunnel floor. It clacked around, then came to rest out of sight.

Leptin grimaced. He looked around and found another stone. He moved to a different angle from the tunnel, and hurled it in, again bouncing it off the floor. It clacked against the wall and hit the floor again—an explosion. A shockwave followed by a short fireball. The blast echoed through the chamber. They covered their ears too late, and grimaced in pain.

When it was over, Gherin whistled. It harmonized with the ringing in his head. "Bigger boom, last time."

Leptin nodded. "Much big boom. Okay look now."

They crept forward, Leptin in the lead, looking over every inch of surface as they crawled into the tunnel. The floor was clean of small rocks, dust, and debris: it had all been pushed out or obliterated by the blast.

"Clues gone," Gherin said.

"Nah," said Leptin. "We find something. Did last time. They good clean, not great."

Gherin considered. "Maybe leave note?"

"Heh. Yah. Leave note on floor."

"Not floor." Gherin pointed. "Wrote on wall."

Just past the tunnel, out into the next room . . . where they could hear the stone scream loudest . . . there was writing in red on the far wall.

It said, in an uneven hand not entirely familiar with human letters:

If you're still alive, we should make a deal.

"Oooooooooh," said Leptin.

"Oooooooooh," said Gherin.

Chapter 11

They emerged from the hole an hour later, and locked the closet door behind them. They heard noises from the south side of the basement, perhaps a janitor pushing a cart outside of the Department of Elections, and left through a small door on the northwest side.

They crawled from bush to bush in the darkness, looking for an alleyway to run to when they were sure no cars were passing and no cultured and domestic humans were stumbling back from a late night show or party. It's easy to hide from culture humans: they only see what they expect to see. They'd find a hiding place for morning easily enough. Perhaps, Leptin muttered, they shouldn't stay with the same two humans again. It was creating arguments. Leptin held up a hand and motioned for Gherin to follow him across the street.

But Gherin was looking the other way.

Leptin turned. Gestured.

Gherin stared at a massive stone building across the street.

Leptin skittered back. "What?" he hissed. "What see?"

"Opera," Gherin whispered reverently.

"Where?" Leptin held his claws out.

Gherin blinked. "Big building. Stone. Pillars."

"Like castle," Leptin agreed.

"Yah."

"Bad castle," Leptin said. "Easy invade. No good choke points."

"Is where opera play," explained Gherin.

"Ahhh." Leptin nodded, understanding. "Opera weak. Easy conquer."

Gherin shook his head. "Heard stone scream tonight."

"Yah."

"What think it takes make stone sing?"

57

Leptin scratched his head. "Alchemist? Maybe hammer?"

Gherin shook his head. "Go now."

"Maybe bottle wine?" Leptin said.

"Can go now," Gherin repeated. "Just wanted look."

"Yah," said Leptin. "Go now. Think maybe . . . ," he stopped.

Gherin waited, his ears pricking up.

"Gherin?"

"Yah?"

"Got knife in pouch?"

"Yah."

"Give."

"Cheese or war knife?"

"Cheese."

A moment later, Gherin handed him a cheese knife, handle first. Leptin bent it in half and dropped it on the ground. "War," he said.

Gherin slipped a wickedly edged dagger into his hand. "Not good," he muttered. "Butter spread uneven."

Leptin pivoted, facing back toward City Hall, and hurled the dagger into a bush at the edge of the lawn. A squeal pierced the air. But not for long.

Leptin walked over. Lying in the dirt, nearly cut in half, was a large rat. Leptin nodded to himself.

Gherin looked at the rat's tracks. "Follow us?"

"Yah."

Gherin picked the knife up out of the ground and licked the blade clean. "Too bad kill. Learn who sent."

"Know who sent."

"Ah," said Gherin. "Yah." He pursed his lips. "Need oregano."

Chapter 12

The Japanese Tea Garden in Golden Gate Park was created for the 1894 World's Fair by a minor member of the Japanese aristocracy, Makoto Hagiwara.

The humans don't really know this story. The rabbits and dogs have their own version, that they hardly ever tell. Only the rats and the spiders tell it correctly.

There were very few Japanese people in America by the 1890s, and Hagiwara did not have to leave his homeland. But lying on a straw mat, he dreamed of land. Of forests, of rivers, of mountains: in his dreams, he tilled their soil and turned them into perfect gardens, their borders running together so that one could not even say what kind of land it was – only that it was beautiful.

Japan is a very small island – and his family's wealth could not change that. Every acre that he could till belonged to someone else, and had been tended by their family for generations. His dreams were too big for a society so old.

So he boarded a ship. Sailed to the biggest, youngest, state in the biggest, youngest, country in the world. Became its most unlikely frontiersman.

Came to San Francisco.

A wealthy Japanese nobleman settling into a five-dollar-a-week room at the Cable Car Hotel was an oddity. The San Francisco Examiner treated his arrival as though he were a reverse Marco Polo (they thought all Asians were Chinese) coming to learn about their ways, rather than one more homesteader. It was seen as something of a joke, in the Chamber of Commerce, when Hagiwara offered to improve the landscaping behind the San Raphael timber mill for a mere $50. He didn't even need the money.

But he got the job. Why not? It would be funny.

He set to work himself, hiring no help – not even the Chinese laborers they assumed he would pick up for pennies to do his heavy lifting. He took off his shirt and tilled the soil. He felt the soil between his fingers, and every dream he'd ever had came rushing to his head as his soft hands finally became dirty.

He finished exactly on time, and no one laughed. What had once been an angry crag leading to a mill on the Gold River had become a serene path winding through three man-made hills, and each hill served to blunt the angry scream of the mill saw. A perch atop each hill afforded a perfect view of the other two: one whose rose petals perfectly matched the color of the setting sun, one where the scent of lilac flowers blended serenely with the smell of hard woods, one whose cherry blossoms danced in the gentle wind. The mill's workers brought their families on Sunday to picnic. "Yes," they said proudly, "this is where your father works."

Hagiwara was hired to renovate the grounds around the Wells Fargo bank. This time, he was offered $500.

"Baron" Hagiwara, as they now called him, did not disappoint. By 1890 he was designing estates for the wealthy. They called it an "oriental" style because they did not understand how original it was.

When plans for the 1894 World's Fair in San Francisco were being drawn up, Hagiwara approached the city with an offer: let him design America's only Japanese Tea Garden on an acre of land in Golden Gate Park – a tribute to his homeland, and an exhibit no other World's Fair had ever had.

The city agreed, and Hagiwara set to work. Finally he could turn this alien landscape, as unfamiliar to him as the surface of the moon, into the shape of his home. Making it beautiful on its own terms had only been practice for making it beautiful on his. He smiled every day for a year.

The fair arrived and the Japanese Tea Garden was filled with gentle hills and a pond with little rolling tributaries, and women in traditional Japanese robes serving tea with little cookies that contained predictions of the future. It was the first time a "fortune cookie" was ever served in the United States.

The fair went and the city asked if Hagiwara would let the garden stay. Hagiwara made a counter-offer: he would let the garden remain, and even expand it from one acre to five, if the city agreed that he and his family could live on it and tend it for the next 100 years.

The city agreed. John McLaren, the superintendent of parks and the one man Hagiwara considered a worthy colleague, sealed the arrangement with a handshake.

Hagiwara built a small cottage on five acres, and moved there from the Cable Car Hotel. History does not record where his family came from – whether they were other Japanese living in California, or if he finally allowed his parents to make the arranged marriage they had always insisted upon – nor do the animals care. The dogs and the rabbits and the ducks only speak of how much the family loved each other, while the rats and the spiders remember just how carefully Makoto Hagiwara tended every blade of grass, and how his family dutifully, lovingly, followed in his footsteps. He brought in rare plants from across the ocean, and spared no expense on soil. His ancestral fortune dwindled as the garden thrived, and he considered it a worthy exchange.

Then, in 1900, the city took it away.

The dogs and the rabbits and the ducks love this part of the story. To them, this is the most important point: that the city took the Tea Garden away from the Hagiwara family in 1900 because it was extremely successful and because, after all, he was only a slant-eyed foreigner who, rather than tending to their buildings and homes, had isolated himself on a piece of city property. Who, with his devotion to some alien tradition, was surely standing in the way of progress. They don't really understand the reasons the city father's gave, the dogs and rabbits and ducks, only that Hagiwara could no longer afford to live in the Cable Car Hotel, and was forced into a shanty home on H Street. He demanded to see John McLaren, to hold him to their agreement, but McLaren always had an excuse.

At this point the dogs howl and the rabbits stomp their feet, as they are told of the Hagiwara family's suffering: how they turned H Street into "Japanese Village," and cooked for sailors as a way to live, though by this time other restaurants served fortune cookies.

And the dogs laugh and the ducks cackle as they hear how, year after year, the Tea Garden turned decrepit and decayed, until, in 1907, the City Fathers sent John McLaren to Japanese Village to offer to lease the Tea Garden to Makoto Hagiwara for $1 a year if he would return to his little house, now in need of repair, and tend to the garden again.

A bargain was struck, and McLaren vowed never again to let politics interfere with friendship.

That is where the story usually stops for the dogs and the rabbits and the ducks. But the rats and the spiders know better. They know that this is only a prelude. A rehearsal.

For the story goes on.

Makoto Hagiwara died in 1924, and his children spent the rest of their inheritance upon bridges and stones to cross the garden streams, and lived in the small house their father had arranged. The garden was tended by Goro Hagiwara, and then George Hagiwara – who had been born in America.

It flourished for almost 20 years.

This time, when the government came, it brought an army.

In 1942 the Hagiwara family was shipped off to a Japanese internment camp in Arizona, where they stared out of barbed wire at a desert without flowers. Once again, John McLaren – still in charge of the parks – did not remember his handshake. Once again, white businessmen took over their family's work. They renamed it the "Oriental Tea Garden" and brought in Chinese women to serve fortune cookies. When the garden fell into decrepitude and disrepair again, the city decided that perhaps that was its natural state. Had it ever really been beautiful?

By the time the Hagiwara family was released in 1946, their home had collapsed. They petitioned the city to let them return to tend the garden Makoto had built with his own fortune, but the the city refused. The tea concession was valuable. The city refused to pay for their home, or compensate them for their labor. The 100 year agreement had lasted less than 50.

But in 1974 the city put a bronze plaque in the now renamed "Japanese Tea Garden" to honor the Hagiwara family's service. It sits on a rock, little seen, in a garden that every visitor agrees is lovely – but that is unrecognizable compared to what it once was.

The spiders and the rats and their followers gather in the garden every year on the anniversary of Baron Makoto Hagiwara's death, to tell this story and to mock the plaque. This … this! … they remind themselves, is the reward for virtue in the human's world. This is what being good in a high culture gets you. Never forget, they tell their children, if you ever think that human society is ever anything more than accidentally kind: this is all they give to those who give so much.

It is the only celebration of Makoto Hagiwara that San Francisco has. He could never have imagined, when he left Japan, that the people who best remembered him would be rats.

"Life is not fair," said Willie O'Shaughnessy, holding his cards close to his chest.

The duke of rats snorted. He held his cards loosely, so that if someone just strained their neck a little he might be able to see what they were. It was as though the duke wanted you to try and look.

The duke of rats' great-grandfather had once ruled the Tea Garden: it had once been their family seat. Then there had been a revolution.

"What I'm telling you," said Willie, "is that there's not a beautiful spot on this earth that wasn't fought over by someone, some time. A place this good has to have a tragic history."

The duke shook his head. "Land," he says. "It always comes back to land, for you."

They were sitting on a pair of large mushrooms near the giant statue of the Buddha. A Happy Meal carton sat between them, open and empty except for a small collection of scraps of paper.

"No, no," said Willie. "It comes back to who gets to live on it. That's a slightly different thing."

"You do love playing your games," said the duke. "But I wonder . . . ," he picked a scrap of paper out from underneath his royal sash. "What would you say if I were to raise you a two story on Hyde street, near the pier?"

He tossed the scrap into the Happy Meal box.

Willie's whiskers twitched. "Water front," he said. "Must have a hell of a hand."

The duke's tail flipped from left to right. "Naturally you think I'm bluffing," he said. "You think everyone has a price, and so you assume that everyone is always bluffing."

"Does this building have a story?" This was a private game: just the two of them. The other O'Shaughnessy boys were out at a party thrown by a mole who lived under a jazz club. Aaron had seen to it that Bevan would be the guest of honor: it was a way to meet voters.

"The upstairs unit is a spacious apartment. The downstairs is a very sad ice cream parlor that . . . ."

An extra ripple in the pond was all the warning they had that company had come.

"Cards," said Leptin, emerging around one side of the Buddha statue, behind Willie. "Always cards you two."

"Maybe got problem?" asked Gherin, slipping around the other side, behind the duke. "Get help? Maybe try drinking?"

"Welcome back," Willie said, putting his cards down slowly, so no one could see them. "How have you been enjoying my city?"

"Your city," muttered the duke, who slid his cards together into a single row and slipped them in his sash pocket.

Willie frowned. "Taking the cards out of sight cancels the game, your Grace. You know that."

The duke smiled. "I was bluffing. Terrible hand."

"Well played."

"Thank you."

"Our turn," said Leptin. "Play goblin game."

"Yah," said Gherin. "Eat rabbit."

"Rules easy," said Leptin. "Learn quick."

Willie tapped his foot on the ground. "Your problem," he said, "is not knowing that the house always wins."

The duke of rats snapped his claws together. "Let us demonstrate."

From underneath the pagoda shaped souvenir shop, a thousand whiskers rustled. Rats emerged by the hundreds, pouring out into the garden and circling everyone, gnashing their teeth.

"I believe," the duke said, "that this changes the odds."

Leptin scratched his head. "Maybe. Maybe no."

"Rats," said Gherin, smiling, "good with cheese."

The duke's eyes narrowed. "At the very least you must admit that it makes a fight pointless. Even if you could win, by the time you got through the vanguard my friend and I would be long gone. And then what would you have?"

"Food," said Gherin.

The duke's jaw clenched. "The glib response of a doomed man."

"Huh?" Gherin scratched his head. "You no like food?" He turned to Leptin, who shrugged.

The rats stared at them and twitched, waiting for an order.

"Gentlemen! Gentlemen!" said Willie O'Shaughnessy. "Let's not fool ourselves. You're not here for a fight: you came back for a reason. You realized you've been doing things wrong. You realized you can't just come into my city . . . ."

"*Your* city," muttered the duke of rats.

" . . . and start turning over rocks. That's not how things work here. You have to come with a gift. I said we could make a deal, but you didn't want that. But now you see: I know where the mouse went, and I can have him cleaned up after for as long as it takes. You may be hot stuff in goblin town, but this is my city, and you need to acknowledge that."

"Your city," muttered the duke of rats.

"The good news for you," said Willie, "is that we're not here for a fight either."

Leptin and Gherin exchanged glances.

"Let me get straight," said Leptin. "There place named Goblin Town?"

"Where?" asked Gherin.

Willie and the duke glanced at each other.

"That's not the point," said Willie.

"Maybe want visit," said Gherin. "Sound nice."

Willie's ears twitched. "All I meant was—"

The duke held up his hand. "Willie," he said, "if I may. My colleague thought the place you came here from was called 'Goblin Town.' Obviously he was wrong. The important thing is: we know where the mouse is, and we want to make a deal."

"Make . . . deal?" Gherin asked. "With rabbit?"

"A rabbit who knows something," said the duke. "That's altogether different."

"Little different," Leptin admitted.

"Not when got garlic sauce," said Gherin.

Willie stamped his foot on the ground. "You can keep searching and I can keep blocking you! My boys can clean up after the mouse's every move! Or I can tell you where he is. You're the ones in a hurry, not me."

The goblins looked at each other again.

"Okaaaaay . . . ," said Leptin.

"For sake argument, never heard 'bout garlic sauce," said Gherin.

" . . . what want?" Leptin finished.

"Ah, that's more like it," said the duke.

Willie flashed his famous smile. "This is the good part. We want you to start a war."

The goblins looked at each other.

Finally, Leptin asked: "You like fight trolls?"

Willie's smile only fell for a moment. "No no, we'll pick the sides."

"Trolls good," said Leptin. "Got big rocks. Also tusks."

"Sounds lovely, but it won't suit the purpose."

"Okay." Leptin shrugged. "Who want fight?"

Willie's smile widened. "The rats," he said, "and the rabbits."

Gherin and Leptin exchanged glances. Finally, Leptin spoke up. "What you do," he said to the duke of rats, "is punch him. Real hard."

The duke tittered. "No no, dear boy. Not him and me, our respective peoples. Or more broadly, our peoples' peoples."

Leptin shook his head. "Still gotta punch him."

"Please allow me to explain."

Leptin sighed. "Never win war this way."

Gherin hit him in the arm. "Story time," he said.

Leptin scowled, but was silent.

"That's better," said Willie, smiling. "If you listen, you can learn something. I notice you boys always talk."

"That's a common character flaw," said the duke of rats, rolling his eyes. "Even among those who should know better."

Willie's nose crinkled. "What are you saying, Reginald?"

"Absolutely nothing."

Willie showed his front teeth.

"Now then," the duke said. "Perhaps you are aware that it is in the nature of dynasties to rise and fall."

Leptin groaned and hit his forehead with his hand.

The duke smiled wanly. "I appreciate your sincerity. It's so hard to find in politics and poker. But of course that's because it's counter-productive. The very reason Willie and I can be friends is that we are both insincere enough not to let our peoples' well-earned animosity get in the way of our goals."

Willie's whisker's quivered. "That's a very eloquent way to put it, your grace. You're a good talker."

"Touché."

Leptin flexed his fingers and clicked the claws loudly, one at a time, on the Buddha's pedestal.

Willie and the duke looked at each other. The duke cleared his throat. "Look," said Willie, "it's like this. For a long time this city was ruled by the nobility. You got nobility where you come from?"

"Nah," said Gherin. "But know what is."

"Okay," said Willie. "Well, around here, the noble families are the spiders and the snakes and the cats . . . and the rats, like my insincere friend here. They used to own this place tight. History says they got the deed from a Spanish priest, back when that counted for something, and held on ever since. Did all right for themselves. But about fifty years ago things changed. My people got hungry, got organized, and now the rabbits and the seagulls and the dogs and all the rest have a piece of the pie."

"What kind pie?" asked Gherin.

Willie smiled wide. "It's filled with money."

Gherin and Leptin looked at each other skeptically.

The duke of rats sighed. "There is no actual pie. He means that about half of San Francisco is now controlled by the old aristocracy, and half by the descendants of the young rebels, who perhaps, someday, will figure out what to do with it."

"Why no pie?" asked Gherin.

"Why no Goblin Town?" asked the duke.

Gherin scratched his chin. "Huh."

Willie stomped his foot on the ground three times. "Are you paying attention?"

"Must be," said Leptin. "Still bored."

Gherin punched his friend in the shoulder again. "No, is interesting," he said. "Maybe pie. Not sure."

"Maybe war," said Leptin. "Not sure."

"If you want to find the mouse, you listen," said Willie. "If you won't even listen, we can't do business."

Leptin looked at Gherin. Gherin shrugged. Leptin sighed. Gherin sighed. Around them, a thousand rats twitched their tails.

The scent of betrayal filled the Japanese Tea Garden. Everyone was quiet for a while.

"All right," said Willie. "That's better." He took a breath. "The trouble is my highly pedigreed friend here is right. My associates don't really know what to do with the territory they've won. They just sit on it when there's real money to be made. And his people?" He looked over at the duke.

The duke of rats closed his eyes. "I fear the aristocracy is too content to rest on its shrinking laurels. Without bold action, the body politic is in stagnation and we are in decline."

"We're sitting on a gold mine, but they're treating it like a cave," Willie agreed. "Something must be done."

"War?" asked Leptin, his ears perking up.

Willie smiled. "That's right."

"There's so much of mutual interest we could do . . . with the proper positioning," said the duke. "Alas, Rose the spider queen blocks me at every turn due to an old misunderstanding about silk. If I move against her directly, it's civil war. But if she is killed by outsiders I can be a war leader. The pieces are in place."

"It's easy," Willie said. "The only one who might be able to beat my boy Bevan in the election is the incumbent, Handsome Gavin. He's protected by some ugly, ugly, dogs—but I think you'll like that."

"Listening."

"Yes," said the duke. "The only hard part about Queen Rose will be finding her, and I can make that easy. You don't have to make her suffer, but I think after you meet her you'll want to." He tilted his head and considered for a moment. "Honestly, though, I thought her spiders would have found you by now. Are there really no spiders where you're hiding?"

"Nope," said Gherin. "Taste like chicken."

The duke nodded. "That's the spirit. When all's said and done, we'll send agents to take you right to the mouse. You do whatever you want with him, we don't much care, provided that when you're finished you leave and put all this ugliness behind you. Perhaps you can go someplace with pie."

"Listening."

"That's our deal," said Willie. "Everyone gets what they want." He hesitated, then held his paw out. "Let's shake on it like businessmen."

Leptin looked at Gherin, and a message passed between them.

Leptin spit on the ground. "Nah."

"Excuse me?"

"Nah."

Gherin shook his head. "No pie."

The duke's teeth gnashed. "Perhaps you don't understand the issues—"

Leptin spat again. "You think you sophisticated," he said. "You think. You think read book and live building mean no blood when kill. You think we no listen. We listen. You say 'war,' but think 'money.' We listen. Goblin not sophisticated. Got no Goblin Town. Okay. But we listen. Goblins got saying, 'no shake hands with venom maker.'"

"Yah," said Gherin. "Got that. Good saying."

"Is that so?" the duke of rats hissed, his eyes sinking into his head.

"We listen you. We see you. Venom maker. Not stupid."

Willie's foot stomped. "If you turn me down . . . ." His foot stomped. "If you come to my city . . . ."

"*Your* city," hissed the duke.

Willie's foot stomped. " . . .and turn me down," Stomp. "You will regret it. Everyone regrets it when they cross me." Stomp. "Everyone!" His foot started stomping faster than the eye could follow. "I'll sweep the mouse's tracks so clean you couldn't find it with a police bloodhound! And then I'll sick the bloodhounds on you! Do you hear me!"

"Hey Gherin?"

"Yah?"

"Heard rabbit taste like cheese."

"Mmmmmmmm."

The duke's tail lashed, and the hoard of rats charged. The duke vanished within them as Willie leaped away.

Chapter 13

That morning, the custodians at the Japanese Tea Garden were astonished to find the corpses of some five hundred rats fallen around the statue of the Buddha, some of the skeletons licked clean of meat. A newspaper columnist declared that it was the fault of homeless people living in the park, who keep them as pets. Police swept the parks for the next few weeks, with k9 units, to arrest the homeless and have them tested for diseases. The Tea Garden was closed for over a month.

No rabbit remains were found.

The newspaper columnist was hailed as a hero. "Finally," people said at parties, "someone had the guts to tell the truth about homelessness." A former sportswriter who had been given a shot as a political columnist, his career was made. He quickly became a respected man, instead of one more hack banging away at a keyboard in a dying industry. He gained access to the rich and powerful, the doors to closed meetings just seemed to fly open for him, and became known for his theories about what really went on in city politics. Never knowing that his biggest fan, and most influential reader, was a rabbit.

The odd thing, and this bothered him, was that his dog – his beloved mutt – seemed to treat him less respectfully. It ignored his commands and tried to run and … he was sure of this, somehow, though he didn't tell anyone because he knew how crazy it seemed … the dog rolled its eyes whenever he talked about politics.

Come to think of it, he considered one night after drinking Belgian beers in a Lower Haight bar with some friendly competitors, most animals didn't seem to like him much, anymore. He saw dogs on the street come up and lick his competition's hands, then turn their noses away from him. Cats had always been indifferent to him, but now they were aggressively so. Rats on top of municipal garbage cans hissed at him before scurrying away. What was that about? What had changed?

Chapter 14

From the safety of a pair of bushes they stared at the tall white tower for hours, until the full moon rose above it.

"Big tower," Leptin had said.

"Yah."

"Must got wizard."

Gherin shook his head. "Nah. High culture no got wizards."

"But . . . ," Leptin pointed. "Tower."

Gherin shrugged.

"Sure?"

Gherin hesitated, and they stared at the tower again. And again.

Leptin folded his arms. "Why tower like that, no got wizard?"

"Look pretty."

"So?"

Gherin shook his head. "High culture like pretty, no got wizards."

"Sure?"

They stared at the tower again, slipping into the shadows as a homeless man with a rat in his pocket came near, arguing about a newspaper column. They stopped, for a moment, looked around, then shuffled off into the distance.

Leptin watched them go. "World make more sense," he said, "got wizard in tower."

Gherin nodded slowly. "Think wizard got magic spam filter?"

Leptin stared at him. "Internet high culture. No got wizards."

Gherin squinted. "Wizard invent high culture. Yah? So maybe got blog. PayPal."

"Then," Leptin pointed. "Wizard in tower."

Gherin scowled. Scratched his head. "Huh."

"Yah," said Leptin. "High culture got wizard, wizard got email, wizard in tower." He smiled. "Logic."

"Ooooooo," said Gherin. "Where find?"

"Saw uncle use once," said Leptin. "Scary."

"Yah."

They both looked back at the tower.

Leptin took a deep breath. "Gotta have wizard," he said.

"Nah," said Gherin.

"Maybe small wizard?"

"Nah."

At last, when the moon was high, Gherin settled the argument by bolting forward through the trees up to the tower and scaling the wall. Gherin's claws clutched into the white stone as Leptin held his breath. He looked first to the tower's rooftop arches—fire might spring forth from the open arches on top—and then to the sky. Lightning might come crashing down from the sky. But those were only the simple options. Wizards could be subtle. The most dangerous ones were.

But Gherin made it to the roof, stood between the stone arches, and waved. Leptin cursed, licked his pointy teeth, and ran up the side as well. His ears were pitched forward, his teeth bared, his heart still and calm—the way it got before any battle in which he expected to die.

There was no fighting on the roof of the tower. Just Gherin and a few loose boards and a recycling bin.

"See?" Gherin said. "No wizard."

Leptin looked around, and nodded. "No make sense," he muttered.

"High culture," Gherin said again.

"No make sense."

"Look," said Gherin, pointing to the city that now sprawled beneath them. "Safe. No goblins. No dragons. No faceless marauders. Big streets. Tall building. Good cheese. Zagat guide. Opera. See?"

Leptin looked out over the city and bared his teeth.

"No make sense," Leptin said. "Why wizard make high culture, no got wizards?"

"Not know. But ... no wizard."

Leptin looked around one more time. "Yah."

Gherin sighed. "Good view."

"Bridge better."

"Yah," Gherin admitted. "Bridge better."

They looked down at the buildings and the lights, their backs to the ocean.

"Big city," said Gherin.

"Yah."

Far away, a cab and a bus honked their horns.

"Got lots place hide."

Leptin blew air through his teeth. "Find easy, no stupid rabbit."

"You sure rabbit taste like cheese?"

"Not think be hard. Find mouse easy. Not take long."

"Yah," Gherin said, looking back out over the city. "Rabbit enemy, make hard."

"Yah." Leptin bared his teeth at the city again. "Yah."

Gherin's ears went flat. "Give up?"

Leptin's hand shot out and punched his friend, hard. "Nah."

"Ok. But, can't track mouse."

"Yah."

Gherin's ears perched forward. "Got plan?"

Leptin nodded.

"Ooooooo," said Gherin. "Plan!"

Leptin nodded again. "Rabbit hide mouse. Can't track mouse."

"Yah."

"But mouse hunting. Rabbit not know what mouse hunt. But goblins know. Goblins know what mouse hunt."

This time Gherin nodded. Then he smiled. "Goblin watch symbols, mouse show up!"

"Yah."

"Plan!" said Gherin hopping up and down. "Good plan! Stupid rabbit! No even taste like cheese!"

Leptin shook his head and waited for his younger friend to calm down. He looked out over the city, at the tiny human people walking below, at the tall glass skyscrapers looming above. He wondered if there was as much about the world inside them that he didn't understand as there was in the places that high culture had given up. The world he knew was vast and dangerous and beautiful in ways he suspected these frail, talkative, creatures could not see. He wondered if the wizard had understood, when he made the pact protecting culture humans, that someday his descendants would forget he ever existed, deny the very possibility that he could have been real. Leptin stifled a yawn. Maybe. Wizards could be subtle that way.

"Leptin?"

Here it was. "Yah?"

"Not know ancient symbols."

"Nope."

Gherin nodded somberly. "How track?"

Leptin took a deep breath. "Need mapwyrd."

"Ooooooo."

"Yah."

"San Francisco got mapwyrd?"

Leptin shook his head. "Need go find."

"Ooooooo."

"Yah."

Gherin scratched his forehead. "Ever meet mapwyrd?"

Leptin nodded. "Yah. Good soldier need good map."

Gherin nodded. "Me no meet."

"Tricky. How find mapwyrd, no got map? Paradox."

Gherin closed his eyes to think about this for a moment. "Got answer?"

"Got answer. Know is mapwyrd not so far, along thorny path that curl Middle Ages. Live in cave on mountain. Found once. Find again."

"Ooooooo."

"Yah."

"Kay. We go?"

Leptin hesitated for a long time. "Me go."

Gherin's ears fell flat.

"Yah," Leptin said.

"But . . . mapwyrd!"

Leptin leaned forward. "Think good. Find mapwyrd take days. Weeks. Hunt through time, not return exact. Not sure how long. Maybe mouse make move. Maybe peek head up. Maybe chance talk. But goblins gone, find map. See?"

Gherin nodded slowly.

"Maybe goblins gone, rabbit set trap."

Gherin pounded his fists together. "Stupid rabbit!"

"Must keep watch," Leptin said. "See city."

Gherin nodded slowly. "Eat rabbit."

Leptin considered. "Maybe."

"Me stay?" Gherin said.

Leptin nodded. "You see city, high culture, better. Me know mapwyrd is. You go, maybe find, maybe no."

Gherin scowled, but nodded. "Mapwyrd scary?"

Leptin considered for a moment. A long moment. "Nah."

"Okay."

"Okay." Leptin tapped his fingers on the tower's top arch, one by one. "Okay."

They looked out over the city.

"One thing," Leptin said.

"Yah?"

"Need make promise."

Gherin tilted his head.

"Yah?"

"Yah. Know you still see woman most beautiful in world."

Gherin looked at the floor. "Yah."

"Still want kill man, think make woman happy."

Gherin sighed. "Yah."

"Need make promise no kill. No hurt. No touch."

Gherin looked up and stared. "No kill?"

"Yah."

"No hurt?"

Leptin's gaze was firm. "Yah."

"No . . . touch?"

Leptin bared his teeth. "Yah."

Gherin shook his head.

Leptin growled. "Got treaty," he hissed. "Big treaty. You honor. You honor! Gherin listen! Gherin listen Leptin, make promise!"

They stood, nose to nose, tooth to tooth, no space for the city between their eyes. The only difference was that Leptin didn't blink.

Gherin looked away. "Okay," he said quietly. "Gherin promise."

"Promise on . . . ," Leptin considered. "Moors of Lost Memory."

Gherin hissed.

"Gherin listen Leptin! Respect scars!"

Gherin stepped back. "Gherin swear on Moors of Lost Memory, no kill, no hurt, no touch beautiful woman or silly man."

Leptin let out a deep breath. "Okay. Good. Good. Is right."

Gherin nodded. He looked out over the city, and back to his friend, and his expression changed. "What Gherin do?"

Leptin put his hand on his shoulder. "Keep watch. Keep track. Follow enemies. Keep hide."

Gherin flashed his claws. "Yah. Okay."

"Yah. Keep watch for mouse, Gherin. Keep eye on rabbit. Big important."

"Yah." Gherin nodded. "Big important." He hesitated. "Be safe?"

"Yah."

Gherin turned, and this time looked out toward the ocean and the distant mountains across the bay. "When you go?"

"Soon. Come back fast can."

"Leptin?"

"Yah?"

"Before go?"

"Yah?"

"Want eat Indian food."

Leptin stared. "Just ate hundred rats!"

Gherin shrugged. "Need curry."

Leptin sighed. "Okay, yah. Before go."

They skittered down, Leptin swearing to himself that he would never climb this tower again.

Chapter 15

The street twisted back on itself, almost violently, over and over again. Magenta bushes lined its side, and small metal sculptures of dogs looked out from inside them, perhaps guarding the houses behind. Leptin didn't know that this was one of the most famous streets in the world: he just knew it was a good place to start. A lot of things can be hidden in a curvy street.

He cracked his knuckles. He stretched his claws. He picked a piece of rat meat out from between his teeth. His face scrunched up when he realized it tasted like green curry. He looked back down at the street, stretching back and forth into the darkness below him.

He looked carefully.

"Yah," he whispered. "Yah." He started walking, carefully, down toward the magenta bushes and the metal dogs. As the street wound around him, he didn't curve with it. He kept his eyes focused, his feet carefully moving forward in a perfectly straight line, as the road turned. He stepped up onto the curb. He walked through the magenta bushes. The little metal dogs stared. He kept his eyes forward.

Another step . . . another step . . . and another road opened up. A dirt path, even more twisted, that led between buildings where there was no space. Leptin licked his fangs, keeping his eyes focused. The gaps in high culture are everywhere, and this new road smelled like home. One foot in front of the other. Step. Step. Step.

He was through the path between buildings, and now the dirt road was underneath a sky so cloudy the moon was just a rumor. Barren trees were on either side, and small hovels made of discarded boxes covered in tarps: shantytowns where truly lost humans ended up when they had no connection to civilization and only could put one foot in front of another. Leptin suspected they didn't know how to get back. Around a campfire, a dirty faced man with dark eyes and a beard to his knees eyed Leptin. The goblin flashed his claws and hissed. One step in front of another. Follow the new path as long as it's useful. New paths always arc away from culture.

To the left, outside a shack, a furry man with the head of a human baby and the fangs of a bat rocked himself in the dirt and laughed. A hybrid thing: something so lost its form had vanished too. Leptin walked past. There were formless things to fear, but this was not one of them. The trees grew thicker ahead, and the path moved forward. He sniffed the air: it smelled like lavender and raw meat. He could feel the direction time ran, and put one foot in front of the other, faster now. This was a good path.

Green flowers peaked up by the side of the road, green flowers with red berries that dripped like blood. Birds flew across the cloudy sky singing the songs of lost sailors. The ground sloped upwards. Good. Good. Upwards was good. Upwards and backwards. There was a rustling in the trees to his left, and Leptin saw a massive spider sitting in a web covered tree: each branch had stuck to it the perfectly preserved head of one of its victims. Their eyes were wide, their mouths open in silent screams. They swayed in the breeze. The spider hung from its tree between the screaming heads and stared down at Leptin.

The goblin hissed. A creature like this, making nest so close to a high-culture city? "Bad," Leptin muttered. "Bad, bad."

The spider lowered itself to the ground. Leptin showed his fangs and bared his claws. It had been a long time since he'd had a real fight. It had been a long time since he'd spilled the blood that burns your skin and been stabbed by the fangs that blacken your flesh and poison you from the inside. He leaped forward to strike first.

Yes: it smelled like home.

Chapter 16

The tallest building in San Francisco that looks like it might have gargoyles on it used to house a newspaper. But the publishing company discovered that it could make more money moving the newspaper staff to less interesting offices and renting the historic building out to the tech companies whose products were making newspapers obsolete.

Management called this "effective resource allocation." Reporters grumbled that it was exactly the reason everything was going wrong.

Sitting at the top of the building, staring out over the city, Gherin could confirm that there were no gargoyles, and it seemed like such a wasted opportunity. But if he put his ear to the concrete, he thought he could almost hear the argument going on over the building: quality and history verses youth and efficiency. Gargoyles verses no gargoyles.

Gherin sighed and drummed his fingers against the stone. He should be investigating. He should be making sure the mouse wasn't on the move. If the mouse took action, he'd be easier to find for a few hours . . .

Leptin had told him so. And Leptin was right. Leptin was always right. His family had told him to honor the scars. Honor the scars.

It was the right thing to do.

But he had worked so hard, begged so much, thrown his family's influence like a brick, to get here. And now there was high culture all around: thrillingly tall, amazingly colorful, so full of mystery and delicious on the tongue and teeth. Chasing the mouse . . . well, was the mouse really going to do something tonight? Really? And the stupid rabbit wasn't a threat. Nothing that needed to be watched carefully.

Leptin would disapprove.

Honor the scars.

Gherin wanted to. He really wanted to.

But when would he have another chance to see a city like this?

He could hear Leptin's voice, whispering in his ear.

He'd make it up to his friend. He would.

Smiling, he skittered down the side of the building, looking to all the world like a gargoyle in flight.

Chapter 17

When the spider died, the heads it had stuck to the tree fell down—a rain storm of decapitation. Leptin held his arms high as they crashed to the ground around him, howling as the poison blood rippled in a stream by his feet. His chest and thighs were charred and scarred, new wounds lashed on top of old ones, and they hurt so much.

The tree began to crack and splinter. Nothing the spider had done would survive its death. Soon, Leptin thought, carrion birds will come. Soon scavengers will come. Everything would be picked clean. He should leave now, he knew. His training told him clearly: go now. But he waited. He stood, among the heads and the stream of blood that burns, one leg upon the spider's black and red torso, waiting.

When he saw the first flock of birds overhead, when he saw the first eyes in the forest, he stared them all down.

"Tell!" he shouted. "Tell all! Tell all Leptin, killer of spider! Tell!"

Then he moved. Then he ran, hobbling on his weakened legs, dashing into the forest, into the bushes, behind the trees, following the path. Because he had been taught long ago, and it was true, that if a soldier wants to survive the best skill he can learn is when and how to hide. He'd learned it was true. He'd acted foolishly.

But it had been worth it.

There was a long way to go.

Chapter 18

The last stagehand out the backstage door of the San Francisco Opera building stopped for a moment, with the door half open, and caught a whiff of curry. It mingled, strangely, with the image of the set he'd spent the last four days building: four glorious scenes in Renaissance Venice, each of which had its own hand-crafted furniture and carefully painted backdrops that could be lowered and raised by a series of pulleys that were finally working right.

Something about that combination of worlds . . . curry and the seat of European trade, one nothing but a smell, the other an illusion carefully painted on industrial canvas . . . made him realize that the world was bigger than he'd ever imagined. Sometimes that's all it takes.

He began to hum a tune from the opera that had finished rehearsing just a few hours ago. He'd been in a terrible mood all day: now he was convinced that the world contains enough multitudes for him to find something delightful in it. The cold San Francisco air hit him and he wondered if he should call up an old friend and insist they hit a bar. The moon looked down on him as he locked the door behind, and he debated if he should try OkCupid again.

All that, he thought, from curry and painted scenery. Happiness doesn't depend on any of the ingredients we treasure. He walked down the street to the bus stop and got out his phone.

Gherin watched him go through a tiny window in the door. He could see that some alchemy had occurred in the human, changed him. He tilted his head and wondered what it was. High-culture humans were in the grip of so many things he didn't understand, and he had the sneaking suspicion that they were beautiful. What makes people build such tall buildings? Paint things so that they look like other things? Cook such complicated meals? It was fascinating. He burped, and tasted curry on his teeth.

Now that he was alone, he looked around at the backstage in earnest. "Ooooooo," he whispered. There were winches and pulleys and ropes, switches and lighting boards, curtains and loose lumber and tools, big wooden boxes and ladders. It was so big. There were strange shapes up near the ceiling. This, and not a tall white tower, was just where he imagined a wizard would live.

Gherin smiled and ran to the wall. He skittered up it fifteen feet then sprung out to grab a rope. He scurried up higher, higher, toward the ceiling, until he'd climbed up to the catwalk. He didn't hesitate—he understood catwalks perfectly—and hopped over, and stared at the giant painted canvas hanging before him.

"Ooooooo," he said again. "Pretty."

He scratched his chin. It looked like Venice several hundred years ago, but, they'd gotten the canals wrong. So interesting. He ran across the catwalk and leaped over to another perch to see the backdrop behind it. He stared for a while, wondering if just one human painted it all, or if they did it together, and whether they sang while they painted, and whether there was another human with a whip standing over them to make sure they didn't steal each other's food. So many questions.

He turned around to look at the first picture again, and stiffened. He saw, for the first time, that the stage ended and that the entire rest of the room . . . an enormous cavern! . . . was filled with seats! So many empty seats! And so many levels! There were little boxes of seats that climbed up the side of the walls, and a whole different level of seats on the balcony behind it. And there was a giant stalactite of glass and metal hanging down from the ceiling, caressed by the stone, full of sculptures and words. Enormous! Like a sculpted cave!

He leaped back onto the rope and climbed as high as it would go, then sprung to the ceiling and clung there, and worked his way over to the giant glass and metal fixture that hung from the ceiling. It was like one of those things that high-culture humans have that get bright when they flick a switch. The switch, he realized, must be huge. Where could they keep it?

He crawled closer.

He reached out his hand, and hesitantly tapped a claw against the cloudy glass.

It sounded just like a claw hitting thick glass. He smiled, and tapped it again. Then he crawled closer and ran his hand over it. Smooth. He put both his arms around it, hugging it while his talons dug into the ceiling.

He stayed there for a little while, until the rush wore off and he was convinced nothing would happen. Then he planted his claws on the ceiling again and crawled over to the wall. He scaled it back down, into one of the boxes of seats. The seats, he realized, were fuzzy. He ran his hand over them.

"Soft," he whispered. "Like rabbit."

He smelled them. Not good to eat. He shook his head.

Then he stiffened and showed his claws.

"Got ten claws," he said without turning around. "How many want?" It sounded like something Leptin would say, and he beamed inside.

Behind him, a small voice coughed. "Um, none, sir, if that's acceptable to you."

Gherin raised an eyebrow, though he doubted the creature could see it. "Want die?"

"Nope. Nope. Absolutely not."

"Then be no here when turn around."

"I'm just . . . ."

"Gherin having moment."

"I just . . . ," the voice squeaked. "Sure is pretty, isn't it?"

Gherin considered. "Yah," he said at last. "Yah."

"Would you . . . would you like a tour? I could tell you all about the building."

Gherin raised his other eyebrow. He pivoted on his talons and spun around. A bat was sitting on top of the hallway behind the box seats. Its wings trembled with fear.

Gherin's eyes narrowed. "You opera bat?"

"Um . . . well . . . it's not a formal title, no. But, I do live here and watch the place for Mr. O'Shaughnessy."

"Ohhhhh," said Gherin, licking his claws. "You work for rabbit."

"Yes . . . yessir."

"You good taste hoisin sauce?" Leptin never would have said that.

"Puh . . . please, sir," said the bat, shifting back and forth on its tiny feet as its wings shook. "I can't tell you about the opera house if I'm inside your stomach. I really can't."

Gherin stroked his chin. "Why want give Gherin tour?"

"Mr . . . Mr . . . . Mr. O'Shaughnessy said he thought you might show up here, and if you did, I should be nice to you and show you around."

Gherin's lips curled.

"There's . . . there's . . . there's a rat here, too, who has orders to report to the duke as soon as you're sighted, but, but, but, I haven't seen him around anywhere," the bat said, his eyes darting.

Gherin burped.

"You ate Mordecai?" the bat squeaked. "Oh my gosh! Oh no! Oh my goodness!" He fluttered his wings. "The duke's going to be so upset!"

Gherin shrugged. "Opera dangerous."

"No! It's not! It's colorful and beautiful!"

Gherin nodded slowly. "Why rabbit want Gherin get tour?"

The bat's head huddled close to his chest. "He, he . . . he wants to make you an offer."

Gherin snorted. "Eat rabbit."

"He thinks once you've seen the opera house, you won't turn it down."

Gherin tilted his head. "Yah?"

"Yessir."

"Good house."

"Yessir. It's magnificent."

"What offer?"

"No sir! I'm not supposed to tell you until you've seen the whole opera house!"

Gherin flexed his claws.

"I'm not!"

Gherin picked his teeth.

"I'm not!" the bat screeched, its whole body quivering.

Gherin considered, then took a deep breath. He inhaled through his nose, collecting all the scents of the place, and sorting them out. Nothing smelled like a trap, just like a frightened, scared, mammal.

"Okay, opera bat. Show Gherin."

Chapter 19

Leptin waited under the river, holding his breath, as the dark rider's horse paced back and forth along the bank.

He did not know where the rider had come from, or who it served, or why it followed his tracks wherever they led in time and magical geography: he only knew that the path had not been smooth, the way had not been clear, and that the rider had picked up his trail three days back and never let it go.

No sleep, no food, no time . . . this chase had to end. But this was not something to fight. This was something to fool.

The hooves struck the riverbed, sending clumps of dirt and pulverized stone into the water. Back and forth, back and forth. It knew something was wrong, but it didn't know Leptin had carved out a cubby hole under the river bank, just ten feet away.

Back and forth. Back and forth.

Leptin held very still.

Travel between places like the goblin lands and the high culture of humanity was never safe . . . but the trip to twenty-first-century San Francisco had not been nearly so dangerous. Was this bad luck, or were things getting worse? Leptin feared that the mouse's hunt was having consequences: that the dangerous things of the crossroad and the cemetery could feel the ancient sleeping symbols rise and die, and it was bringing them out in force.

He doubted the wizard had prepared high culture to survive such an onslaught. The goblin armies would prevail against the ancient symbols for a while . . . but not if the sun went out. Not if the earth cracked open.

Back and forth. Back and forth. He could hear the horse snort, even through the water, and see that its breath boiled the river's surface. What was this thing? If it could track his footsteps through the water, or if it had magical scrying powers, he was dead.

Back and forth. Back and forth.

It suspects, Leptin realized. It's lost the real trail and suspects he's beaten it. But it's hoping that if it waits here, if it stands and flashes fire and iron hooves, that he would grow scared and bolt. Leptin smiled: it was a futile hope. He was an experienced soldier: he didn't give in to nerves. The right strategy is the right strategy. And he could hold his breath for a very long time. But all the same his brow furrowed: if he was right, this creature was subtle too. The monsters who understand their prey are the most dangerous.

Back and forth. Back and forth.

You have no power over me, Leptin thought. But he would never howl it out loud.

In his weakest moments, he thought that the only reason he's still alive is that he's a coward.

No one had ever told him that, but he'd outlived too many comrades whom he'd admired for their bravery not to think it now and then.

But now was not the time to be weak.

Back and forth. Back and forth.

Now was not the time to be weak.

If you respect scars, respect wounds earned honorably, everything else falls into place and becomes clear. Leptin had many of those.

I am hiding, he thought, but I am not a coward. I am a good soldier. You have no power over me.

The horse reared on two legs. The rider howled and the surface of the water burned. The horse leaped over the river and began following Leptin's false trail into the desert of tenth-century Utah.

Leptin waited a long time, to make sure it was not a trap, and then slipped out of the lake and back toward the Renaissance. His mind was quiet: momentarily at peace.

Chapter 20

The hardest thing for Gherin to accept had been the prop room.

He had stared, open mouthed, at the stone work and vast marble stairs in the lobby, the high windows of the mezzanine level, and the colorful frescos on the ceiling. But the prop room had stopped him cold.

The Opera, he declared, must be extremely powerful to have so many swords and shields and guns lying around.

"But," the bat had protested, "they're not real!"

"Huh?"

"They're . . . they're . . . they're not real! They're props! Like those wooden flowers, or that plastic clock."

Gherin had inspected. "Look clock."

"But it doesn't tell time!"

"Broke?"

"No! It never worked."

Gherin laughed. "Opera bad builder."

It had taken a long time to explain, and it didn't really take until Gherin leaped over the table for a Parisian café and picked up a shining sword made of wood and paint. He held it, recognizing that the balance was all wrong, feeling in a way he couldn't see that not only was it not a sword but it could never have been a sword, or even intended to be a sword.

"Trap?" he asked.

"Prop," the bat said.

"Prop," Gherin repeated, and tossed the sword away.

"Yeah," said the bat. "Let's . . . ."

"Prop," said Gherin again, and he sounded angry.

"Um . . . let's go onto the stage," the bat said, and started flapping out of the prop room and over toward the curtain. Gherin stayed behind for a minute, hissed at the prop room, and then followed. He crept through the backstage area he'd been in before, looking overhead to see that the hanging backdrops were still there, wondering for a moment why they were so beautiful when the prop sword was so vile, and then pushed his way through the thick velvet curtain.

He stood on the stage, looking out into the empty house, and it was stirring.

"Isn't it amazing?" said the bat, flying around the stage at eye level. "They put on eight operas last year! Cosi fan Tutte was especially good!"

"Yah," said Gherin, though he didn't understand most of that. But standing here made him agreeable. "High culture."

"What?"

Gherin frowned. "Every opera got opera bat?"

"Well . . . ," the bat flapped around the stage in the other direction. "I don't know. I'm sure every opera house has animals in it."

"Yah," Gherin said, carefully. "Wild animals live inside high-culture place. Get exposed art. Still wild. Got culture, still talk. Strange. Strange. Not sure."

"Oh no sir! We're not domesticated! Not by any means! My family's lived here for twelve generations," said the bat. ("So had Mordecai's," he muttered.) "And we come and go as we please. We stay because it's got lovely, dark spaces and high ceilings and there are so many delicious insects coming through. And . . . and . . . because the opera's beautiful. That's all."

"Opera bat live two worlds."

"I, I . . . I guess so. I never thought of it like that." The bat fluttered over to hover uncomfortably in front of Gherin. "Now, sir, Mr. O'Shaughnessy would like to make you an offer."

Gherin licked his claws. "Yah?"

"Yessir. He'd wants to know if you'd like to come back this Saturday and see an opera."

Gherin's jaw dropped. "See . . . opera? Alive?"

"Yessir. He'd give you a box all to yourself. He can arrange it. You could see the whole production, without interruption. It's . . . it's a tremendous experience. I really have to tell you. If you like, I can give you a few details about the current season."

"See opera?"

"That's right, sir. He hopes you'll accept."

Gherin took a deep breath. Reluctantly, he asked "What cost?"

The bat smiled. "Nothing sir. This is free."

"Nothing?"

"No sir. Mr. O'Shaughnessy just wants to emphasize how much you have in common, and how much you have to offer each other. That's all."

"Free." Gherin tilted his head. "No trap?"

"Oh sir! No sir! No no no sir!"

Gherin tilted his head the other way. This was a terrible idea. Even if it wasn't a trap, which it almost certainly was, it wasn't right. It was probably a trap. Leptin wouldn't approve. But . . . those curtains, the frescos, the hanging crystal light, even the prop room . . . all these strange and beautiful things were in the service of something greater, something he couldn't even imagine because they had no operas or orchestras at home.

"Yah."

When would he ever get another chance?

Chapter 21

At the foot of a mountain, two ogres sat hunched by a blazing fire under a young moon. The logs in the fire were the massive rafters of what had once been a great mansion. They burned high and they burned slow. Everything else was rock; boulders that had fallen from the great peaks above.

One ogre reached his hand toward the fire and removed a piece of meat sizzling on a sword. The blade was red hot. "Think it's done," he said morosely.

"Yeah," said the other, reaching in to pull a steel spear from the fire. It held what had once been the thigh of a mighty animal in place: the melted fat dripped down into the fire and sizzled. "Probably won't taste good."

"Nah," said the first ogre. "Never does."

The first one held the sword up to his bloated face and sniffed at the meat. It was still too hot. "I think we leave it in the fire too long. Every time."

"It's a big fire," said the other, and left it at that. He looked away from his food and up at the stars.

"I thought I smelled a plague yesterday," said the first ogre. "Or maybe the day before. From England."

"Huh."

The first one opened his cavernous mouth and sank his stubby teeth into the meat. He chewed slowly. "It's terrible," he reported. "All burned."

"Don't talk with your mouth full."

The first one shook his head. "What good has being polite ever done 'ya?"

"I'm trying to improve myself, Gurk."

Gurk chuckled. "And I'm trying to . . . ," he paused. "Hey Bosh."

"Yeah?"

"There's a goblin over on the path."

"Yeah?"

"Yep." Gurk thought about it a moment, then took a deep breath. "HEY GOBLIN!" he shouted. "I CAN SEE YOU! WHY DON'TCHA COME OVER HERE BY THE FIRE WHERE IT'S WARM?"

The base of the mountain was silent. "Interesting choice," said Bosh.

"Well, I coulda thrown something at him," Gurk admitted. "But, honestly, you're not such good conversation these days. I'm sorry, but it's true. You're taciturn."

"I'm polite," Bosh muttered. "Don't speak unless spoken to. Trying to improve myself."

"Yeah well . . . HEY GOBLIN, GOT FOOD HERE, IF YOU'RE HUNGRY! CAN TELL YOU ANYTHING YOU WANT TO KNOW ABOUT THE MOUNTAIN! I PROMISE NOT TO THROW ANYTHING AT YOU, OR BASH YOU ON THE HEAD!"

Leptin's response echoed across the stone landscape. "Take oath?"

Gurk nodded, the muscles in his meaty neck bulging. "Yeah, I'll take an oath. What on?"

There was a pause. "Hounds," Leptin said.

"Oooh," said Bosh. "Good one."

Gurk looked over. "You good with this?"

"Well," said Bosh, "we're not gonna eat him, right?"

"Nah. Wasn't planning to."

"So we won't bash him."

Gurk nodded. "Okay." He switched the sword that held his dinner over to his left hand, and raised his right hand into the air. "I swear," he called out, "by the hounds of the Archduke Mazerick that you shall be our guest and no harm shall come to you while you sit by our fire!"

Bosh held up his hand. "I, too, swear."

"Let our bones be forfeit to their hunt if we lie," Gurk finished.

The wind picked up and carried the words away.

A moment later, Leptin stepped cautiously into the firelight. He sized them up carefully. "Big," he said.

"Want some meat?" Gurk asked.

"Yah." Leptin didn't want to appear eager, but hunting had been scarce on this trip.

Bosh looked at his companion curiously. He looked back at the goblin. "It's terrible," he warned.

"What got?"

"Well," said Gurk, "there's a couple of weapons with their blades in the fire there, and each one has a good chunk of meat on it. Help yourself."

Leptin stepped forward and looked into the massive blaze. There were, indeed, a number of weapon handles sticking out, each attached to a blade that ran through sizzling flesh and held it in place.

Leptin looked back up at the ogres and hissed. He bared his fangs.

"What?" asked Gurk.

Leptin hissed again. "Cursed!" he spat. "You want trick!"

"Ha!" laughed Gurk, chuckling from his hard belly. He hit Bosh on the shoulder. "He's smarter than he looks!"

Bosh shook his head. "Yeah," he said to Leptin. "You probably shouldn't eat that."

Leptin took a step away, his claws in a defensive position. "You swear oath!"

Gurk shrugged. "I didn't think it would actually hurt ya . . . exactly. Don't know for sure, really: might not do anything to 'ya. It's our curse, not yours."

"Cursed food!"

Gurk nodded. "About as cursed as you get. How'd you figure us out?"

Leptin spat on the ground.

"Look, we swore not to hurt you, and you're not gonna eat anything, so, you're safe now, right?"

Leptin stood where he was.

"C'mon, just tell me. How did you figure it out? I really . . . I'd really like to know."

Leptin scowled. His eyes flashed back to the path: the ogres were big, with enormous legs, but were heavy and he was fast. He thought he could make it, as long as he had a head start. He bared his teeth. On the other hand, maybe he could kill one of them: if he were fast, and accurate, they had big veins in their wrists and their necks. He'd have to be accurate, and avoid hitting muscle, but those were their weak points.

Bosh turned and looked Leptin in the eyes. "Look, that was wrong," he rumbled in his deep ogre voice. "I should have said something. I had a chance to be better than that, and I failed. I'm sorry."

Leptin's ears twitched.

"Give me the chance," Bosh said, "to treat 'ya like a true guest, and make up for a mistake."

Leptin stared back, deep into Bosh's eyes. He took a deep breath. He stepped forward again, and walked around the ogres to the other side of the fire.

"Thank you," said Bosh.

Leptin sat, out of arms reach. "Be better."

Gurk laughed. It was a good natured explosion. "Goblins are always so serious," he said to Bosh. "'Ya know?"

Bosh shook his head.

"So c'mon," said Gurk. "How'd you figure it out?"

Leptin blew air through his lips. "Easy. Logs not burn right."

Gurk nodded. "True. Good eye."

"Ogres always hungry," Leptin finished damningly. "Ogres no share food."

Gurk laughed again, but it didn't last long. "Yeah," he said, rubbing his stomach. "Yeah."

"So, probably curse. Figures."

"Yes, little creature," Bosh said. "We are an accursed pair."

Leptin nodded. "Smell okay."

Gurk smiled. "I'm glad we have that going for us."

"What happen?"

They said nothing.

Leptin rolled his eyes. "Want sit fire, no talk curse? Really?"

Gurk sighed. "Okay."

"Long ago," Bosh rumbled, "this was the site of a great manor house in the estate of a noble lord." He paused, and looked over at Gurk. "Are we in Scotland or France?"

"France," said Gurk.

"Scotland," corrected Leptin. "Kinda."

"Huh," said Bosh. "Well, it's not important. He was spending the winter here with his wife and children and their servants and a company of guards and the keeper of the lands. And . . . ," the words grumbled in his throat. "And . . . ."

"And we were passing by," Gurk said. "And we were hungry. Really hungry."

"There were so many of them," Bosh mumbled.

The fire crackled and spit.

"So?" Leptin asked. "What problem?"

"We knew better," said Bosh.

"This was . . . after Dee's treaty," Gurk said softly.

Leptin inhaled sharply. "Wizard," he hissed.

Gurk nodded, but Bosh shrugged. "Don't know," he said. "We didn't see him."

"Wizard dead. Wizard dead."

"Don't know," said Bosh. "We didn't see him. It just . . . ."

"We ate the lady of the house last" Gurk said. "She was plump in all the right places, and it was polite. And when we were done we were sitting on the floor by their fireplace. There was a flash of lightning without a storm. Darkness descended upon night. And the bones we'd tossed in the corner rustled, and shook, and screamed. It was . . . ."

Their hands reflexively moved to their ears.

Leptin waited as long he could. "What happen?"

Gurk opened his mouth, then stopped, and shook his massive head.

Bosh took a deep breath. "These beams," he said, pointing to the fire, "are the last of the manor house, and we can't leave the scene of our crime until they burn out. The only food we have to eat are the bodies of our victims, magically returned, which taste of fear and betrayal. The burns they get from the fire never go away, they become tougher and harder over the centuries, blackened and brittle, and we can feel our own teeth marks in them from long ago."

"They're not worth eating anymore," Gurk groaned. "And I'm so hungry."

"I think," Bosh said sadly, "we have a very long time to go."

"Sad," said Leptin.

The ogres nodded.

Leptin scowled. "Why want me eat food?"

Gurk lowered his head. "I thought it might make you stay here too. I . . . wanted somebody else to talk to."

Leptin looked at them both, and his lips quivered. "What wrong him?" he asked, pointing to Bosh. "Him got mouth."

The ogres looked at one another.

"You're quiet all the time!" Gurk roared. "We haven't had a good conversation in a hundred years!"

Bosh grumbled under his breath.

"We're starving! The least you can do is tell a joke!"

Bosh looked away. "I don't want to tell a joke."

"Tell a story!"

"I've run out of stories. I don't want to be funny. I'm trying to think about my life. I'm trying to improve myself."

"There's nothing wrong with you!" Gurk roared.

"We're here," Bosh said, staring into the fire.

"We made a mistake!" Gurk pounded his meaty fist on the ground. "That's all!"

Leptin looked between them, and slowly nodded.

"No, Gurk," said Bosh. "I think we're monsters."

Gurk roared into the night. Leptin scooted away. Gurk turned. "You see?" he shouted. "You see? He's gone mad!"

"We were hungry," Bosh said, perhaps to himself. "That's all. We made too much of it."

"I'M STARVING NOW!"

"I'm trying to be a better person."

Gurk pounded the ground with both hands and howled. Bosh sat, stony faced and silent.

Leptin stood up and slowly walked around the fire, behind Bosh, and back toward the path up the mountain.

"WAIT!" shouted Gurk. "Wait!"

Leptin shook his head. "Need go."

"Wait!" cried Gurk. "Please! Before you go, tell me a story! Say something new! I need something new to think about! Please!"

Halfway to the path, Leptin stopped. He turned, and scratched his head.

He had never seen an ogre beg before.

He pounded his chest. "Leptin," he said proudly. "Son Endocran. Father soldier. Great soldier. Kill king. Make children. Many children. All go war. All Leptin brother, sister, soldiers. Leptin soldier. Like father. Go war. Fight together. Claw to claw. Blade to blade. Battle Glom canyon. Battle Naga River. War of Rites. All together. Youngest brother die first." His voice rose: he began to howl, as goblins do when they tell their stories by firelight. "Head eaten wind shark in Kesber Pass. Great sad! Oldest brother die: neck slit in burning woods. Big tears. Oldest sisters die together, back to back, at Demon Hearth. Brother die from giant club in coldest north! Sister lost dwarf tunnel; brother caught, sacrifice by Black Hand; sister breathe troll smoke; youngest sister, little sister, lead charge into plague wall, never come back. Gone! All gone! Great sorrow—mother bury self alive! Gone! All gone!"

He took a breath and held his hands high, reaching for the stars, as the fire spit. "Leptin, father, left. Still fight. Draw swords! March to Battle of Goren Vaj!"

At the mention of that name Gurk leaned back. Bosh looked up.

"When the moon died," Bosh whispered.

"Moon die! Trolls die! Seelie die! Demons die! Goblins die! Dark General Excior ride from Skaris Cragg with flaming sword and earth turns to dust! Angels fall and armies ride over corpses! Die! All die! Endocran die! Father die! Leptin see shield wall, see Excior with flaming sword, see truth: Leptin hide in corpse! See father die with corpse eyes, hear father scream with corpse ears, see corpse trampled by army, fall into flaming crag when ground spit. Gone! All gone! Alone! All alone! Leptin hide, Leptin survive! Alone!"

His howl echoed through the night. For a moment, all was still.

The goblin looked into the fire. "Leptin still fight. Sent human lands, high culture. Stop mouse: mouse end world not careful, world fall into sun. Must win. Leptin still fight." He took another breath. "Leptin tired. When world save, go home. Maybe find woman, make new soldiers. Maybe. Maybe sit by fire. Be old. Feel scars. Maybe. Maybe. Leptin tired." He pounded his chest and ended his howl. "Leptin tired. Want go home."

There was silence in the night.

"I heard," Gurk said softly, "there are less than twenty veterans of Goren Vaj alive."

Leptin took a deep breath. "Yah. Know on sight. Make pledge: no matter army come from, never kill each other. Survivors. Respect scars."

Bosh took a deep breath. "Excior no longer rides. What happened to him?"

Leptin took a deep breath. Chuckled to himself, remembering his delusion about the human. The resemblance was real, but . . . Leptin understood now why he was seeing things. "Leptin like think Dark General tired too. Find place far away battlefield. Look for new life, find fire to sit next to. Maybe woman."

Yes, that was what he liked to think.

Bosh nodded. "He's trying to improve himself."

"Oh shut up," hissed Gurk.

Leptin spat on the ground. "Done," he said. "Go save world."

He turned and ran before they could say another word. He did not like to spend time around the cursed and the damned. He did not want to rest before he got home. He thought of the pain on their faces and Gurk's wail, the terrible punishment for crossing forbidden lines, and he hoped . . . hoped . . . that Gherin was keeping his promises. The boy had no discipline: he had no idea how close he was to stepping into an abyss.

Chapter 22

James did not notice the single claw reaching around to the front of his throat, almost tapping at his soft skin, almost ripping his life out. He slouched on the futon, his back against the armrest, his laptop propped up against his knees, and played his game. He was deep, deep into a key battle between his dark elven armies and the dwarves of another player whose ISP said he was in Korea and whose handle was "DarthMaulCloneD." According to message boards, he was competitive with the world's top players.

Gherin inched his claw back and forth, back and forth. The most beautiful girl in the world had gone to bed a long time ago. She and James had fought, again, about whether it was fair to split the rent evenly even though she used so much more closet space and had the bedroom all to herself, since he almost always slept on the futon now. It was a particularly ugly fight, because they were teetering on an edge and knew it. Any fight now could be the last.

She would not miss him, Gherin thought, perfectly still except for his claw that inched back and forth, back and forth. She would not miss him at all. The most beautiful girl in the world would be happy he was gone. It would be a clean kill: no noise. Lots of blood, but that could be cleaned. Lots of meat on James' body: Gherin could eat it all by morning and have the bones and the bloody mattress out on the curb. So easy: all the man paid attention to right now was his game, and this war.

He held perfectly still.

Leptin wouldn't approve, Gherin knew. But Leptin wasn't here.

Still, he waited. He wondered why.

At least, he decided, James was good at this game. He ran his armies like a real commander would (or at least, the way Gherin imagined a real commander would): he had a particular maneuver Gherin liked in which he'd send scouts out to discover enemy territory, and then have them flee at the first sign of a superior force. They wouldn't flee very fast, though, and so the enemy would come after them and fall right into an ambush the dark elves had set up just out of sight behind their scouts. Very effective. He was very good at determining when to use archers and when to use melee fighters too, Gherin noticed.

The only trouble being that it was a stupid game: unfit for a man who had slept with the most beautiful girl in the world. The very thought made Gherin shudder.

Why, Gherin wondered, wasn't James dead yet? Surely the rules of nature operated even in high culture: a male this pathetic with a woman that beautiful would be killed by other, stronger males. What possible objection could culture have?

Leptin wouldn't approve, that was true. But he wouldn't approve of the opera either. Some things were worth doing.

There was always the wizard to consider. He was a very clever wizard, even when he was dead. Maybe especially when he was dead. But ... Gherin inched his neck upward to get a look at James' bulky body arched half-way up the futon ... surely even the wizard would see that this one had to die. Just look at him: the wizard who had safeguarded high culture for humanity wouldn't want someone like this in it. Wasting beautiful women's time. Making them go to bed crying. No: any sensible wizard would be on Gherin's side. It only made sense.

His finger tightened.

But then there was the opera.

Gherin could kill James any time, but the invitation to see the opera was tenuous. It could be revoked. It was probably a trap. Anything could go wrong. It made sense, didn't it, to see the opera first and then kill James?

James' forces had found a crack in the DarthMaulCloneD's mountain defenses, but instead of pressing the attack they were letting the dwarves almost repair it, until the dark elven archers tore it down and massacred the dwarven repair forces from a safe distance. More dwarves dead, more enemy resources spent, at no cost to James.

Gherin was puzzled by this line of thought: he had never before used one good thing he wanted as a reason not to do another good thing he wanted. It fit together strangely. It made his head hurt. But it seemed right. First opera, then kill. That's how it should be done. Yes. Yes. He smiled, and felt very high culture.

Then he remembered that James had made the most beautiful girl in the world cry, and snarled silently. His hand tightened.

From outside Mari's bedroom Caramel the cat screamed. James jerked, almost impaling himself. Gherin vanished under the futon. Disgusted, he slipped out the window as James opened the door to let the bad cat out.

The cat, Gherin decided, didn't know whose side to be on. He was going to find a really good steakhouse, eat bloody meat raw, and see if he could figure out what a Caesar salad was.

Chapter 23

The pile of rocks looked like half a dragon's head, one eye and a row of teeth scattered on the winding mountain path. Leptin remembered it: he had arrived. The way was different—the very act of traveling through the thick muddy currents of time changes the world in your wake—but this was it. He'd wondered, the first time he'd seen it, if these rocks were a deliberate warning.

Back then, he'd decided that they were too subtle. If you make a warning it has to be obvious: if you want people to know you can kill a dragon you need to put its whole head in an obvious position, on a pike or attached to a wall. Otherwise they might miss the point, and then why warn them at all?

These were just rocks.

"Just rocks," he muttered now. But up here the whole mountain side seemed to be overflowing with hidden meaning, just under the surface, waiting to burst out. The cracks in the path below his feet almost looked like an ancient rune (he assumed, not actually knowing anything about them). The sound of the wind whipping over the peaks could maybe have been a distant battle cry. The small green twig slowly growing in the shadow of a boulder made him think of a new world waiting to be born.

But they weren't. He shook his head. He was here. This is how you know you've reached the home of a mapwyrd: everything looks like a symbol of itself, showing you the way to something greater.

"Kkkkkkcccccckkkkkkkhs," Leptin muttered. He walked forward, around another curve, and saw the cave entrance up ahead. It vaguely looked like his mother's mouth, open to sing a song. That he did not remember.

He took a deep breath. It had been a long time. Those had been better days, younger days. He walked up to the cave mouth. Slowly, he raised his hands to show that he came unarmed. Slowly, he held a pouch into the air, a pouch filled with colored pebbles from the river. He poured them into his hands, and tossed them up.

They landed on the ground in a perfect order, forming a diagram of the cave. A line of light blue pebbles snaked through it, showing the way he had to go. They ended at a reddish piece of sandstone, the only one in the pouch. That was where he had to be. He stared at the pebble diagram, memorizing it carefully. There would be no second chance. If he threw them again, they would show him the way to something else.

He'd heard a story, once, about a wild human who had offended a mapwyrd and found that all roads took him to a great garden of glass with no way to leave. It had been a wizard's paperweight, and the glass bauble, with its prisoner, was given away each year as a trophy to the best troll singer in a fetid swamp.

Leptin took one last look at the pebble diagram, and then scattered it with his foot. He walked into the cave. He had to go through five caverns to reach his goal. Far away, water was dripping from a stalactite down a very deep hole.

The first cavern was big and filled with green moss. Something scuttled. Drip. Drip. Drip. There was an easy way off to the left, but Leptin walked carefully toward the hole ahead of him, and then veered off to the right. The descent here was so steep he would almost have to fall down it, but it was smooth with no moss: it had been traveled recently. Even if it hadn't, he would follow the map. You survive magic by knowing which rules to follow and which rules to break. There is no other way.

He slid down the ravine and into the second cavern. It got smaller and smaller, rock closing in around him. It leveled suddenly, buckling his knees. There was a splash. He was in standing water. Small eyeless fish darted around him. Leptin staggered. The eyeless fish seemed so significant, the patterns they swam in so meaningful, the presence of water in the cave of the mapwyrd so indicative, signs and portents pressed in on him from every side, he swam in symbolism, it seemed like all the world's secrets would be revealed if he could just decipher this code—he stopped breathing.

The pain in his head was white hot before he noticed it. He yanked his gaze away from the water and closed his eyes and stumbled forward, scraping his shins on a row of rocks, stumbling.

"Means nothing!" he told himself. "Means nothing!" His lungs filled with air and it burned. He took another breath. He did not open his eyes. He crept forward on his hands and knees. His head ran into a wall. He suffered in silence, except for his deep breaths.

He didn't open his eyes until some part of him stopped looking for patterns in the darkness. It had been easier, last time. For some reason the mapwyrd had gone deeper into the cave.

He glanced back at the pool, just quickly: he had to picture the pebble map in his mind again. He had to get his bearings. This was still the second cavern. There was a long narrow path ahead.

"Going potionwyrd easier," he muttered. "Walk in hut. Say 'want potion!' Easy. Swordwyrd simple. Like swordwyrd. Got lotsa sword."

He'd never liked maps. Wanting to find something you couldn't track was a bad idea. But complaining wouldn't help. Complaining never helped. Bad ideas are sometimes the only ones we've got.

He crept forward into the long narrow tunnel. There were paintings on the walls. He didn't look at them. Art was always a trap.

The ceiling of the next cavern remained low. Skeletons lay along the walls. Here in the cave of the mapwyrd they weren't just corpses: they represented all the corpses Leptin had ever regretted in his life. He passed the bones of his father on the left, his brothers on the right. It seemed as though his mother was reaching her sad hands out to him, and he longed to lie in her embrace. He bared his teeth at his mother, the way he always had when she was alive. There would be time to regret it later. Now forward, forward, past the last of the corpses.

"Probably looked at paintings," he muttered. Served them right. Or maybe they were the painters, in which case he hoped they suffered.

The ceiling rose suddenly and the walls grew wide as he entered the next cavern. The floor was uneven and stalagmites covered it like spears standing on end. There was a path that hugged the walls and wound up around the room to a ledge on the right. He moved carefully, touching nothing, over to the beginning of the passageway, stepped forward, and then stopped.

There were footprints on the passageway.

He knelt down to look closer.

Goblin footprints.

His eyes widened. Something about them caught his eye. Perhaps it was the spacing between the toes, or the size of the talons. He looked at his own feet carefully.

Yes. He nodded as though he understood what was going on. They were his footprints.

"Bad," he hissed. "Bad bad."

He looked around carefully: he saw no time streams that might carry him across his own path; and even if there were, they'd have to move awfully fast, and spin in a circle, and then get sticky. No. No. The problem wasn't time. Was this magic? Could these really have been his footprints from his last journey to this cave, even though he'd never stepped into this particular cavern?

He had to go along this path: the map had said so. But what were the rules? Should he step in his own footprints, or avoid them?

He stroked his chin. He flexed his talons. And then, slowly, he put his right foot in the first footprint. A map, he decided, is something you follow. It was his best judgment, and he had to trust it.

He put his left foot in the second footprint, and then his right foot in the third. Behind him, with a small blue glow, the first footprint disappeared.

He walked carefully up the ledge, his footprints vanishing behind him, taking away all trace of his presence in this room. As he reached the ledge far up the other side of the cavern, he saw the last footprint ahead of him and wondered if, when he got there, he too would disappear.

Had he read the magic wrong?

Four steps to go.

This is how it works, isn't it? You walk your own path and then . . . then . . . are you free to take a new path? Or do you fade away when you reach the end?

Three steps to go.

Could he just disappear like that?

Two steps.

Yes: he could just disappear like that. But if he left a footprint behind, wouldn't that mean his journey was never finished? His task incomplete?

One step.

"Stupid mapwyrd," he muttered.

He placed his foot in the last footprint, stepped forward, and then took it out. It vanished like all the rest. A cold wind blew through the cave, but nothing else changed.

Leptin sighed deeply. Footprints, even his own, are just another kind of map, and not to be confused with the destination.

He walked forward, into the fifth cavern.

Pieces of parchment with the world drawn in many colors were scattered across the floor; the wrecks and skeletons of globes sat in every corner; the walls were a map of the cave itself, its every nook and crevice carved into its own stone walls. There was light, green light, emerging from two open scrolls that sat on two wooden tables at the far end. The mapwyrd sat on the floor between the tables, sketching furiously on the skin of an animal with a fountain pen.

His hair was long and thin and grey like an old man's; his skin was thick and gnarled like the bark of a tree; his fingers long and nimble; his eyes were milky white with pupils the color of burning coals. "You have come here before," he said in a hoarse and faltering voice. "I remember."

"Yah," said Leptin. "Long time."

"You sought a map of the Winterblood Forest, and after you left the map changed. That is how I remember you: the goblin who broke the symmetry of the trees."

"Bad trees," Leptin said. "Bad trees."

"They were beautiful," the mapwyrd croaked. "That is how I remember you: the breaker of something beautiful."

Leptin shrugged. "Okay."

The mapwyrd chuckled. It sounded painful, like it opened a crack in his throat. "Now you return. What would you like to break this time?"

"No break," said Leptin. "Save."

"Well look at you," said the mapwyrd.

He paused in his frantic drawing, his pen quivered, and then added some final strokes to the animal skin. He put the pen down and brought the skin close to his eyes. "This," he said, "is your life. All mapped out. Would you like to see it?"

Leptin hissed. "Not what here find."

The mapwyrd's cracked lips smiled. He held the skin forward. "But you want it."

"Get take two maps?"

The mapwyrd grinned and cackled his sore cackle. "Just one."

Leptin shook his head. "Not what here find."

"But it's what I'm offering," the mapwyrd said. "Anything else you'll have to pay for."

Leptin nodded. "Got whiskey," he said, producing a brown glass bottle.

The mapwyrd licked his lips. He leaned forward, and his coal eyes strained. "Goblin?"

Leptin took a deep breath and shook his head. "Human. High culture."

"You disappoint me."

"Smokey," Leptin said. "Taste like bog."

"Little goblin . . . little goblin."

"Big bog."

"You have come with less than you had before. It has not occurred to you that I would ask for more."

Leptin's eyes narrowed. "Why mapwyrd want big payment make map? Got plenty. No run out. Good practice."

The mapwyrd chuckled again. "The world is different."

Leptin bit his lip. "You lot deeper in cave now."

"Oh yes." The mapwyrd crawled forward on his hands and knees. "Do you not see the world coming apart around us? Reality twisting off its axis, unmoored? Can you not see it? I CAN!"

Leptin nodded.

The mapwyrd crawled closer. "I ask myself: what would I need to survive if the world spins into the sun and is engulfed in flame? Or falls out into space and eternal night? How would I live?"

Leptin scratched his head. "Already got nice cave."

"I ask for more because the world demands more!" The mapwyrd was right before Leptin now, his hand reaching out, just inches away from the goblins face. "And you have come."

The mapwyrd smelled of ink and paper and skin. Leptin held his breath. The mapwyrd's fingers almost touched his ear, almost traced his jaw. The mapwyrd's eyes stared into his.

Then he crawled back, back to his pen and his scattered papers, back to the animal skin with the map of Leptin's life. Back to the tables with the open scrolls, and the green light that shone from them.

Leptin inhaled.

"You come in a time of need, and so I drew your life to see what you might have of use to me. I will give you whatever map you seek. But in exchange, I may change a line on the map of your life. One line, and send it wherever I choose." He picked up his fountain pen. "Do we have a bargain?"

Leptin blinked. "Not . . . not work that way."

The mapwyrd tittered. "Oh, you think you know something about maps, do you?"

"Map . . . ," Leptin struggled for the words. "Map show life. Map not life."

The mapwyrd pointed his pen at Leptin. A drop of ink fell onto the cave floor. "Do not presume to tell me of my craft! Go!"

"Wait," said Leptin.

"Go!"

"Wait!" Leptin shouted. "Yah! Yah! Got deal!"

The mapwyrd's breathing was heavy. He wheezed and hissed. "Very well." His breathing slowed. He smiled again. "Very good." He pulled a blank sheet of paper from the cave floor and sat on a smooth rock. "What do you wish to have laid out before you, as though you were a god looking down upon the world?"

"San Francisco." Leptin didn't hesitate. "Early twenty-first century. Hiding place of mouse. Pitter Patter Pounce. And resting place of ancient symbols. All living ancient symbols."

The mapwyrd's eyes widened. His lips moved, but no sound came out. "The ancient symbols," he finally sputtered. "So that's . . . is that—"

"Make map," Leptin said, folding his arms.

"Yes. Yes. Of course." The mapwyrd set bottles of ink around him in a dozen colors, and suddenly his pen was moving faster than the eye could follow. A city sprang up on the parchment, and details began filling it in. Deep, deep, underground, were ten remaining ancient things, buried but in the mind's eye of every living creature. They grew solid. All but one, under a decommissioned navy base, which began fading away.

Leptin pointed. "What that? What that?"

The mapwyrd didn't look up. "It is . . . dying," he said. His voice cracked with fear.

Leptin snarled. The mouse was on the move. Right now. Hundreds of years in the future, at this very moment, the mouse was on the move, killing another thing that must not die.

Gherin had failed to stop him.

Had Gherin been fooled? Had there been a fight? Was he wounded, or imprisoned?

Was he dead?

What had happened to his young friend to keep him from his duty?

Chapter 24

The lights went down.

The audience clapped as the conductor, dressed in a tuxedo, stepped in front of the orchestra. Gherin clapped too, because it seemed like fun. He shivered with anticipation. Perhaps there would be a fight.

The conductor raised his baton, and eighty instruments followed.

When he lowered his baton, music exploded.

Gherin's jaw dropped. He stared, dumbly.

All of those instruments, playing at once, and yet none of them went their own way. They all stayed together, somehow—carried along by a rhythm they heard and obeyed.

He noticed the harmony next, the strings and the brass playing notes that were not the melody, yet somehow added to it, soaring and diving and returning to the tune. So much variation, but it all made the theme stronger.

He had never imagined the universe contained such sounds.

Only then, then, did he realize it was beautiful too.

"Ooooooooooo," he heard himself gasp. His body was numb. His mind whirled.

When the curtain rose, he saw the backdrop from backstage in its rightful place, and understood what it was for. When the humans came on stage, accompanied by music, they were in costumes that matched the place the backdrop was pretending to be. They carried swords that were not swords, but now . . . somehow . . . were swords again.

The humans opened their mouths and did the most unexpected thing. They sang . . . sang melodies and harmonies together that mixed with the music as though they were coming from one singer, one mouth. Then they sang harmonies too, with the music and with each other—at the same time.

Gherin wept.

Chapter 25

When the final curtain fell, and all the clapping was over, and the lights had come back up, and the many, many, humans in their pretty clothes had left, and the lights had gone down again and the stage was dark and the auditorium was quiet, the opera bat found Gherin sitting alone.

He was in the nook in the second-story wall that was cleverly concealed between box seats, where he had been put hours ago and given a chair and a sandwich.

The opera bat hung from the ceiling and coughed.

"Ex . . . excuse me, sir?" he asked. "Did you like the music?"

Gherin didn't look at him. "Yah."

"The score was marvelous, wasn't it. And those duets!"

Gherin said nothing.

"Did . . . did you like the costumes?"

"Yah."

"And the set?"

"Yah."

"And the story?"

Gherin looked up at him. "Was story?"

The opera bat's eyes widened. "Y . . . yessir! Of course!"

Gherin looked back at the stage. "Where?"

"All . . . all through the m . . . music, sir! The whole thing told a story!"

Gherin put his hands on his head and shook it slowly. "Miss so much."

"What . . . what did you think was happening?"

Ghein looked down at the ground. "Thought music."

The opera bat fell into the air and flew around in front of Gherin. "Oh. Well . . . you see . . . the music helped . . . tell . . . a story."

"Story good?" Gherin asked.

"Oh, well ... I like it, sir. Yes."

"What story?"

"You ... you mean ... what happened in it?"

"Yah."

The opera bat fluttered its wings alarmingly. "Oh, well, it's ... it's ... somewhat complex ... sir ... it ... it's a story within a story ..."

Gherin scowled. "Huh?"

"A ... story ... within ... a story ..."

"How fit?"

"Oh dear." The opera bat flew in tight circles. "The main ... the main character is a poet ..."

"Ooooooooo," said Gherin, appreciatively.

"And the other main character is his Muse. Do you ... do you ... know what a ... muse is, sir?"

Gherin nodded. "Yah. Uncle ate once."

The opera bat nearly flew into a wall. "Oh no sir! No sir! You don't eat a muse!"

Gherin shrugged. "Not poison. Taste like troll."

"No no, sir! A muse is a mythological being!"

"Yah. Hard catch."

The opera bat let out a moan too high for the human ear to hear, and landed on the seat of a plush chair. "It ... it ... it doesn't work ... like that ... sir ... you can't just ... eat ... a muse ..."

"Nah," Gherin agreed. "Cook on spit."

"Are ... we ... even ... talking ... about the same thing?"

Gherin tilted his head to the side and considered. "Not sure. Opera hard understand."

The opera bat rested his body on the soft padding, and muttered something muffled into the seat.

Gherin leaned forward and put his head across the seat, so that his breath enveloped the opera bat. "Tell Gherin opera story."

The bat shuddered. "Oh sir ... it's very complicated ..."

Gherin bared his fangs. "Now."

The bat leaped into the air and fluttered around Gherin's head, squeaking at the top of his lungs. "In the opening sequence the muse disguises herself as the poet's best friend ... they're in a tavern ... and the poet's rival in romance, who is a Count, asks that the poet entertain students with the tales of his three lost loves ..."

Gherin shook his head. "Big confuse."

"Sorry! Sorry! It ... um ... in the first act, which is the first story, the poet explains how he fell in love with a woman he only saw in a window, not realizing that she was an automaton made by a man who is played by the same actor who plays the romantic rival ... the Count ..."

Gherin looked at the bat blankly, and stretched the claws on his right hand.

"Oh! Oh! Oh!" Squealed the opera bat. "Well ... you see ... the same actors play multiple parts, each act is a different story within a story ..."

Gherin stretched the claws on his left hand, and shook his head. "Make short."

"But there are three more acts!" wailed the opera bat.

Gherin snarled. Even from this distance, the opera bat could feel his breath.

"It's ... it's ... " The opera bat saw his life flash before his eyes. "IT'S ABOUT A POET WHO LOVED FOUR BEAUTIFUL WOMEN IN HIS LIFE, BUT THE MUSE SABOTAGED HIS CHANCE WITH EACH OF THEM, SO THAT HE SPENDS THE REST OF HIS LIFE DEVOTED TO POETRY!"

The opera bat collapsed into the chair.

"Ohhhhhhhh," said Gherin. "That's good. Scary." He sighed. "Opera got it all."

"I'm glad you like it," moaned the opera bat.

"Yah."

The opera bat muffled something into the seat cushion.

Gherin's ears raised up. "Wha?"

"Oh ...sorry ...sir. I just ... I didn't know I had that ... had that in me."

Gherin nodded. "Yah. Good with pressure." His ears tilted forward. "Every opera same story?"

The opera bat lifted its pale little head. "Oh no, sir. Ever opera is different!"

Gherin shook his head. "So much learn." He leaned down in front of the opera bat. "How many operas? Four? Five?" He raised his eyebrows. "Six?"

"Oh ... oh no sir. There are hundreds!"

Gherin leaned back against the wall. "So many," he whispered, staring at his hands, trying to count them all. He stared down at his feet. It didn't help.

The opera bat cleared his throat. "How ... excuse me ... sir ... how many stories do your people have?"

Gherin looked up at him. "Two."

"Wha ..." the opera bat blinked again and again. "You only have ..."

"Yah," Gherin said. "Goblins got two stories." He closed his eyes and smiled. "Good stories."

"What …if I may … ask … sir: what are they?"

Gherin looked over at him, and held up one claw. "War." He held up a second claw. "Love." He nodded and put his hands down.

"That's … that's it, sir? War … and Love?"

"Yah. War. Love. Only two stories. Story different every time tell, though. Never same twice."

"I see, sir," said the opera bat, thinking deeply. "I see."

After a while, Gherin stood up and sighed. "So many stories." He looked over at the opera bat. "Glad not eat."

The bat flew up into the air. "S … sir … Mr. O'Shaughnessy would like to know if … if … you'd care to join him to discuss … ," he spoke slowly, trying to remember the exact words, "coming to an arrangement whereby a number of cultural amenities, such as the opera, may be put at your disposal on a permanent basis."

There was silence in the opera house.

"Yah."

Chapter 26

The City Hall of San Francisco is one of the most beautiful government buildings in the world. In the city council room, underneath a dome of pink marble trimmed in gold, there are eleven leather seats, one of which is raised above the others: the president's chair.

Willie O'Shaughnessy had never sat in that chair before. It was a risky proposition for his boys to take over city hall, even at night when all of the humans were gone. He didn't want to be an elected official, anyway. Let other animals beg for votes: let his brother. An animal who needs votes will never know rest.

But city hall was right across the street from the opera house, and he had an important guest to impress, so it was worth the risk. He didn't know anything about goblins, but he knew the look in Gherin's eyes: he could picture the goblin walking into the main hall, under the magnificent dome, staring up at it and getting lost in the spire. He could hear the goblin's talons clacking on the marble floor now. Such sharp claws he had. A natural predator.

Willie had a rabbit's stomach, and it clenched at the thought of those claws. But his breathing was steady. He closed his eyes and thought of the ax: the terrible ax. He'd come up from nothing. He'd been born in a cage in Texas, and a human in overalls had taken his mother and father and cut their throats with a hatchet before his eyes. He knew what had happened to their meat, and one of the trucks that kicked up dust when it parked outside of the house had carried their pelts away.

Willie's stomach had clenched at the sight of that ax and the things it did, but after his parents were gone he had seen the look in his brothers' eyes, and known that they would never listen to their stomachs again. He had gathered them together. Aaron had figured out a plan to escape. Jake and Gerardo had bled to break the cage. Sean had carried Bevan on his back, pretty little Bevan who'd needed to be protected from the truths of the world, as they ran away from the house and into the dust. They survived coyotes and highways and a terrible pack of wolves, and by the time they'd reached San Francisco they were men.

No one had thought a family of rabbits could be a force to contend with—but they lived in their new home with the same determination it had taken to get out of that cage.

Yes, Willie's stomach flipped as the door to the council chamber was pushed aside and the fiercest predator he'd ever seen walked from the marble hallway onto carpet. But he knew the look on the goblin's face—he could always tell a man who wants something badly enough—and that's sharper than any claw. Someday, Willie thought, I will own every cage in the city and put the children of my enemies in them.

He had to admit: the chair felt good.

Gherin had lingered in the main courtyard. The last time he had been in city hall he had gone straight down: now he was looking up. Up was better. It seemed to go on forever, yet the end could just be seen far above. He shook his head and wiped his eyes.

The opera bat flew ahead, and Gherin's claws clacked on the marble stairs up to the second floor. A gang of raccoons was waiting at the top, smirking. They eyed him warily through their fur masks.

Gherin scratched his head. "Expecting rats."

The raccoons just tittered and four of them stood on each other's shoulders so that the top one's deft hands could work the doorknob and open the way into the council chamber.

"Rats better," Gherin muttered, and walked in. One of the raccoons made an obscene gesture at his back. They followed him into the council chamber, and when they were all through pushed the great wooden door closed behind them. It latched with a click.

Gherin looked around. There were four raccoons behind him, and another four in the back of the room, leaning against the wall. One was smoking a cigarette. The only other animal, sitting on a chair high above every other seat in the room, was Willie O'Shaughnessy. The rabbit grinned broadly and hopped from the chair onto the desk in front of it.

"Glad you could make it," Willie said. "You know, if you like the opera, I bet you'll love the symphony. And movies. Oh yes, you're going to love movies. I think we should see a movie together. Would you like that? All you've got to do is tell me if you'd rather laugh or cry. Then I'll pick the right film."

Gherin looked around. "Where rat?"

Willie shook his head. "I'm afraid our last bit of unpleasantness has convinced my colleague that you can't be worked with. Apparently there's some kind of bad blood between your species and his. Did you know that? Do you have any idea what your people did to his?"

Gherin shrugged. "Eat? Think eat."

Willie nodded. "Could be. Could be. In any case, he's now intractable. Much like your friend: a man who can't figure out a way to get what he wants. But we're not like that. You and me: we're going to get what we want, and everyone will be better off for it."

Gherin nodded slowly. "What movie?"

Willie's eyes brightened. "What's a movie? It's life—put right in front of you, in all its glory, for two hours. It's everything you can imagine."

Willie's stomach was turning so hard it almost brought tears to his eyes. But he stood up straight, tightened his legs, and leaped down from his high perch to the floor below—right in front of the goblin. He looked him in the eyes and smiled like it came naturally.

The raccoons gasped.

"There's so much to show you," Willie said. "You know, I was new to the city once, a long time ago. I came in off the highway with briars in my fur and no idea where to get a good *tikka masala*."

Gherin's eyes narrowed. "What that?"

"It's delicious. I've spent my whole life doing what you want to do. And I got there. I've got the life you want. I can see it. But you . . . I'm gonna be honest here . . . you've got an advantage over me. You're useful. You're obviously useful. Nobody looked at me and said 'I can make money with that rabbit.' But you: you're one of a kind. Two of a kind, if you count your friend—but he's going away. You're staying. Don't try to deny it. I've been watching you. You're looking around and some little part of you is wondering: what neighborhood should I live in? And that means I can help you. That means you won't have to work as hard, or sacrifice as much, as I did to get here." He clapped his soft paws together. "We are going to have a great time. Season tickets to the opera, free movie passes, fresh organic rhubarb pie. Seafood and fireworks on the Fourth of July. Cocktails at a Prohibition themed speakeasy."

Willie laughed. "You have no idea what I'm talking about. Okay. But it's all yours, kid. And that's just the first few weeks. We can start tonight."

Gherin's ears were flat against his head. His tongue was dry. "You . . . you rabbit," he said.

Willie smiled proudly. "That's right."

"You animal."

"Yeah."

"This human high culture. How get so much?"

"That's what I'm trying to tell you!" Willie punched the goblin in the shoulder with his soft paw. It was a mistake, and he hurried to cover it up. "You've got to know how to work the system! It's easy, once you know how. Learning's the hard part. Learning's impossible, most of the time, unless you've got somebody to show you how: somebody who's already plugged in and doesn't make the worst mistakes." He smiled broadly.

Gherin nodded slowly. Something was becoming clear. He could almost put words to it. "High culture got holes."

Willie shrugged. "You just gotta play the system."

Gherin nodded again, still trying to put it together. "Holes. Animals get in. Sometimes humans get out. Maybe one foot each side, like opera bat."

"Opera bat?" said Willie. Then he chuckled. "Oh, right. Alvarez. He's a good kid, isn't he. You like him?"

Slowly Gherin nodded. "Like opera bat."

"We'll keep him around," said Willie. "This is gonna be fun."

Gherin took a deep breath. "Want me kill, yah?"

Willie's smile didn't move. "Only a little. After the first few, I don't think you'll need to do much more than wave at someone to get them in line."

Gherin shrugged. "Okay. But, no kill at opera."

"That's fair," said Willie. "That's fair. No killing anybody at the opera. Good rule."

"Yah." Gherin nodded slowly, trying to think clearly: trying not to wonder what *tikka masala* and movies tasted like. "Yah. And . . . find mouse."

Willie kept smiling, but waved that away. "Aw, forget about the mouse."

Gherin's eyes narrowed. "Mouse need stop."

"But—"

"Big part deal."

Willie started to sigh, then covered it up. "All right," he said. "Sure. If it's important to you, it's important to me. We'll find him. I can find anybody, and you can stop him."

Laughter peeled through the room.

Willie's face froze.

A high heroic voice cried out: "Oh, how the corrupt have feet of clay, Willie O'Shaughnessy!"

All eyes looked up to the window sill. There, standing with his chest puffed out, was a bold mouse with a sword belted to his side, leather boots upon two feet, and a fine felt hat upon his head.

Willie's smile fell. "Well, this is embarrassing."

The raccoons hissed and leaned back. The one with the cigarette quickly snuffed it out and held it behind his back, standing in the corner like nothing had happened.

The mouse smiled at their fear and picked up a pack of dental floss beside him. He tossed it high, high, impossibly high into the air, and it latched around the chandelier on the ceiling. Clutching the other end in his hands he leaped from the window and let the dental floss swing him to the ground, right between Gherin and Willie.

He stared up into the goblin's eyes. "You have sought the mouse; and you have found him. But know, creature, that I have been watching you as well, and see that this is the sort you collude with. It does not speak well."

Gherin stared and the little mouse, with his chestnut striped fur and little nose and bright eyes, and a strange expression came over his face.

"Mouse!" Gherin gasped. "So . . . cute!"

Pitter Patter Pounce's expression soured.

"So . . . so . . . cute!" Gherin said again. He couldn't help it. He reached a hand out to pet the little guy . . .

. . . and found his palm on the point of the mouse's sword. In less time than it takes to blink the little thing had pulled it out and placed it, perfectly, where it could do damage if pressed a hair further.

"Do not judge the power of a bite by the size of the teeth," Pounce warned.

But Gherin's expression didn't change. "Got little sword!" he gasped. "Forged good!" He looked at it closer, and gasped again. "Spanish style! Ooooooo!"

Pounce sighed.

Willie nodded glumly. "I can sympathize," he said. "As a rabbit, I get that all the time too. No matter . . . ."

The sword was at Willie's throat. The rabbit's ears fell.

Through his haze of adoration, some part of Gherin realized just how impressed he should be by the mouse's speed and accuracy.

"Do not presume to compare us, Willie O'Shaughnessy! Though you claim to be a power broker you are nothing but a politician, who shall try to take my credit when the world sings my praises. A man who only stands for himself has a fool for a conscience."

Willie slowly backed away. "I'm just saying: people don't see past the fur and floppy ears. That's all. It's a curse." He looked over at the raccoons, gesturing with his eyes that they should come closer. Form a line of defense.

They looked at each other, and hesitated.

Pounce turned back to Gherin. "What you must understand is that he is irrelevant: there will always be vultures, and some of them will fancy themselves eagles. But I have mud on my boots and blood on my sword from fierce work this night, and you have traveled far through time and space to speak to me, giving a message to good men that I might hear it. So, creature, speak: what would you say to Pounce?"

Gherin blinked. "Ah," he said. "Okay, yah." He realized, for the first time, that he and Leptin had never really discussed what they would tell the mouse when they found him. It had always been assumed that Leptin would do the talking. And . . . mud on his boots? Blood on his sword? What had he been doing tonight? Gherin was supposed to know, had been supposed to be watching, searching . . . ."

The mouse coughed. "Perhaps it's written down somewhere?"

"Nah," said Gherin. "Goblins not good writing. Better howling. More fun." He cleared his throat. "Okay. Talk now. Good good. Here problem."

Pounce nodded and gestured with his free hand to go on.

"You killing lots ancient symbols. Got stop."

"What?" asked Willie.

Pounce took a step closer to him, the point of his sword just touching Willie's nose.

"Naturally you'd want me to stop," the mouse said, "for evil protects its own. But—"

"Uh-uh." Gherin held up his hands and waved them. "No do that. Evil no protect evil. Evil . . . ," he searched for the appropriate word. "Ignore evil, mostly. No care. Goblins do own thing, trolls do own thing, demons do own thing. Not friends. No care. Mouse want kill trolls, demons? Okay. Goblins point and laugh. Good time."

Pounce leaned forward toward him. "Then . . . why?" he asked. "For these symbols are the most ancient of the fundamental evils that plague our world. Their destruction is the beginning of a better one. Surely you can join me in supporting that!"

Gherin sighed sadly. "Nah. Got problem. Is no better world. Just this world. Kill symbols, world stop turning. Go off axis. Endless night. Endless fire. No good humans. No good goblins. No good mouse."

The mouse scowled. "Oh, I have heard that tired refrain played so often by instruments of corruption. The world cannot be changed, we must learn to live with injustice. It is the song that the powerful sing to the weak, the poetry that the large teach the small. And it is a lie. It has always been a lie."

He stood tall in his little boots. "Every battle I have won has proven that the small and powerless can make the world a better place if we resolve to change it."

"Yah!" Gherin acknowledged readily. "You big hero." He stopped and scratched his chin. "Okay, small hero. Tiny. But big courage, make big fights, win good. Yah. But . . . ," he tried to find the words. "Ancient symbols make world go. Maybe no good, maybe devour what touch, but, presence make world go. Kill, world not go. See?" He shook his head. He knew it wasn't enough. "World powered by big forces, terrible energies. No other way. Not fair. But, no other way."

Pounce's eyes sparkled. "It is always convenient for the powerful to tell the world that their excesses are necessary, but we will find another way. If the world stops spinning, we will spin it. If fire burns, we will put it out. If night falls, we will be beacons of light. We will find another way! This is the essence of heroism, fell creature: to find a better way in a fallen world!"

Gherin's eyes widened. He scratched his head. "But . . . but . . . can't!"

"I have been told that a thousand times by a thousand different despots, yet here I stand while their crowns have been beaten into plows. For the small can conquer the large and the just can vanquish the wicked. We will find a better way!"

Gherin shook his head. "Take chance bad. Like world. Not want burn in dark."

Pounce gestured around to the room: to Gherin, to Willie, to the raccoons huddled against the wall. "There we have it: the stark difference between good and evil. Good will take a chance on the small, on the weak, on the suffering—knowing that we have something to contribute. Knowing that we can change the world. Evil likes things just the way they are, thank you."

He twirled his sword in the air in a glorious display of skill. "Well, I shall always stand with the small—a fact that should bring you great comfort, for in the scale of the universe, goblins are very small indeed."

Three of the raccoons started clapping.

Willie looked over the mouse's sword at them and brought his paw to his neck. The clapping slowed down. He made a slashing motion, and the clapping stopped.

But Pounce saw his opportunity. "Join me," he said, extending a hand. "Join me, and we will make a difference. Join me and we will make a better world! We need fear no tyrants, nor live by their rules: join me and be free!"

He looked straight at Gherin. "You can do better than the path your feet are set on. You can do better than cast your lot with this rabble. Change your footsteps. Join me, and do better."

Gherin was surprised at how long he was quiet.

But he shook his head. "Can't save world this time. Not all wounds heal. And like opera. Want taste movie."

"That's my boy," said Willie.

Pounce turned. "One more word from you . . . ."

Willie hopped back onto a city supervisor's desk. He pointed at the raccoons. "Fight him and I'll get you scraps from a steakhouse! If you don't, I'll have your den set on fire before morning!"

Pitter Patter Pounce shook his head sadly. "Oh Willie O'Shaughnessy, . . . you strain the quality of mercy with such enthusiasm."

The raccoons looked at each other. Some of them shrugged. Some of them slumped their shoulders. The three that had clapped looked down at the floor.

"It's just business," Willie said, motioning with his paw.

The raccoons charged.

Gherin slapped his head as they bounded toward the mouse. "Fight not good," he muttered. "Talk better."

A raccoon sprung at Pounce, but he ducked below it as though bowing to a king and stuck upwards with his sword as it passed, ripping a long scar along its stomach. It howled in pain and lay where it landed. Another raccoon grabbed at the mouse, only to find its paw pinned to the ground by his sword.

"Ah Willie," Pounce sighed as he sprung into the air, pulled his sword from the raccoons paw, and kicked it in the face, knocking it on its back. "That lie is old and lazy, what rich men say when they have little conscience and no fear." A raccoon snapped its jaws at him, only to find Pounce standing on its nose. He struck the raccoon in between the eyes with the hilt of his sword and it staggered back onto the floor, howling.

He vaulted from its head onto the head of another raccoon and pinned its ears together with his sword. "A man who says 'it's just business' means, 'I don't want to try.' A man who says 'It's just business' means 'you are not a member of my tribe.' He means, 'I have no imagination.'" He pulled his sword out and struck the raccoon on the head with its pommel, then jumped onto the shoulder of another raccoon as it fell to the floor.

The next raccoon grabbed for him once, twice, three times, and somehow he eluded its grasp. Then he leaped away as another raccoon jumped for him, claws extended, and the two fell down in a tangle of claws and teeth. Pounce walked calmly away.

A raccoon tried to tackle him and crashed to the ground, bleeding from both feet. "As for you curs," Pounce said gently, "I heard his threat, and my blows will not kill you this night."

Two raccoons lunged, teeth snarling. He leaped from one's snout to the other's shoulder, and then back to the first one's head, and then onto the other's back, leaving fresh gashes each time. "But," he said, thinking it over, "I advise you to stay down."

They collapsed, whimpering.

With all the raccoons on the ground, Pounce sheathed his sword and dusted off his hands.

Gherin jumped up and down clapping.

Willie stared at Gherin, his lips trembling. "What are you . . . why are you . . .CHEERING?"

"Huh?" Gherin gave him a puzzled look. "That great!" He pointed at the mouse. "Him fight and talk same time! That hard!"

Pounce smirked, and bowed.

"Goblin like good fight," Gherin explained. Then his face turned serious and he turned to Pounce. "How you learn fight so good?"

"Practice."

"Oh."

"Now," Pounce stroked his chin. "The question becomes whether to kill Willie O'Shaughnessy."

Willie remembered the way the ax on his neck felt, and snarled at it. "It's not so simple, mouse."

"On the plus side," Pounce said, stepping back and forth, "he tried to have me killed this night, is a force of incalculable evil in this city, and a manipulative snake of a rabbit who will spend his life aiming at vengeance if he survives. On the other hand . . . ."

He paused.

He scratched his head.

He looked at Gherin. "I can't really think of a downside."

Gherin shrugged. "For you? Nah."

Pounce drew his sword. "That's what I thought."

Gherin stepped between them. "Me want him live, though."

Pounce sighed. "You are young and thoroughly seduced. I can sympathize, even if I cannot admire it. But you have seen me fight, and must surely understand: you cannot stop me."

Gherin hissed through his teeth. "You want kill ancient symbols. Got stop you anyway. Stop you now, get rabbit too."

Pounce nodded slowly. "I suppose that makes sense."

"Yah."

Pounce raised his blade. "In the words of my first swordmaster, Don Estabon Rosicrucis de Seville: May you fight like you love."

Gherin raised his claws. "Goblins got saying: Die quick."

"It lacks poetry."

Willie said "Not gonna happen." He threw a grenade between them.

They recognized it in flight, and leaped away—each in a different direction. It exploded, ripping desks apart along with the wooden barricade that separated the public area from the city councilors' desks.

"I do NOT bet my fate on a fight between other people!" Willie shouted. "I make my own fate! And I am NOT going to risk my new boy on you!" He leaped into the air, high up in the air, and reached the nearest wall. On the way down he caught the handle of the emergency fire alarm, and pulled it.

Claxons sounded. Sprinklers lowered, and water filled the room.

"First responders will be here in under two minutes," Willie said. "You wanna be here when that happens?

He bolted through an open door that lead into a hallway that lead to the city councilors' offices. "C'mon, Gherin!" he shouted.

Gherin and Pounce eyed each other, muscles tense.

Then Gherin struck.

His claws swept the floor where Pounce was standing—Pounce leaped over them like a runner over a hurdle and landed on Gherin's forearm. Gherin swiped with his other hand, and it stuck on Pounce's sword, the blade buried all the way into his palm. He couldn't move the hand.

He pulled his hand back and shook his arm violently. Pounce pulled his sword out and fell off the arm, landing . . . sword down . . . on Gherin's right knee. Again the blade went deep. Gherin's leg buckled and he fell to the ground, snarling. He kicked at Pounce with his other leg, but Pounce vaulted over Gherin's foot in a graceful summersault and landed on his shoulder.

He scampered up to Gherin's ear. "It will take you years before you're ready to face me," Pounce whispered. "For right now, just remember: you're on the wrong side."

He leaped off Gherin and over to the line of dental floss hanging from the chandelier. He climbed up it fast as lightning, and leaped from the lighting to the window, where he disappeared.

Gherin heard sirens in the distance. He stood up, tested his leg, and winced. He lowered himself to all fours, giving him more support, and dashed after Willie. He followed the rabbit's scent around the hallways and into a broom closet with a hole in the floor. He squeezed through into a crawlspace that led to a maintenance hatch that led underground, and when he emerged into a sewer tunnel he found Willie, Jake, and Gerardo waiting for him.

Willie smiled. "Glad you made it! I was starting to worry."

Gherin scowled. "You got lots explosives."

Willie's smile grew. "I thought I might be fighting you tonight, and if that happened I knew raccoons weren't going to cut it. Pity about those boys. The ones that survive will be okay: I've got connections in animal control. On the other hand, word gets out that the mouse killed them, it might turn a few of the right heads. That's all you gotta do sometimes." He whistled. "This was a big screw-up. The humans are going to be trying to figure out what happened for years. If they decide it's terrorism, life gets harder for everybody. But there's this newspaper columnist, I'm sure he can be put on the trail of a more convincing story. And ... ," he shrugged. "I've got a new friend. And that's what's important in life, isn't it. It's who you know."

Gherin nodded slowly.

Willie noticed Gherin's wounds. "You take a swing at him?"

"Yah."

Willie chuckled and pat his brothers' arms. "How'd it go?"

Gherin considered. "Draw," he said at last.

"That's good!" said Willie. "That's real good. To think I spent time hiding that bastard from you. I can't regret it, because it brought us together, but I'm real sorry about it all the same."

His eyes narrowed. "Once you've run a couple errands for me, you can have him. I'll help. And then ... oh, you're gonna love this town."

Chapter 27

The map of San Francisco was nothing like the map of the Winterblood Forest. That map had been heavy and dark with dashes of white illuminating the paths and hidden places. This map was thin, nearly translucent, yet with the illusion of depth so that it seemed to Leptin that he wasn't so much seeing through it as into it.

The ancient symbols that kept the world in motion were the only things he couldn't see through.

Leptin nodded at it, then stared through it at the face of the mapwyrd. "Technique changed."

The mapwyrd smirked and shuffled over to one of the tables, picking up his ink and pens and placing them down near broken rules and compasses. "Why do you think I live in a cave bordering the Renaissance, but for the chance to practice my craft in silence?"

Leptin shrugged. "Cave nice?"

"No. It's not nice."

"Renaissance got good eats?"

He snickered. "Goblins are always hungry. Always think with your stomachs."

"Nah," said Leptin. "Think claws too."

"Indeed."

Leptin took another look. "Good map," he said, satisfied. "Shows where things is."

"Yes." The mapwyrd shuffled back over quickly with a bone tube, rolled the map up, and placed it inside. "My technique is much improved." He gave Leptin a quick nod. "I appreciate you noticing more than it might appear."

Leptin nodded, took the map, and stuck out his chest. "Yah," he said. "Pay now."

The mapwyrd blinked. "What?"

Leptin stared ahead. "Pay now. Make change Leptin life map. One line."

The mapwyrd smiled. His teeth were rotting. "I already have."

Leptin blinked. "Nothing happen?"

The mapwyrd chuckled. "It will. You just haven't gotten there yet."

Leptin thought about, and nodded. "Okay."

They stared at each other for a moment, each looking at the other's teeth.

"Go," said the mapwyrd. "Now."

"Yah."

Leptin turned around. It was going to be a long trip back.

Chapter 28

The moon reflected dimly in piles of hubcaps and leaky transmissions and an engine sometimes used as a stool. The discarded puzzle pieces of technology, rusted and battered, waited in a junkyard by the Bay for broken cars to be hauled over, and for human hands to lift them up and see if they fit: see if they could bring the dead back to life, for a little while longer.

Most wild animals avoided this place, afraid of the spirit of rust and decay that can make broken metal roar again. But it was the home of Junkyard Ed, who knew nothing ever comes back from the dead.

He was not the biggest dog in San Francisco. It was known that there was a domesticated black lab that had grown to truly gargantuan size: he belonged to an internet billionaire, who kept him on an entire floor of a skyscraper downtown.

Junkyard Ed, however, had the biggest jaws, and he belonged to no one. Let the black lab have his castle in the sky, looking out enormous windows at a world of opportunity and waiting to be fed: Junkyard Ed kept court on the ground, in the dirt, and ate whatever he wanted.

Junkyard sat on the open bed of a desiccated Ford truck and watched his pack chase the bones of a homeless man that he tossed from his enormous mouth. He enjoyed this game. They'd found the wild human, nearly dead, drunk on a corner a week ago. The opportunity had been too good to pass up.

To be a leader, Junkyard knew, is to never be alone. It is to play games that remind everyone who the winner is. When Junkyard laughed, a dozen smaller dogs who surrounded him laughed too. When he barked, they bared their teeth. When he was finished eating, they fought each other for the scraps. And they frolicked when he tossed them the bones of a man.

He clamped down on an elbow joint, tilted his head back, and hurled it from his jaws out past the pile of windshield wipers. Three pit bulls chased it down and pulled it between them. A femur bone next, thrown from his massive jaws out to a family of mutts. A rib-and-a-half, sent flying: he watched two Dobermans charge straight into a fence trying to grab it, and he laughed.

Suddenly the wind smelled wrong.

He dropped the fingers in his mouth and sniffed.

He bared his teeth.

He looked around, trying to get a lock on the scent. He leaped off the truck bed and whirled in a circle.

The other dogs bared their teeth and barked and looked, and for a moment he felt confident . . . until he realized that they didn't smell a thing. They were just following his lead. Useless.

He howled for quiet. The junkyard grew still.

He lifted up his head and walked in a slow circle. "I know you're there," he growled. "Whoever you are. And I know why you're here. It doesn't matter what you smell like: people only come here for a fight."

The voice, so unlike an animal's yet so unlike a man's, came from on top of the roof of the truck. "Yah. Good dog."

The pack turned to look. Junkyard Ed put his front paws on top of the truck bed to get a better view. He leaned forward, his body taut, and showed his massive teeth while he looked the intruder over.

For a moment, he lost his breath.

"Well, well," Junkyard said at last. "I'd heard rumors, but I hadn't believed it. Not really."

Gherin shrugged. He was eating an apple. "Yah," he said between bites. "But true: organic taste better."

Junkyard blinked. "What are you talking about?"

"Produce," Gherin said. "Human culture got more kind apples. More kind apples! Crazy."

Junkyard considered this, and shook his head. "Aren't there supposed to be two of you?"

Gherin took another bite and chewed slowly. "Nah," he said. "Maybe tomorrow."

"Is that so . . . ," said Junkyard. No, the rumors had been clear. There were two of them. That meant an ambush was coming. Or this was a distraction. "In all of the city, you've come here. Where," he chuckled, "we don't even have *apples*. Are you trying to hire me or kill me?"

Gherin took the last bite. "Kill."

Junkyard nodded. "Okay. Why?"

Gheirn though about it. "Like opera," he said at last.

"What's like opera?"

"No, no. Me like opera."

"You do?"

"Lots."

"Oh." Junkyard's tongue hung out for a few moments in a way he'd never been comfortable with: it made him look less fierce. "Stranger," he said, "I don't understand you at all."

Gherin nodded. He didn't understand why the dog needed to die either. Willie had tried to explain it: something about how if he was going to stay in town, he couldn't just kill the mayor, so he had to kill somebody else that would send the right message. Willie had tried to draw it out on a chart for him, but that only made him angry at the chart. Politics was confusing.

"Well," said Gherin, "there five lines. One red, and one got dots. You on chart. Mayor on chart. Green line. Yah?"

"The Mayor?" asked Junkyard. "This is about Handsome Gavin?"

"Well, green line connect black line."

Junkyard's breathing was heavy. "That preening runt."

"Yah," said Gherin. "Got blue line. Goes in circle."

"So that would mean you're working for . . . the spider queen? The rabbits?"

Gherin lost track and tried again, using his fingers this time. "There five lines. One red, and one got dots . . . ."

Junkyard shook his head. "No, I get it now."

"Yah?"

"Sure. It's business."

"Okay," said Gherin. "You explain?"

Junkyard's tongue fell out again. "To . . . to you?"

"Yah. Big help."

Junkyard leaned forward and in a low growl explained, "Stranger, this is all you need to understand: there are bodies buried under the piles of axles and tires. Do you really . . . really . . . think you're anything but one more grave in my home?"

Gherin stretched his claws and cracked his knuckles. "That easy understand." He smiled.

Junkyard shouted back to his pack. "Guard the perimeter! The other one's around somewhere!"

"Other one what?" asked Gherin.

"You know," said Junkyard, turning his full attention to Gherin, "I've never killed a goblin before."

"Good try new things. Ever go opera?"

Junkyard paused a moment. "Actually, I've lived my whole life in this city and no, I never have."

"Too bad."

Junkyard shrugged. "Never been to Alcatraz either." He leaped forward in a mighty rush.

Gherin had not been prepared for a dog that big to move that fast. Junkyard's body knocked him off the roof of the truck and they fell onto the ground.

Junkyard landed on Gherin and clamped his massive jaws down on the goblin's left arm. The teeth pierced through skin and scale.

Gherin shouted and swiped with his right hand. The claws ripped along Junkyard's nose and into his neck, but the dog didn't let go. Gherin pulled his feet to his chest and lashed out with his talons as junkyard did the same. His hind legs left a gash on Gherin's chest while Gherin's talons cut through fur and left a trail of blood.

Still the dog didn't let go.

Gherin pushed himself into his foe, and bit Junkyard's right ear off.

Junkyard screamed—he couldn't help it—and Gherin was free. He whirled around and scrambled to his feet as Junkyard recovered from the pain. The dog's eyes were bloodshot.

Junkyard growled and leaped. Gherin hissed and spun aside, his claws lashing out and cutting through the dog's side as he passed.

Junkyard pivoted and lashed out again, his teeth reaching for Gherin's neck, but the goblin was too fast, and by the time Junkyard closed his mouth on empty air Gherin was on his right flank, his fangs in the dog's back leg.

Junkyard screamed and tried to pull away, but this time Gherin wouldn't let go. He bit down further as Junkyard lost his balance and crashed on the ground. Gherin's feet lashed out and left the deepest gash yet: Junkyard's belly was shredded.

Gherin bared his fangs and stepped back. "No seen opera," he hissed. "Make you soft. Make weak."

Junkyard looked around at his pack for help, but saw the way they were watching: they'd chased after too many of his bones, laughed at too many of his jokes . . . and now they were giddy at the sight of his blood.

Worse, they were more afraid of the goblin now. Useless.

Gherin stepped toward him. Junkyard'd spent his whole life owning his corner of the city, his whole life as the master of life and death, and yet now, in these final moments, he realized that perhaps there was only one thing he'd ever really been good at.

He charged, again: fangs forward, claws extended, hard and fast and bloody, shouting his war cry.

Again he was faster than the goblin expected: the goblin didn't have his experience, hadn't seen this coming. His teeth sank into the goblin's shoulder, his front claws scratched at the goblin's chest, his back legs scratched at the goblin's legs. He pushed with all his might, ignoring the goblin's claws, ignoring the goblins fangs . . . pushing harder, and harder, and harder, the way he had his whole life, his size and bite the only things that never left him . . .

. . . until he died in the goblin's deadly embrace.

Gherin disentangled himself from Junkyard's corpse. His wounds were deep, but not intolerable—only the bite in his left arm, the first blood of the battle, caused him great pain. He spun around and looked at the pack, daring them to defy him.

Then he howled at the moon. And the pack howled too.

Chapter 29

Crossing a river near a Seelie glade, Leptin had seen a mighty flock of pterodactyls float across the horizon and circle three times, far, far, away from their home and hunting grounds. Two nights ago strange lights had soared across the sky, stopping and starting in impossibly swift motions: the skyboats of some unknown people trying to find their way.

There were tracks, on the ground, in shapes that did not belong here. They were fresh.

21st Century San Francisco was not where it was supposed to be.

The world was confused. Leptin rubbed his eyes and let out a deep breath. He finally understood the problem. He thought.

Leptin stared at the night sky from on top of a small mound. His people had built this place, shortly before the treaty. It wasn't, strictly speaking, in the land of human high culture: it was on the border, and a high culture human would have to get very lost, or turn wild, before finding their way here. Still, it was close, inviting an accident, and so the goblins had abandoned it when they pulled back from high culture in all times. But crossing the rocky plains it had been a beacon to him, standing out to his senses, drawing him to it across a timescape that made no sense.

He had hoped to find another goblin here ... though it was absurd to think that one would be camping in this abandoned place. But it had been a long journey, and many days since he'd spoken to anyone. It seemed to him that if he could meet another goblin perhaps it would mean that Gherin was all right – although he knew that made no sense. He slapped his head. That was stupid troll thinking.

He shouldn't have stopped here. He knew that. Never, he'd had it drilled into him, rest on the plains when you're alone. But he'd needed to get his bearings. Another ancient symbol had just died. That had to be the root of the problem.

Something moved. He saw it out of the corner of his eyes, and looked down from the heavens. A series of shapes, far away, were dashing across the rocky plain, glittering in the moonlight.

He hissed. He counted 1 ...2 ...3 ... 4. Four animal shapes – probably hounds. And then another shape, taller, right behind them.

"Bad."

They stopped, then turned suddenly. Coming straight towards the mound.

"Bad bad."

He calculated their speed: they were much, much, faster than he was. No point to run. He was on a plain – so there was no place to hide.

"No stay on plains," his father had told him, again and again, "unless got big strength. Lots'a goblins. No got big strength, no stop. Run day, run night, get place camp hide."

The one time he hadn't listened, it had gone wrong. Which probably meant it was very good advice.

He decided to stay on the mound. The symbolism appealed to him: making his stand on a place that had once belonged to his people. But it was more than that.

This enemy was being led by dogs: that meant it was a hunter. The best way to avoid being attacked by a hunter is to not act like prey.

Leptin dug his talons into the mound.

The shapes advanced beneath the starlight, faster than he could have thought possible. The taller being ran behind the dogs, holding them on leashes: it was human shaped, long legged, wearing armor of metal plates held together by leather straps.

A moment later he could see he had made a mistake. They were not dogs: they were wolves. Enormous wolves.

He should not have stopped here.

The hunter led the wolves up to the base of the mound, then raised a hand. The pack stopped, as though paralyzed in mid step. Leptin could see now that the hunter, underneath the helmet, was a human-looking woman with long brown hair.

"Goblin!" she said, and it was both a greeting and an exclamation of surprise.

He shrugged. "Yah. What you?"

She smiled at him, but the wolves growled fiercely, staring at him with shining eyes.

"Sit!" she said.

As one, the wolves fell to their haunches. "Very good," she whispered. She let the leashes go and they hovered in the air. She stepped around her pack and walked up to the border of the mound. She stopped.

"Tell me, goblin: do you know where we are?"

Leptin blinked, then scowled. "Yah."

Her grin widened. "Then we have something to talk about. May I approach?"

Leptin showed his fangs. "Polite. Like. You swear leave when ask?"

She raised her right hand, held in a fist. "I so swear."

Leptin's scowl twisted. It was traditional to swear to a powerful being or a place. Surely she knew that? An oath taken to nothing was a vault without gold.

She was testing him, he decided. She was seeing if he was afraid. Or … perhaps … she has that much pride.

"Yah," he said, gesturing with a talon. "Come."

She strode up the mound to stand beside him. She was over six feet tall, and graceful. She removed her helmet, and held it in her left hand. "I am Hela," she said. "Once of the Militant Tomb."

She looked human to him. Didn't smell that way, though. She smelled like her wolves. Or was it the other way around?

"Nice pack," he said, pointing at them.

She smiled proudly. "They are my children."

He smelled again, then raised his eyebrows.

She met his gaze, and held it. "It is the reason I am favorably inclined towards your people, and my pack is not," she said. "You know, I assume, of the wolf Garm?"

Leptin spit on the ground. "Yah. Grandfather helped bind to cliff. Lost fingers."

The wolves shrieked in rage.

She nodded. "Your family did me a good turn. I nearly died too many times collecting bounties because I could find no partners strong enough to hunt my foes and honest enough to guard my back. Since your people had imprisoned the world's greatest hunter, he was easy to find … and his appetites easy to satisfy." She shook her head and smiled down at the snarling wolves below. "Family really are the only ones you can trust."

Leptin shook his head. "Tribe," he said. Almost instinctively. "Trust tribe."

She stared down at him while her children snarled. "Really? And yet I notice you are here alone."

Leptin sighed. "Complicated," he said. "On mission, human high culture. Gotta sneak. Tribe too big come."

"I see." She shook her head. "In my experience, people always have a good reason not to join your struggle and make your enemies their own. There is always a good excuse. Only blood binds."

"Huh."

They stood together on the mound as the wind blew and the wolves howled.

"I cannot find my way," she said. "We are tracking a false prophet of the Nightshade Road, and while we have his scent I do not understand where he has taken us, or how we have come to this place. You on the other hand, goblin without a tribe, seem knowledgeable."

Leptin nodded. "Yep."

Her eyes narrowed. "I will not threaten you, goblin without a tribe, though there is bad blood between your family and the father of my children. Nor will I beg or bribe you. I will only ask you to extend me the courtesy of one traveler to another."

Leptin licked his lips, and then grinned widely. "Yah," he said. "Like you. Got steel in bones."

"Thank you."

Leptin pointed at the ground. "Norway. 9th century."

She gasped. "Impossible."

"Listen Leptin." He pointed to his left. "Border high culture two leagues, maybe one and half. Border shallow. Time get solid fast, easy step through."

She blanched. "One and a half ... I could have crossed right through into the lands of high culture and not even known."

Leptin nodded. "Big danger."

"We would be doomed ... the treaty ..."

"Dead wizards keep treaties," said Leptin. "Magic thicker blood."

Her expression hardened. "You mock me."

"Yah, little."

"Have you no family, Leptin of the goblins?"

Leptin slowly shook his head. "All dead."

"Ah," she said. "Forgive me."

"Okay."

She waited a moment, to see if more would be said. It would not. "Tell me, then: how have I not realized how close I was to catastrophe?"

Leptin looked at the wolves and then back at her. "Wolves track, yah?"

"Of course. They are my guide through time's many rivers."

"But ... steel woman navigate by stars, yah?"

"Naturally."

Leptin shook his head. "Bad bad. Stars wrong now."

"What do you …" she looked up at the sky. "How can the stars be …wrong?"

"Look," said Leptin. "See close constellations. Not right." He pointed to a line of stars. "Hunters's arrow no hit fleeing dragon now."

"But that's …" her helmet fell out of her hand and rolled down the mound, where her children sniffed it eagerly. "By the One Eye …"

"Look," he said again, pointing to a spiral series of stars. "Coiled serpent reach poison nectar now."

She stared for as long as she could, then turned away. "What does this mean?"

Leptin shrugged.

Her eyes hardened. "Do you know what has happened?"

"Symbol die. Ancient. Big."

"This means nothing to me."

Leptin sighed. "Mouse not understand. High culture humans not understand. Great changes always begin with symbol. Only way happen. Symbol change first, then world. Symbol get born, symbol get die, symbol add pair eyes. But change first. Then world. Every time. Symbol change, world shudder."

She stroked her chin. "I'm not certain that's true."

Leptin bared his fangs and pointed to the sky. "Symbol die! Now stars change, time hard track! What you got?"

She raised her hands and held them before her. "I apologize, Leptin of the goblins. I accept your explanation. I did not mean to offend. The stars are subtly different, and you have done me a good turn by pointing this out."

Leptin nodded slowly. "Yah, okay," he said.

She put her hands down.

"Anything navigate by stars now, get big confuse. Eyes lie. Leptin need close eyes track through time now, and Garm-consort need trust wolves now, let other senses guide."

She nodded. "They will not steer me wrong."

Leptin shook his head. "Be slower. Stars pull time, like moon pull tides. Little change make big ripples. Everything off course now."

She pursed her lips. "That will be difficult. My hunts require speed. My livelihood precision."

"Life hard."

"Indeed it is," she muttered. She took a deep breath. It sounded like a growl. "The world becomes more dangerous."

"Yah."

Slowly she smiled. "I find that brings out the best in me."

"Huh."

She stared down at him. "You disapprove?"

He scratched the dirt with his talons. "You find Garm, make children, go hunting. You plenty dangerous now."

She laughed. "I do like your people so."

"Uh huh. Know why Goblins so great?"

She smiled. "Tell me."

"Tribe better family."

Her smile froze. "I think not."

His ears rose. "Yah. Tribe choice. Come age, face tribe, make choice: decide if belong. Ask get duties, ask get obligations. Yah! Choice good! Mean carry tribe's burden, carry own burden." He spat. "Not family. Family never ask: want wear chain on neck? Want pull mother cross time? Family duty slave duty. Blood not choice. Blood merciless. Tribe duty choice made: this who am. This who want be. Tribe better."

She stared at him. "I have been unfailingly polite, Goblin without a family, and yet you mock me at every turn." She bared her teeth. "You understand that my good will is what keeps Garm's children from avenging the imprisonment of their father."

Leptin shook his head. "Nah. You no fight. Fight stupid. You got prey. Got move slow. Not waste time. Fight Leptin, maybe child lose eye, lose foot. For what? You win, get nothing. Prey further away." He bared his fangs back at her. "Fight stupid."

Her eyes flashed. Her smile deepened. "Cruelty can be its own reward."

Leptin's skin went cold. "Then fight stupid fight," he said, trying to keep his voice fierce, his ears straight. "See children hobble, hear children scream, bury one more in Militant Tomb. Leptin's grandfather waiting say hello. Got thick blood!"

The wolves were perfectly still, their own ears perked up, waiting for the command.

She threw back her head and laughed. "I saw that, Leptin the Goblin without a Tribe! I saw the fear cover your warrior's heart, and that is the only gesture of respect I require. Dislike me if you must, but we both know you do not take me lightly."

Leptin held very still, waiting to see if her expression changed, if the command would be given all the same. Eventually he covered his teeth. "Yah. Okay. Fair."

She nodded, and then smiled. "Where are you going, Leptin of the Goblins?"

"San Francisco. Twenty-first century."

"Ah ... a long way away then. But I've heard it's lovely."

Leptin shrugged. "Meh."

"They say the buildings in the wizard's high culture are the tallest beneath the sky, and that even the lowliest peasant can whisper to the world."

"Think so."

"Perhaps someday, then, I shall see these marvels for myself. In the meantime, you have my thanks for straightening my course and assisting my work."

"Okay, crazy steel woman."

"Hela," she corrected him, walking down to the base of the mound.

He tapped his head. "Leptin remember."

She held out her hand and her helmet flew to her from the ground. "Good hunting."

Leptin said nothing as she took the leashes in her hand. "Hunt!" she cried, and the pack leaped forward like a star shooting across the plain.

Leptin let out a deep breath. It was nice to know he had family enemies. He wished he'd known his grandfather better. He hoped, if he ever met those wolves again, he could end them.

He did not think that this conversation bode well for Gherin. Stupid troll thinking.

She was too selfish to have ever belonged to a tribe, he thought. If she had, she could have told him exactly what's wrong with them. That they are susceptible to politics, that they can play favorites. When the tribal elders had told him that he must take Gherin with him … that had not been a duty he had felt on his own. But that they had come to him at all, that they had turned to Leptin in their hour of need to fulfill this most difficult of duties … that had been an honor the children of Hela and Garm would never know. His whole family had not died selfishly for themselves – they had died for their tribe, which had made their lives selfless.

No tribe is perfect. But if it's yours, then less than perfect will do.

When Hela and her brood were out of sight, he stepped off the mound, sniffed the air, and felt the ripples of time around him. The border with high culture was a still lake where time grew fetid and still; but he could feel a thin ribbon running through it that, if it came out properly on the other side, would connect him with 19th century London.

Cutting through high culture was always dangerous, but it would be the least impacted by the changes to constellations it did not even see – and he would spend no more time on the plains. His father had been right, and he would not make that mistake again.

Chapter 30

The most important of the spider queen's subjects lived in Chinatown, direct descendants of the animals that had come over with the railroad workers from China. They'd been called "vermin," then—treated as pests, purged over and over again no matter what good they did for the city's ecosystem—but they had endured.

After a time, the ability to endure is a highly sought after skill. The descendants of China had merged with the remnants of the old Spanish aristocracy that had come on the ships and trails of missionaries, and a newer, stronger, dynasty had been born. The most important members of the court lived in Chinatown.

But not Queen Rose.

The queen lived in a house high on a hill in North Beach, looking down on her subjects from a third floor tower. To rule, she had learned, is to hold very, very still and let the world bustle around you. Feel its vibrations and position yourself at the center so that everything comes to you eventually. Never act for trivial reasons: only act when your decisions will be decisive and devastating. Do this, and the potential for action ... the idea that you may do something . . . is enough to keep your subjects in line.

She knew her kingdom was trembling. She saw the wave of change coming. It had been so nice to have Handsome Gavin as her enemy—a preening, narcissistic show dog who deep down fancied himself a prince. He was far more impressed with the pomp and loyalty she commanded than he was by any of the trappings of his own democratically elected office. It would have been even better if he were stupid, but intelligent and vain is almost as good as stupid much of the time.

Soon, however, Handsome Gavin would be swept away. She could see it, even if he couldn't.

The murder of Junkyard Ed, that vicious outlaw whom every mayor had needed to cut a deal with, had sent the message clearly. There is a new power that cannot be stopped. The rabbits were on the march.

Well, she knew what would come next. She watched the traffic on the dark streets beneath and listened to her guards die on the floors below. She had never understood the migratory patterns of humans and their wagons. They did not cluster around food, they did not cluster around water, they did not cluster around prey. It made no sense: they had a sense of purpose she could not fathom.

Her guards were not doing well. But of course they had been prepared for very different threats. No one in San Francisco, except that interloper mouse, had apparently stood a chance. She bit her lip, just slightly: they should have come to her first. But then, she'd made herself harder to find. A queen cannot simply be approached: it defeats the whole point.

She hoped they didn't damage the house too much.

Her steward had just been sliced in two on the floor below. She was sure of it. This was quite exciting, really. But the stakes were low. The few courtiers and servants she really needed had been moved to safety days ago. If you are at the center of all vibrations, no footsteps can surprise you. The only real question was her own safety. And that would be very interesting indeed.

Footsteps on the stairs, and no one left to challenge them. The door to the tower creaked open.

Gherin stepped inside, his wounds still healing. He looked around the tower, saw it was empty except for webs. Empty except for her.

He stared.

"Ah . . . ," he said. "Maybe got wrong tower?"

She turned from the window, now, to look at him. So that was a goblin. She tilted her head. "Aren't there supposed to be two of you?"

He shrugged. "Get that lots." He looked at her carefully. Ah . . . ," he tried to think of the appropriate way to say this. "Why you human girl?"

She was. Or almost was. Seven years old, with dark black hair and big eyes. She smiled, because she understood that to be the appropriate response. "People are often confused by the title, 'spider queen,' and jump to conclusions."

Gherin nodded slowly. "Easy mistake. Yah. Think maybe change name?"

"But in fact the body you see is only the host."

He scratched his head. "Oh. That okay, then."

She held her left hand forward, as though it were to be kissed, and showed him the ring. A golden setting holding a block of amber, which had perfectly captured and preserved a large female spider. "The spider queen," she said. She pulled her hand back. "The host." She smiled again. "Do you understand now?"

Gherin's face tightened. "You queen long time, different bodies."

"Yes."

"Make easy set up human city."

"Yes."

"But ... take girl ... break treaty!"

"My people signed no treaty. We were beneath the great wizard's attention."

He nodded. "Lucky."

"Yes ... lucky. You can say that, having never lived at the mercy of humans."

He shrugged. "Food good."

"They build on our homes."

Gherin shook his head. "Build opera house on homes. That okay."

She frowned, just a bit. "We do agree that the web of culture is worth the death of flies."

He grinned. "See? Happy ending."

"I'm afraid not," she said. "I have lived long enough to know that there is no such thing."

Gherin scowled. "As happy?"

"As an ending."

He considered this, for a few moments. "Okay. Good tip. Maybe kill you now."

"If you think so."

He looked at her closely. "Not afraid?"

"I've lost hosts before."

He nodded, scowling. "Yah. Not sure what do ring. Give big think. It ...."

The floor trembled. They both looked around. Rats leaped from every corner of the room. They chewed their way through the walls. By the hundreds they leaped onto Gherin. Reginald, duke of rats, fell from the ceiling and onto the little girl's shoulder.

"Protect the queen!" he shouted.

Gherin staggered under the onslaught as his wounds were re-opened by gnashing teeth. The only thought he had time for was a stab of betrayal: weren't they on the same side?

Rose the spider queen turned her head slowly to look at the duke. "I had a suspicion, she said, "that you would be my loyal subject this week."

He shrugged. "The unfortunate fact, your majesty, is that Willie O'Shaughnessy has a goblin now, and I do not."

"Still," she said, watching Gherin writhe and strike and whirl. "You could have profited by my death."

"To what end, your majesty, if it cannot be kept? The rabbit is not a reliable ally when he has an advantage. Your authority and command of intrigue are no longer optional."

"Interesting choice."

He bowed deeply on her shoulder. "May I have the honor of saving your life?"

"You may proceed."

As he slaughtered rats, Gherin heard the window smash. A minute later, when the fight was over and he stood among the bodies he saw a rope ladder had been attached to the window frame and the queen and the duke were gone.

"Skkksssssksss hssskkkkk!" he hissed. The rats had opened up every wound he'd received from Junkyard Ed, he'd been betrayed by Willie's friend, and the queen was still alive.

No one had told him there would be rats.

"Bad day at office," he muttered, and winced.

He sat down against the wall and looked out the window onto the city, and watched the traffic on the dark streets below. Everyone had someplace to go in the city, and he wanted to see them all. But first he would rest here, for a little while. Then he would get a steak. At a good restaurant. Then he would have a talk with Willie.

Chapter 31

Willie was talking with Aaron when Gherin arrived at the tea garden. No poker game tonight: just family.

Willie waved and held up his paw, taking a moment more to finish his conversation of twitches and whiskers and stomps. Gherin waited by the pond, breathing heavily, as Jake and Gerardo hopped over.

Gherin was beginning to think he could tell the difference between the rabbits. He could recognize the quality of their character in the nits of their fur, seeing clearly that Gerardo would stand next to him, solid and quietly, while Jake would punch him on the shoulder as hard as he could.

"Hah!" said Jake. "You got real banged up there, didn't 'cha? Got put through the ringer! I hope you got the other guy!"

Gherin nodded slowly. "Yah."

"Hah! It's good to see you can take it the way you dish it out!" Jake still wore deep scars on his stomach from their first encounter.

"Yah," Gherin said quietly. "Gherin hunter."

"Bet 'ya are. Bet 'ya are. Hey," Jake leaned in close. "Did'ya know there's a herd of bison in the park?"

"Nah."

"It's true! The humans put 'em in a fence! Bison! A whole herd of 'em!"

Gherin nodded slowly. "Good know."

"'Ya know what I've always wanted 'ta do?"

Gherin didn't say anything.

"Eat a bison!"

Gherin raised his eyebrows.

"I know, I know—I know what'cher thinking!" Jake repeatedly stamped his foot on the ground. "Impossible. No rabbit in history has ever eatin' a bison! But that's what would make it so incredible! Imagine it!"

Gerardo sighed. "You can't eat a bison."

"I could maybe if he helped!"

Gherin looked around to see who Jake was pointing at. No one else was there.

"You could help with the stabbing and the clawing!" Jake said.

"You can't eat a bison," Gerardo repeated again.

"We'd be a team," said Jake. "Like Kirk and Spock, or Leonardo and Davinci!"

Gherin scratched his head.

Jake pointed his thumb at his brother. "This guy? He doesn't even want to try!"

Gerardo's scowl deepened. "A rabbit . . . can't . . . eat . . . a . . . bison."

"Hah! What's the point o' livin' if you ain't tryin'? That's what I say! You with me, guy? Are 'ya? It'll be great! And . . . ," his eyes gleamed as he gently scratched his belly. "I figure 'ya owe me one."

"Huh," said Gherin.

"Hey! Hey!" Suddenly Willie was in between the little crowd, pushing them all in separate directions. "Come on, let's not waste the man's time! He's our angel of death—and you treat angels with ritual and respect, right?"

"I'm just getting' to know him, Willie—"

"I know you are. But Sean needs help stocking the bar. Okay? Gerarado, help me out."

Gerardo grabbed his brother by the tail. "Come on, Jake: we'll get you a cold one."

Jake pointed at Gherin as he let himself be dragged away. "You think about it, huh? A whole bison! Just you and me—a whole bison! Hah! It'll be . . . ."

Willie gently turned Gherin around to face the pond. "Sorry about that. He's excitable. So, I—"

"Him really want eat—"

"Forget about that," Willie said impatiently. "It's something he says just to screw with people. He takes 'em to the bison pen and has them start laying into one, but it turns out they're smart and they're herd animals so the minute you hurt one they all charge at you. It's pretty deadly. Jake's 'friends' have had a lot of accidents that way. A lot. But sometimes, I think he really means it. I don't know. But you . . . ," Willie pat Gherin on the back. "I know you got Junkyard! That makes you, me, and Bevan legends in this town. It's a whole new game now. I need to take you out for a steak."

These rabbits, Gherin noticed, liked to put their paws on him. "Had steak."

Willie looked concerned. "Where?"

Gherin scratched his head. "Name of drink. Bourbon."

Willie slapped his forehead. "Ah no no no! This . . . this is a travesty! I'm taking you to Bocca. No question. Once you start taking less than the best, people start treating you as less than a king. I am not going to let that happen. But . . . ," his eyes narrowed. "I haven't heard a thing from Reginald. So I need you to tell me: are we at war too?"

Gherin tilted his head and thought about it. "Yah. Think so."

"You . . . think so?" Willie asked. "You think we're at war?" When Gherin nodded he made a motion to Aaron, who silently nodded and hopped away. "Is she dead?"

Gherin took a deep breath. "You sure rat duke friend?"

Willie opened his mouth and almost asked a question, then shook his head and saved his breath. "Well, it's not the war I wanted, but it's the war I've got."

"Sorry."

Willie pat him on the back again. "That's okay. It's not a knock-out punch, but it's still a hard shot. We're way ahead of where we were this morning, and you and me are eating steak."

"Ate steak."

"You want another one?"

Gherin hadn't thought about it that way. "Yah."

"Good. This'll be better. Can I tell you something? Nothing tastes as good as a fine steak in the middle of a war. Fact of life. And we better enjoy it quick because this won't last very long." He stopped and looked up at the goblin. "She is still alive, right?"

He looked down at the ground. "Yah. Rat duke save."

"Pick a side Reginald, pick a side," Willie muttered. "You're going to tell me everything over dinner, and then we'll see a movie. A real celebration. Now, let me tell you what the secret to a good steak is: it's the marbling."

Chapter 32

Movies had been deeply disappointing.

"How can you not see it!" Willie had shouted at him. The rabbit was a real cinephile.

Gherin had only shrugged. "Nothing there," he'd said, pointing at the screen. "Just flicker lights."

"But . . . ," Willie's face had turned red as he tried to find the words.

The argument had been interrupted by a band of cats who bounded into the theatre shouting the name of Her Majesty Queen of Spiders. Gherin had let Willie stutter about directors of photography as he ripped the felines apart.

It had been like that all night. First they had eaten a steak at a closed restaurant that Gherin had to admit was far superior to the one he'd snuck into, but had been attacked by a small legion of poison spiders and snakes. The resulting fight had ruined dessert, and Gherin never got to try crème brulee.

"Some other time," Willie had said.

Then they'd gone across town and been ambushed by an elite squadron of rats, none of whom (Gherin was sure) tasted like caramelized sugar. At last they'd reached a small movie theatre in the Outer Richmond where Willie could arrange private screenings through his influence over the owner's parakeets.

They'd gotten popcorn, which was delicious, sat down in the comfortable seats, and Gherin had clapped his hands when the room went dark, because that was still a good trick.

But then the movie had started, and he hadn't seen a thing. "Just flicker lights."

The cats had jumped in shortly afterwards, and they were good fighters. By the time Gherin had finished them off, he was bleeding again and Willie had eaten all the popcorn.

"Look at that!" the rabbit said, pointing to the screen. "It's a whole story unfolding right in front of us!"

Gherin squinted his right eye, and then his left eye, and then both at once. "Nah," he finally decided. "Just lights go flicker flicker."

"No! Well . . . yeah," said Willie. "But, it's so much more than that! The lights add up to something!"

Gherin scratched his head. "How?"

Willie stomped his foot against the chair. "They just . . . do!"

"The spider queen shall eat your entrails!" one of the cats hissed as he died.

"It's . . . it's like reading," Willie said. "Sure, all those letters are really just squiggly lines, but, they're also letters and words when you know how to see 'em right."

"Ohhhhh," said Gherin. "Can't read."

Willie blinked. "But . . . you haul that Zagat guide everywhere!"

"Yah yah! Like book. Tells yummy places. But not read. Goblins no read. Go human land, get enchanted. Wyrd cast spell, let goblin speak human tongue, know what letters say." He held up a battered copy of a Zagat guide from ten years ago. "Look at pages, like voice whisper words in ear." He looked at Willie to see if he understood. "Yah?"

"Huh," said Willie.

"Yah." Gherin opened the guide to a random page and wiped off cat blood. "See?" he said, holding a section on cheap hotels toward the rabbit. "Just squiggle lines." He pointed at the movie screen. "Just flicker lights."

"That's actually a really terrible hotel," Willie said, looking closely at the pages. "In fact, they all are. Never stay in any of these places."

Gherin squinted. "Not point."

"No," Willie said, nodding slowly. "No it's not. I didn't realize. I'm sorry. I had no idea. But . . . Gherin . . . if you stick around you're going to need a whole new way of looking at things."

Gherin sighed. "Just want find yummy places. Got béarnaise sauce."

"Don't worry. You're best friends with the rabbit who can fix you up. Now c'mon," said Willie. "Let's go pay a visit to a few watering holes."

Gherin scowled. "You notice," he asked, "how go place, get attack? Yah? So . . . maybe stay home?"

"No, no, no . . . ," Willie pat him on the back. "That's the point!"

Gherin scratched his head. "Point get cat fur in teeth?"

"No, the point is that I can go anywhere with impunity. They can't touch me. Look: they're not going to attack Golden Gate Park. That's my stronghold: I've got it locked down. Just like I'm not going to attack North Beach: that's her stronghold. It's sewn up tight. Everybody knows it. What I'm doing is proving that I can go anywhere else in the city I like in the middle of a war: . . . eat a steak at a fine restaurant on the east side, see a movie at my favorite theater on the west side, . . . and drink a beer on the south side, and still be safe. That's the kind of message I want to send. You see?"

Gherin scowled and tried picking some of the fur out from between his teeth with a claw. "Not like this game. You eat all popcorn. Gherin get furball."

Willie chuckled. "If you want to rule the world, you gotta make sacrifices."

"Just want béarnaise sauce."

"Come on. I'll introduce you to Belgian beer. You'll love it. It's made by monks." He grinned while Gherin paused. "Trust me. I know what you like."

"Not movies."

"But popcorn!"

" Yah . . . ."

Gherin followed the rabbit out of the theater. The movie went on, watched only by the corpses in the darkness.

Chapter 33

The most beautiful girl in the world was holding her stupid boyfriend's hand.

Gherin was crouching on a tree branch looking through the window into their living room. It was obvious what they were doing. Sitting in front of a television, watching a movie, holding hands.

Gherin snarled and ran his fingers over the places where Junkyard Ed's teeth had left a mark. In the last two nights he'd been ripped up by Junkyard and chewed on by rats, bitten by snakes and scratched by cats, and he could feel each set of wounds as a separate layer on his skin.

He'd also eaten better than he ever had in his life: Willie was good about that. Fine steaks, Chinese pork ribs, Belgian monk-beer, popcorn, mashed potatoes, garlic bread, Caesar salad . . . he could still taste every morsel.

The movie had been disappointing, but the opera still was the most beautiful thing he'd ever seen. When he closed his eyes at night he heard the sounds and saw the sets and felt himself covered in the singers' voices again. There was so much to think about. So much to process. He was going to see it again next week.

Yet it wasn't all coming together right. He'd woken up at twilight faintly sick at heart, and snuck away from Jake's babbling about bison and Sean's discussion of the latest issue of *The Economist* to clear his head. He just wanted to look at something beautiful again. He'd come here.

And here she was, holding her stupid boyfriend's hand. They were smiling together, watching something that everyone could see but Gherin.

He scowled and licked his teeth. What was the point of having high culture if he couldn't have the girl too?

The ugly stupid man said something that made her laugh. It was intolerable.

Gherin held a dagger in his hands. He tested the blade with his fingers.

"Sharp," he hissed. Good craftsmanship. Forged by a firbolg. Firbolgs were good at that sort of thing.

One throw, even through the window, and it would all be over.

But to kill James in front of the girl . . . even angry, Gherin suspected she wouldn't like that. Women are complicated. And she was so gentle.

Mari pointed at the screen, and he said something else, and they laughed together.

Gherin growled.

Tonight, then. This waiting was over. Over. He would kill the ugly stupid man tonight, as soon as she was asleep. Whatever the curse did to him, it would still be worth it.

That resolution made, something settled inside him. He leaned back against the tree trunk and exhaled. He smiled dreamily and looked through the window at her red hair, and her dark eyes, and her smile—the way it peeked out from her mouth as though to say "is it okay to be happy?" and then answered its own question.

Yes, Gherin said to her quietly. Yes. It is okay to be happy. Whatever you have to do.

He heard a squirrel rustling in the tree. That was okay: squirrels were usually on Willie's side. Or the side that Willie was on, anyway: the side that elected their leader. Gherin wondered how that worked, exactly. He'd already killed the spiders in this tree. He hoped there weren't more: he'd hate to be ambushed here, of all places. Stupid war.

They stood up. Perhaps the movie was over? They turned off the television. Talked a little more. Mari went into the kitchen and began to putter there while James walked over to some high culture devices that Gherin didn't recognize. Maybe computers? What was she doing? Gherin watched her carefully, watched her slender hands and delicate fingers intently. She put big gloves on. Very silly looking gloves. She opened the oven and pulled out . . .

Bread! She'd been baking bread! Gherin swooned. The scent of it filled their apartment: he picked the smell up immediately. She was so wonderful. They would be so happy together . . .

The stupid ugly man pushed a button, and suddenly the apartment was filled again: this time with music.

With . . . opera.

Gherin stopped breathing.

It wasn't the same opera, but Gherin knew what it had to be. So many instruments, rising and falling around each other to make harmonies—playing and teasing each other with tone and sound. It was . . . it was . . . .

Gherin leaned back against the tree, holding on tight so as not to fall. Trying to take it all in. His eyes moist.

Then the most amazing thing happened. When the singers began singing, the stupid ugly man sang too. With them. Same tones, same rhythm, even same words, though they were not his language.

His voice was rich and big and inviting. He made it look easy; he made you think you could sing along too. He matched the invisible singers note for note, his voice carrying out of the apartment and into the street, making the whole block part of stage. So beautiful.

Gherin's jaw dropped. The dagger in his hand slipped and cut his palm. His whole body went numb.

The most beautiful girl in the world was looking at her James, surrounded by the smell of fresh bread. Looking at her stupid ugly boyfriend adoringly, her eyes wide, her hands clasping each other behind her back, her smile wide and bright and all for him.

No no no no no . . . .

Gherin couldn't raise his bleeding hands or the bloody dagger. He could not snarl or hiss. His eyes burned and he looked away even as his ears held on to the sound, that beautiful, beautiful sound, that he knew he would never forget.

Gherin had never felt so helpless.

How many operas did the ugly stupid man know? How many did he have in that box? How many could he sing?

Gherin dropped out of the tree and landed on all fours. Like an animal he skittered into the dark street, running where his instincts took him.

Chapter 34

The dogs howled gleefully among the ruins of the junkyard, chasing meat and bones thrown from the bed of a truck. Their master had returned! Their true master!

They had been lost when Junkyard died: a pack without a direction, a ship without a wind. Unsure where to go, pangs of hunger had begun unraveling the ties that bound them. Cats and raccoons and packs of rats had begun invading their territory. Snakes had begun inhabiting the shelter.

But all was well now! All was good! Their savior has shown mercy! They would follow him forever!

Gherin sat on the truck bed, casually tossing what was left of Junkyard Ed to his former pack; watching them leap and dance and howl and play.

Nothing, nothing, he had done could get the sound of James' voice out of his mind, or the way his song had carried and soared, displaying casual mastery over the beauty Gherin would give up his life to experience.

What hurt Gherin most was that, deep down, he didn't want to forget it. He wanted to hear it again. If someone threatened James, Gherin would hurt them to make sure his rival would live to sing again. He did not understand.

He tossed a bone at the pack, harder than he should. But so what?

He did not understand.

At least he had a fierce pack of dogs now. Willie would like that. Wouldn't he?

Lost in thought, he did not smell the wind change. The pack sensed the intruder first.

They turned and spun and saw the shape standing by a hole in the fence that they sometimes crawled through. They sniffed. They snarled. They bared their teeth.

One, a mutt with matted hair and rancid breath, howled to Gherin that he would bring him the bones of his enemies, and leaped forward.

Only then did Gherin look up. Only then did he see claws flash and Leptin slice the mutt's throat in midair with one clean motion and walk forward into the pack, licking his claws.

Leptin stared at the young goblin, and did not blink. The rest of the pack circled him, growling, but his eyes did not move. "Play with dogs?" he asked.

"Leptin?" Gherin hesitated a moment, then jumped in the air and clapped his hands. "Come back! Good good!" He hopped off the truck bed and motioned the pack away. "Friend!" he barked. "Back!"

Leptin did not move. He kept his voice cold. "Why play dogs, Gherin?"

Gherin stopped walking. "It . . . it . . . ." How to explain this?

"Where mouse, Gherin?"

"You got map? Map say!"

Leptin's eyes narrowed. His lip began to tremble. "Yah . . . Leptin get map. Leptin sacrifice line of life to mapwyrd so get map. Come back, find Gherin playing dogs! Gherin playing dogs, and one more symbol dead!"

Gherin's ears flattened. "Not know—"

"One more symbol dead, Gherin not know! Gherin . . . play with dogs! Gherin . . . eat fine food! Gherin . . . peek at pretty human girl! Gherin have fine time—only Leptin sacrifice! Gherin go vacation, while symbol die and Leptin sacrifice! Gherin . . . ," Leptin's lip curled. "Play with dogs."

Gherin looked at the ground. "Good dogs . . . ."

Leptin's hand lashed out and shoved. Gherin fell over and landed on his back by the truck.

Gherin blinked, stunned.

The dogs growled and circled.

Leptin pointed, his fangs bared. "Leptin sacrifice life while Gherin . . . dine with rabbit!"

Gherin paled. For a moment, his heart stopped beating.

"How know?" he whispered. And knew immediately it was the wrong thing to say.

"Leptin know what war look like!" The elder goblin's eyes flashed a deeper red. "Leptin come back, see city change. War hang over. So grab rat and dog, grab duck: ask what happen." He hissed and stepped over the prone goblin. "What happen Gherin? What happen!"

"Got . . . ," Gherin stuttered. "Got . . . ." Something occurred to him. "Talk to mouse!"

Leptin hesitated. His finger dropped, just a bit. "Yah? And?"

"Tell him!" Gherin said eagerly. "Tell him symbols need live, world not end."

Leptin didn't budge. "Yah?"

"Him no believe, but try explain! And . . . and . . ." Gherin hesitated realizing this was not going to go where he wanted it to.

"Yah?" Leptin's hand clenched into a fist. "Then?"

"Then . . . ," Gherin couldn't stop the words from coming out, however quietly. "Then Willie throw grenade and start big fight and Gherin get stabbed in knee."

Leptin leaned forward. "Willie?"

Gherin hung his head. "Rabbit."

Leptin howled. He raised his claws to his neck and drew his own blood and held it up at the dead moon and screamed at the sky.

The dogs ran away. They did not even look back, and they would never return to the junkyard.

Leptin pointed his bloody hands at Gherin. "Mouse think goblins work with rabbit. Mouse knows rabbit venom maker! Mouse think goblins venom maker! Gherin make mouse think goblins lie!"

"Leptin—"

"You fail Leptin! You fail goblins! You fail world!" Leptin turned his back, and began to walk away.

Gherin scrambled to his feet. It hurt: wounds still fresh. Then something occurred to him.

"Leptin!" Gherin shouted. "Gherin got scars!"

Leptin stopped.

Slowly, he turned around.

"Show," he barked.

Gherin spread his arms to show his wounded chest and walked forward slowly. "Big fights," he said hesitantly. "Got scars. Carry for life."

Leptin was still, his gaze intense. He stared, up and down Gherin's body. He wasn't just looking at the scars, Gherin realized: he was reading them, like a map. Like a book. Like someone was whispering an account of each battle into his ears.

He could not be fooled.

Leptin's voice was a whisper. "Scars . . . not . . . earned . . . for . . . goblins," he hissed. "Scars . . . earned . . . for high culture."

Terrified as he was, Gherin was also in awe. His friend really understood. "It . . . opera so beautiful," he said. "Food so good. Buildings so great. Art so . . . arty. First thing in life Gherin see worth fighting for."

Leptin nodded. "Gherin not failure. Gherin traitor."

Gherin's breath caught.

Leptin turned away.

He'd walked halfway out of the junkyard before Gherin found the air to speak. "Leptin! High culture got holes! Got holes! Can live in hole, be goblin! Can be opera bat! Opera bat!"

Leptin didn't turn around.

Gherin chased after. Got closer to his friend. "Not traitor! Like opera bat! Live in high culture hole!" Reached out to touch his shoulder.

Leptin whirled. Grabbed Gherin's arm, pinned it behind Gherin's back before he could blink. Pain shot through Gherin as Leptin pushed his arm into an unnatural angle, his fresh scars threatening to open again. A moment later Gherin was flying through the air, landing in a pile of tires that scattered around him and pinned him beneath.

Leptin shook his head. "Warned you," he hissed. "You choose wrong scars. Now live with."

He turned again, as Gherin pushed and scrambled through the tires, and was gone.

This time Gherin howled.

Chapter 35

Craig lit a cigarette and took an ash tray buried under sticky-notes out of a drawer. He took a deep drag.

Since seeing the goblins, he'd started up again. He knew it was going to kill him, but . . . but . . . he couldn't explain it. Somehow he'd been set back. Somehow he needed to quit all over.

It was closing time. He'd taken a week off, without explanation. The owners were worried, but what could he tell them? More and more, it seemed like the only people who understood his life were the talking animals. Maybe there was something to this "wild human" idea. Maybe you couldn't live in both worlds at once.

He walked over to the front door and locked it, then turned to the register to count the bills.

Leptin was sitting on the counter, eyes red and mouth stern.

The cigarette fell from Craig's mouth. He absently ground it out with his foot. It would leave a permanent mark on the floor.

"Want talk," Leptin said.

Craig held very still. "Okay."

"Come peace," said Leptin.

"Okay."

"Show you." Leptin held up bottle of Lagavulin single malt scotch. "Want drink glasses or bottle?

The tension fell from Craig's body and he chuckled.

Leptin tilted his head. "What funny?"

Craig held his hands up and walked over to a pile of hats sitting in the corner. "I had a feeling you'd come back. Just a feeling. I didn't know if it would be good or bad. Still don't. So I prepared." He reached down to the very back and picked up a bottle of Ardberg. He smiled. "Aged for twenty-five years," he said.

"Ooooooo."

"You'll like it."

Leptin made a come hither motion with his hand.

"I'm going to get us glasses," Craig said, and stepped into the back room.

Leptin shrugged and eyed the back room casually, his ears pitched forward, curious if Craig was going to try and run.

Craig emerged a few moments later holding two shot glasses.

Leptin grinned. "You handle this good, Craig."

Craig took a deep breath and shrugged. "I don't trust you never to kill me or hurt me; but, I trust you to tell me if you're planning to. And you said you weren't."

"Hah!" Leptin's grin widened. "Talk sense! Okay, drink stupid glasses."

"Thank you," said Craig. He held the bottle out to Leptin, who removed the foil around the top with a quick slice of his claw. Craig pulled the top out and poured the amber liquid, then put the stopper back on.

"Why think Leptin come back?"

Craig shook his head as he picked up his glass. "I don't know. I didn't believe it. But somehow I knew it." He held his glass up. "Here's to hunches."

They drank.

"Good, yeah?"

"Ahhhhh."

"Good as the goblin stuff?"

"No be crazy man Craig."

"Okay." He poured them another round. Leptin drank his down at once, while Craig sipped it. A few sips in, he took a deep breath. "So . . . why did you come back?"

Leptin nodded. "Know where mouse be next," he said.

Craig's face stiffened. "I can't—"

Leptin waved his hands. "No no, not need you tell. Leptin know where mouse be."

Craig nodded, just a little. "I'm not saying anything."

"Leptin know when. Two nights. Leptin know what too. Great symbol. Ancient symbol. Bad, bad, symbol. Slumbers deep, tentacles in every mind. Tentacle wake up, mind see it, go mad. Symbol too much. Represent too much. Ugly truth. Bad bad." Leptin took a deep breath. "Sure dead nice, but must no die. Must no die."

Craig ran his thumb around the rim of his shot glass. "You're putting me in a difficult position."

Leptin spit on the floor. "Think, Craig! Leptin not ask keep secret! No position. Craig got easy job. Tell mouse! Leptin want tell mouse!"

Craig frowned. "But then he'll know you're coming to stop him."

Leptin nodded. "Yah. But also know Leptin give warning. Not must fight. Can try talk." He eyed Craig's half-full glass. "Gonna drink?"

Craig raised his glass and downed it. Leptin held up the bottle to pour two more.

When Craig's glass was full, he picked it up and took another sip. "I . . . ," he hesitated, "talked to Pounce about you two. He . . . decided he doesn't think much of you."

Leptin sighed. "Yah. Mouse meet Gherin. Go bad."

"Oh," said Craig. "Yeah, I can see that. I think he'd like you better." He took another sip.

"Yah," Leptin muttered darkly. "Yah."

"He . . . ," Craig wasn't sure how far he should push this. "He said something about Gherin working for an evil rabbit who wants to be mayor? Which, I've got to be honest, I didn't understand at all. I had a hard enough time with animals talking. I'm still kind of adjusting to that. The rest is . . . ," he made a fluttery motion over his head. "Do you have any idea what that's about?"

"Yah," said Leptin. "Rabbit bad." He downed his shot.

"Right, but . . . ," Craig poured more into Leptin's glass. "Bad like juvenile delinquent bad or bad like Hitler bad? Or—"

Leptin's hand shot out and crushed a styrofoam head sitting on the back wall. Its hat fell to the ground. Leptin opened his hand and let the head's remains fall too. "Rabbit bad."

Craig shuddered. "O . . . okay. Got it."

Leptin took a deep breath. "Rabbit get Gherin. Now Gherin bad."

"Wow," said Craig. "Wow." He finished his glass.

Leptin started pouring again.

"Wait," said Craig. "Wait. I'm . . . this is too much. I need a little time."

Leptin growled.

"I'm just saying—"

Leptin's hand shot out again and ripped another styrofoam head to shreds.

Craig raised his hands and let Leptin pour. He looked at the goblin's face. "Are . . . are you okay?"

Leptin picked up his cup. "Yah."

Craig said it before he knew what he was doing. "You lost a man."

Leptin put his cup down. He scowled. "Lost men. Had honor. This different."

"Okay."

"Just want drink."

"Okay." Craig hesitantly reached for his glass. If he'd known this was coming he wouldn't have smoked tonight: nicotine and whiskey always meant a mean hangover in the morning. And why shouldn't they? Why shouldn't the things that kill you feel like death?

But whatever their bond—and he could not believe he felt any sense of loyalty to this creature of fang and claw and glowing eyes—he had to honor it. This monster had called him a brother in arms, and not tortured and killed him when he was at its mercy. "Respect scars," he had demanded of the wounds on Craig's body. It was a whole lot more than most people had done for him.

Craig raised the glass, knowing it would hurt him badly. Leptin raised his. They drank again.

"Leptin sacrifice part of life," the goblin hissed as he poured another round. "Leptin sacrifice! Gherin play. Gherin leave everything Leptin fight for . . . for opera. For cheese."

Craig took a deep breath before saying what was on his mind. "When someone does that it . . . it dishonors us all."

Leptin looked up sharply and stared into Craig's eyes. He leaned forward. He put his hand on Craig's shoulder. Craig could smell his breath. "Leptin know you not want leave unit, Craig. Leptin know."

Craig waited a long time. Took a drink. Poured another. "Thanks."

Leptin smiled and drained his glass. "Drink good. World probably end now, Craig."

This would be a long night.

Chapter 36

"NO FAIR!" Gherin shouted into darkness. "No fair!"

He stood on the stage of the San Francisco Opera. He shouted again. Nothing answered.

Not long ago he had seen a human on this stage, dressed in colorful clothes, filling the room up with his own misery—singing it out in a deep bass voice. It had seemed to help, and when he was finished everyone clapped and it had been so beautiful that Gherin had whistled and gaped and cried.

But it wasn't working as well for him, although surely his grief was every bit as great as the singing man's—for the singing man had only lost his wife, and she wasn't even really dead. Gherin had seen her again, taking a bow, at the end of the show. The sword that wasn't really a sword hadn't killed her.

But Gherin, he had lost his friend and his home.

"NO FAIR!" he howled. "No fair!"

He sat on the stage and wondered why the opera didn't make it all better. The singing man had had an orchestra: maybe Gherin needed an orchestra.

From high up in the ceiling, the opera bat squeaked. "Sir? Excuse me, sir?"

Gherin raised his head.

The opera bat came wafting down. "Sir? I don't mean to interrupt sir, but . . . but . . . Mr. O'Shaughnessy has been looking for you. He'd like your attendance at a meeting with some out of town mercenaries he's brought in. Very big and fierce. He's going all out, sir. He says he intends to be known as an unstoppable force. He mentioned something called the 'Powell doctrine,' but I don't know what that is. But he says you need to get back, sir . . . ."

Gherin scowled. "Why rabbit need animals? Got hand grenades."

The opera bat hovered. "Sir? What do you . . . you mean the human weapons?"

Gherin didn't respond.

"Oh no, sir. Those are very hard for even him to get. Very rare and precious. There just aren't enough of them to win a war, sir. You need soldiers for that. Vicious soldiers. Can you . . . can you . . . stand up, sir? Or . . . is there anything I can get you?"

Gherin was still for a while. "You got name," he said. "Alvarez, yah?"

The opera bat fluttered above the stage. "Yes . . . yessir."

Gherin nodded. "How Alvarez be opera bat?"

"Ex . . . excuse me, sir?"

"Alvarez got two worlds. Wild animal and got high culture life. How do that?"

"Oh my! I . . . I . . . ," the bat circled around the room twice and then flew down closer to Gherin. "I don't know, sir. I've just been like this. My whole life. I've never been domesticated, sir. No never. No one in my family has . But . . . but we've always lived here too, sir. We just have. And . . . it doesn't seem like two worlds to me. No, in fact . . . in fact . . . I would say it's impossible to cross from one world to another. Yessir, I would say a man can't do that. Except that . . . except that . . . except . . . ."

"What?" Gherin snarled.

Alvarez flew a little higher. "Except that you have, sir. You've come to live with us. So I guess it is possible."

"Huh," Gherin said. "Huh."

"It's something I . . . I never spent much time thinking about, sir. I just tried to be the best . . . um . . . well . . . opera bat I could. I never thought of doing something else."

"Yah," Gherin said. "Opera bat good job." He stroked his chin and then looked up. "What opera think?"

"Um . . . sir? The opera isn't . . . ."

"You opera bat. See all operas. Yah?"

"Oh, well, I'm hardly the mouse of the Met, but, certainly I've seen every production that's come through these doors in recent memory, and many of the rehearsals. And . . . and . . . and . . . I would go so far as to say I've committed much of the canon to memory. Although I do draw the line at operettas. They're just . . . well . . . I mean . . . Gilbert & Sullivan, sir. Very catchy tunes, but—"

Gherin held up his hand. Alvarez fell quiet. "Some time got explain Gherin what all that mean," he said. "But, you see all operas. So, what opera think living two worlds?"

"Oh. Oh. Oh—yes, I see sir. I see. I . . . ." He fluttered up again, and then back down. "I . . . ," he circled a bit, then came to a stop, landing on the stage in front of Gherin. "I think, sir, that perhaps the truth is that it doesn't matter what you feel. It matters what you do. That's what determines what world you live in. And if you want to live in two, you have to work to keep your balance. They're not just going to stand still for you."

There was a long silence.

"Huh," said Gherin.

"I . . . I . . . I hope that was helpful, sir."

Gherin smiled. "Glad have opera bat friend."

Alvarez leaped up into the air and flew close to the ceiling. "Um . . . um . . . no, sir. No. Sir. We are not friends."

Gherin's face fell. "Why?"

"Because, sir, you ate Mordecai."

Gherin nodded slowly. "Okay, yah. Sorry. Still like you."

Alvarrez said nothing. Saying that had been, perhaps, the bravest thing he'd ever done. "Mr. O'Shaughnessy wants to see you sir," he said.

Gherin nodded and got to his feet.

Chapter 37

High in a tree, high on a hill, Leptin stared down at the crags where the ocean reached the shore. Wave after wave battering the rocks.

Here, he thought. Here. The mouse was going to make his next move here. Somewhere down there was an entrance to a vast and terrible tomb.

Stupid mouse, he thought. When your enemies are sleeping, don't wake them up.

All that remained was to find the door. Leptin shuddered.

Something in him stiffened before he heard the wings. Big wings, coming this way. Coming for him.

He did not turn around. Let them think they'd catch him by surprise. Let them be surprised, when the time came. He slipped a wickedly curved dagger into his hand.

But there was no attack. Instead, a massive vulture landed on a tree across from Leptin. Sitting on its back was the duke of rats.

Leptin smiled viciously. "Delivery," he said. "Fresh."

"Oh, come now," called the duke of rats. "I'm not here to fight, and as fast as you are, you'll never outrun my steed. So let's not posture, yes? Let's have a civilized conversation instead."

"Not civilized."

"No . . . no indeed. That is the problem. You are filthy and ignorant, vile and uncompromising. You think with your stomach and your claws. Your presence here has thrown off the balance of power in a way that has led to the worst kind of war: an unprofitable one." He leaned forward. "The others don't remember as well. They tend to be more solitary creatures, with smaller families, and no truly great tradition of oral storytelling. But we remember. We still tell tales of the time before John Dee's treaty, exactly as they were told by our ancestors, when we fought you over every scrap of wasteland. We may be rodents, but your kind will forever be pests."

Leptin shrugged. "Fight now?"

"Cretin." The duke shook his head. "You know your companion is working for the rabbit."

Leptin scowled. "Yah."

"Can you imagine—working for the rabbit? It's a disaster for everyone: Willie thinks he can be controlled, can be civilized, and his mad attempt will ruin so much of what we've built here. So, if you'll pardon me for asking . . . ," his whiskers twitched. "Will you be removing him after your work here is done?"

Leptin took a deep breath. "Not know."

"Yes, I thought not." The duke removed a cracker from a small sack and began to nibble on it. "Friends are nothing but trouble, really. Family's all you can trust."

"No got family."

"Well, then you truly are alone in the world. My heart bleeds. You know what I find mitigates the despair that comes with living in a world of rogues and traitors? Really enormous wealth. But I digress. It would be better for all concerned, if you took him with you."

Leptin considered this. "Why?"

"Because he is an imbalance to our ecosystem, because he is helping plunge the city into chaos, and because if he stays long enough he will eventually do something to violate the wizard's treaty. You know that. You know how he is. Impetuous, greedy, with no sense of the consequences of his actions."

Leptin nodded slowly. "Got point."

The duke smiled as he finished his cracker. "How nice. There are other reasons as well, of course. How would it look for you, leaving a goblin behind? What would you say to his family? What would you tell your superiors?"

Leptin growled. "Wondered that."

"You have refused to do business twice before, but now that you are alone, and your friend is in Willie's pocket, I suspect the calculation has changed."

Leptin spit. "No shake hands venom maker."

"You misunderstand, again. I imagine it must be impossible for goblins to organize a picnic. I'm not offering you a deal wherein you scratch my back and I scratch yours. I'm asking you: what can I do? How can I marshal the considerable resources at my disposal, and those of her majesty queen of spiders, to help you get him out of here? What can we do to make this convenient for you? Because, I assure you, we're motivated to do it. So you don't need to shake my hand at all: I'm surrendering. I'm asking for your orders, which I shall carry out. Do you see?"

"Huh," said Leptin. He tilted his head. "So I say, you do."

"Yes, so long as it helps you to take your young associate back where he belongs."

Leptin smiled. "Got deal."

"Excellent!" The duke of rats clapped his hands together. "What would you have us do?"

"Die." Leptin pulled his arm back and threw the concealed dagger, striking the vulture and severing its long neck.

The duke of rats screamed as he fell down the trees, landing roughly on a branch and running, running, running, out of the forest quickly as he could. Leptin stared down at him, admiring how fast he moved. "Not think him athletic."

He hopped over to the tree and pulled his dagger out and held the headless bird in the air. Dinner. This wait was turning out to be easier than he'd thought.

Chapter 38

Alvarez led Gherin deep into Golden Gate Park, past the waterfall and the open meadows, past the tea garden and past camps of homeless men trying to conceal themselves among the bushes, to an area of dense thickets where Willie, Gerardo, and Jake sat huddling.

Willie smiled when he saw Gherin, the way he always did, but this time the goblin thought he saw relief in Jake and Gerardo's eyes too.

"Good, good," Wilile said. "We couldn't wait much longer, I was starting to worry." He looked Gherin over. "You've been kinda missing the last few days, you look like you haven't slept. You doing okay? You eating right?" He narrowed his eyes. "I don't think you're eating right. When all this is done I think I need to introduce you to southern food. I think it might just be your favorite cuisine yet. And if the park isn't suiting you as a place to sleep, you should have said so. We'll get you hooked up with something that's to your liking." He shook his head. "Anything's got to be better than Junkyard Ed's old place."

Gherin nodded. "Okay." He looked around. "What happen here?"

Willie nodded and motioned Gherin closer into their circle. Then he looked over at Alvarez. "You can go," he said. "Have you got our friend here set up for the opera next week?"

The bat bobbed up and down. "Oh yessir, Mr. O'Shaughnessy. This time I'll make sure he has a program and a complimentary box of chocolates too. The royal treatment."

"Bottle of champagne?"

"If ... if he wants it, sir."

"Of course he does. He wants everything. Get outta here."

Alvarez flew away.

Gherin watched him go. "Opera bat not Gherin's friend," he said.

Willie gave Gherin a sharp look. "Is he giving you trouble? In anything?"

"Nah."

"Then what?"

Gherin sighed. "Ate his friend."

Willie nodded. "Oh, yeah, I heard about that. Suited me fine: Mordecai was trouble, if you ask me. But . . . yeah . . . I guess you do have to watch who you eat if you want to make friends."

Gherin nodded. "Guess so."

Jake tittered. "Just think of how many friends you've made because you've eaten people. Like us! The food's better too."

Gerardo slapped his brother, and Jake stopped laughing.

"A man's got to learn how to socialize," Willie said. "There's an art to making friends, and it involves being loved a little and feared a lot. You ever hear of Machiavelli?"

Gherin thought about it. "Discover America?"

Willie chuckled. "Okay, this is a conversation for another time. We'll figure out ways we can find you some new friends after we've introduced you to a few boys who are nobody's friends. These guys are all professionals, but, it isn't a good idea for rabbits to have these kind of meetings without backup, and raccoons weren't going to do it. They need to see who's side they're really on. So, be fierce kid. Fierce. Can you do that?"

Gherin nodded. "Yah."

"No, see, you still look like you're not eating right. Like you're a little sad. I need you to look like the guy who killed Junkyard Ed, the guy who fought the mouse to a standstill. You got that guy?"

Gherin took a breath and bared his fangs. "Who you want Gherin eat?"

"That's the spirit!" said Willie. "Just keep quiet unless you need to back me up, and if something goes down don't be afraid to get rough."

Jake laughed again.

Gherin nodded. "Do what always do."

Willie motioned, and they followed him across a human street into a small clearing where six coyotes waited, eying each other warily.

They turned. Now the coyotes, the rabbits, and the goblin stared at each other.

"Glad you boys could make it," Willie said, walking closer to their teeth as though it was natural. "As you know I'm paying top of the line, so I expect punctuality."

One coyote sneezed. Another pawed her feet through the grass, digging up dirt. The rest kept staring.

"So," said one in a rumbling voice, "this is the goblin."

"The *legendary* goblin," corrected another.

"Yeah," said Willie. "That's him."

"Hmmmm," said another, sniffing the air. "He doesn't smell so tough."

"Why doesn't he talk for himself?" said the coyote who pawed the dirt.

"Oh he does," said Willie. "When it's important."

"That so," said the one who'd sneezed.

Willie leaned forward, even closer—as though he were stretching his neck out before an ax. "Boys, I'm not paying you to sit around asking stupid questions."

The fangs held their ground. "You paid enough to get me here. Nothing more."

"That so," said Willie. "Gherin, k—"

Gherin had already leaped over Willie, wrapped his feet around the coyote's neck, and squeezed until his talons ripped the head apart.

The body fell to the ground.

"See," said Willie, "it's like that."

"Hmmmmmmm," the coyote who had pawed the earth said, smiling. "I like him."

"The money's good and the teeth are sharp enough to win," agreed the coyote who'd sniffed the air. "I'm in."

One by one the other coyotes nodded in agreement.

"Machiavelli," Willie whispered with a smile.

Gherin cleaned his talons against the dirt.

Willie turned to him. Leaned in close. "You know," he said, "I think you might have met some friends. Why don't I let you get to know these kids for a while. They're all professionals, been through hell, still have teeth; so, I think maybe you guys might have a lot to talk about. Just have them ready by tomorrow night. I want to make sure everybody knows I've got overwhelming force before Sean sits down at the negotiating table."

"Yah," said Gherin, looking back at the coyotes. They seemed . . . nice. Two of them smiled at him. One the way Willie did, another the way Jake did.

"Tea garden," Willie said. "Tomorrow night. When the moon is high."

"Yah."

The rabbits began to hop away, but Gherin reached out and grabbed Jake by the tail.

"Hey!" Jake called as the coyotes laughed.

Gherin leaned into him. "You, me, got talk. Need favor."

Jake smiled. "Oh yeah?" he said. "I'm listening."

Chapter 39

It was dark, the moon was high, and the waves were fierce. Three vans pulled up to the coast of Land's End. The doors opened and a ragtag band of men and women leaped out. They were mostly unwashed and unshaved but still disciplined in their movements and quick to follow orders. In formation, guns drawn, they began navigating a narrow path down toward the water and, just when it seemed they were going to drown, slipped inside the cliff itself, walking underground.

Leptin watched from the trees. This was it, he knew. This was the mouse's army. Not bad, he thought. Not bad. He counted ten . . . eleven . . . twelve humans, many probably former military. He did not see Craig with them, and a part of him he would not admit to was relieved. He did not see MacDuff either.

What he did not see that was important was the mouse. Leptin scowled. Surely the mouse wouldn't have sent his men on a mission like this alone? No . . . either the mouse had gone on ahead, and Leptin has missed it, or he was in one of his soldiers' pockets, or . . . something. Mice were so little: they had a lot of ways to sneak into a place.

If he had seen the mouse there, Leptin might have leaped out of the trees and approached, in front of the whole squad, as a gesture of good faith. But seeing only soldiers he held his ground. There were too many who were too well armed: this was not a good fight. Wait and a better opportunity will come.

He watched as they marched down, disappearing one by one into the cliff just before it met the water, and saw that they left one guard out by the vans and another by the door, almost perfectly hidden from view.

Almost.

Leptin slipped down from the tree and crept silently over to the human road to the vans. One human there to guard. A scruffy man with a long beard that was tied into braids, wearing the remains of a military jacket with Vietnam patches. He was resentful at being left to guard the vans, sure that this meant the people who he respected didn't respect him as much.

Leptin leaped down on him from the van's roof and knocked him out with a tire iron he found in back.

Leptin sighed, threw the tire iron by the man's unconscious form, took his pistol, and slipped down the path along the cliff. Better not to kill any of the mouse's men until he could be sure, absolutely sure, that this had to end in death.

Although, he muttered, it seemed likely.

The guard hiding in the entrance of the cavern was a woman covered in tattoos. She didn't hear anything. She was thinking about an upcoming eviction hearing she knew she couldn't win, and where she was going to live, when her legs buckled and her head hit the cavern wall and she was beaten until she fell unconscious.

Leptin looked down at her and shook his head.

He took her pistol too, and looked into the entrance to the cavern. It was narrow and ran a long way, longer than he could see. He cracked his knuckles and took a step into the darkness, then stopped. His ears grew stiff. He sighed, quietly.

"Leptin wait," said Gherin from behind him.

Leptin turned.

"Go," Leptin said. "No want. No need."

"Leptin no need," Gherin said. "Leptin no . . . want. But listen. Got big thing say Leptin."

Leptin's face tightened. His eyes narrowed. "Gherin got human scars. High culture scars. Gherin pick side."

"Maybe," said Gherin, "but—"

"No maybe!" Leptin hissed. He pointed to the deep ridges cutting along Gherin's chest. "Got scars!"

"Yah!" Gherin hissed back. "Got high culture scars! Want goblin scars! Need goblin scars!"

Leptin's ears lowered, just a bit.

"You right," Gherin said. "Gherin make choice. Big choice. Maybe not think good, but Gherin choice. Okay—Leptin angry. Okay. Yah. Understand. Leptin right. Okay. But . . . fight mouse last chance Gherin have get goblin scars. Like Leptin. Need goblin scars. Need. Need chance, fight like Leptin say, for goblins. Fight like Leptin show, for tribe. Need chance. Last chance ever get right scars. Let Gherin fight."

Gherin opened his arms. "Please."

Leptin stroked his chin. Flexed his muscles, felt his own scars, how they went deep, deep down through skin and into bone. How they reminded him of where he had come from. He looked at Gherin, remembered how the young goblin had used his family's influence to be sent along, and recalled that Gherin had never said anything like this before. If the boy was staying, Leptin thought, maybe he would need something to remind him of where he came from.

He took a deep breath. "Close enough," he muttered. "Better nothing."

Gherin's face lit up. "Gherin can fight?"

"Yah."

Gherin smiled.

Leptin turned. "Come. Tomb below. Mouse here. No kill yet. Wait Leptin say."

"Wait."

Leptin turned back. "What now?"

"Got present Leptin."

Leptin's face twisted. "Present?"

"Yah."

"No got time games, Gherin."

"Wait. You like." Gherin shuffled back outside the cave entrance then dashed back, holding a brown cloth sack.

He held it out.

Leptin took it gingerly and looked inside.

A smile crept across his face. "Ooooooo."

"Yah!" said Gherin. "Good good!"

Leptin pulled out a grenade belt, fully loaded, and strapped it around his chest. He had to circle it twice to get it to fit, but it did.

"Where get?"

Gherin smiled again. "Rabbit."

"Steal from rabbit?" Leptin grinned wider.

"Yah. Rabbit crazy brother know how get stash, help Gherin get trade: kill bison next week."

"But, Gherin work for rabbit."

"Feh." Gherin waved that away. "Rabbit get mad, but Gherin big important rabbit plan. Rabbit live."

Leptin nodded. "Good present. Good good."

Gherin smiled. "Give goblin grenades. Is what Gherin want stand for in life."

"Good good."

Leptin motioned, and as one they crept into the tunnel and the darkness.

The tunnel was long and winding, but there was no question where the humans had gone. Even if there had been open spaces off the path big enough for them to get through, the scent of fresh human where none belonged was overwhelming. They would never lose this trail, however much it wound down into the impenetrable dark. They feared no ambush either: for the humans would need their light to see in the dark, and it would give their positions away.

Leptin took deep breaths, smelled the cave air. Felt Gherin stepping behind him. It was good. Hunting should be done in packs.

The next sound they heard was a torrent of rushing water in the distance. They looked at each other, Leptin shrugged, and they kept creeping forward. The sound grew louder, almost painfully so in the confined tunnel where it bounced off the walls over and over again and mixed with its own echo. Then the tunnel abruptly ended at an enormous cavern, and down below flowed a massive river rushing from the ocean into the depths of the world.

They stopped at the mouth of the cavern, looking not at the river but at a small stone bridge, sculpted out of a single piece of rock, that crossed the entire span of the water. The humans had set up lights there, battery powered lamps to illuminate the span, and a guard stood on the other side of the bridge.

"Hmmmmmm," said Gherin.

"Tricky," said Leptin. "Good vantage point. See bridge easy."

"Take out lights?" Gherin asked.

"Nah. Lights go out, still sound alarm."

Gherin nodded thoughtfully. "You got guns," he said.

Leptin nodded and held up the pistol he'd taken from the guard by the van. He held it forward, carefully fitting his claws around the trigger, and lined up the shot. He nodded. "Long shot for pistol. Maybe." He shook his head. "Better idea."

"Yah?"

Leptin nodded. "Follow. Stay in dark."

Gherin nodded. "Yah." But he looked disappointed.

Leptin gave him a look. "What?"

"Want you throw grenade."

Leptin nodded. "Want to. But . . . patience." He set off into the cavern and crossed toward the bridge, carefully staying out of the lamp's light. Gherin followed.

They reached the bridge and then, setting his claws in carefully, Leptin crawled along the cliff face and under the bridge, then began crossing it on the underside, his claws white with the effort of holding on above the mighty river.

Again, Gherin followed.

It was a long crawl, and they could not hear each other speak above the river's roar—although, this meant the guard would not hear them coming too.

Leptin kept focused, putting one claw in front of another, his progress steady. Gherin stopped, for a moment, to look down into the water.

He had never seen a river this big. There seemed to be shapes in it, slowly following the current—it looked like a small fleet of underwater boats sailing from the depths of the ocean to the depths of the world. Gherin blinked and they were gone. He shook his head and saw that Leptin was now far ahead. How long, Gherin wondered, had he been staring? He worked to catch up.

By the time Gherin arrived at the other side, Leptin had already snuck up behind the guard and battered him unconscious, his face a mass of bruises. Leptin scowled and shook his head as Gherin crawled over.

"Got keep up want scars," he said, holding the guard's assault rifle.

"Leptin," Gherin asked. "Who build bridge? What river this?"

Leptin shook his head. "Ancients. Built tomb around symbol while slumber. Comfy tomb. Soft blankets. Sound of river help lull it sleep. Not know more. Thought maybe Gherin know, had good tutors."

Gherin took a deep breath. "Am 'fraid river, Leptin."

Leptin shrugged. "Sure. Okay."

Gherin shook his head. "No no, not understand. River scary."

Leptin shrugged again. "Sure. Deep river in underground tomb ancient symbol. Why not scary?"

Gherin sighed. "Just saying."

Leptin motioned them forward.

The tunnel beyond the bridge was spacious and carved, the walls smooth, the floor even. They heard the humans at the same time they smelled them: the remaining nine soldiers in Pounce's army had walked down a narrow path below into a huge cavern, and they were running around a massive sarcophagus, setting up explosives.

Even at this distance, it was possible to see that the mouse himself was standing on that stone coffin, giving directions in the dim lantern light.

"Ohhhhhhhh," Leptin moaned. "Bad."

"Bad bad," Gherin agreed.

Leptin fingered a grenade.

"What do?" Gherin asked, trying not to get excited.

Leptin took a deep breath. "You say met mouse?"

Gherin hesitated. "Yah."

"Not go good?"

A long wait. "Yah."

"So mouse see Gherin, mouse think fight."

Gherin looked at the ground. "Yah."

"Okay. Leptin go in, negotiate mouse. Try talk sense. Gherin stay back. Keep quiet."

Gherin's face fell. "But . . . scars!"

"Mission first!" Leptin said. "Besides, mouse no listen. So Gherin hide . . . ," he looked over the surroundings " . . . there." He pointed at a small ledge twenty feet above the cavern floor below.

"Gherin no want hide!"

"If fight," Leptin said patiently, "Gherin shoot."

Gherin blinked. "What?"

Leptin held the assault rifle up.

Gherin gaped. "Gherin never fire gun!"

Leptin showed his teeth. "You want high culture!" He held the rifle forward.

Gherin took it, carefully. "How work?"

Leptin rolled his eyes. "Semi-auto. Fire fast. Lots ammo. Look down scope here, see target here," he pointed at the various parts. "Got recoil, so, keep arms loose. Easy. You learn quick."

"But . . . but . . . no get scars."

Leptin shook his head sadly. "If fight, plenty scars. Promise. Gherin first shoot any humans by explosives there, there." He pointed to the piles of dynamite being set on each side of the tomb. "Then shoot anyone shoot Leptin. Yah?"

"Yah," Gherin said, without confidence.

Leptin pat his shoulder. "Be fun!" he said. "Like time you kill big dog!"

Gherin shook his head. "Not fun," he said softly. "Not fun at all."

Leptin nodded. "Okay, no fun. But mission. Yah?"

Gherin closed his eyes. "Yah."

"Okay. Sneak position. When there, Leptin walk down."

"Yah." Gherin turned to go.

"Wait!" Leptin said.

Gherin turned hopefully. "Yah?"

Leptin reached over and flipped the rifle's safety off. Then motioned Gherin to go.

Gherin crawled through the darkness, hugging the cliff wall, crawling across the rock down to the ledge Leptin had found. Gherin wondered if he'd ever be that comfortable before a fight that he didn't know he could win. What, he wondered, had it been like for Leptin at Goren Vaj?

He settled on the ledge and looked through the rifle, practicing lining up humans in the scope. It suddenly occurred to him to wonder if Leptin thought he was going to survive. The thought made his palms sweat. He had come back to make peace with Leptin, not watch him die.

Then it occurred to him that he might die, and for a moment the world seemed too much to bear.

Leptin watched Gherin get into place and practice aiming with the rifle. He nodded approvingly. He could not understand the young goblin's choices, but it seemed that something about getting scars for high culture was good for his character. He fingered the grenades again. Ah, high-culture weapons—so loud and powerful and noisy. So ridiculous and ugly, but so effective. Only magic can stand against it. It even seemed magic, in its way: if fellow soldiers had not told Leptin that a machine gun was high culture instead of a magic wand, he might never have known. High culture came from a wizard, so maybe there was a connection.

The grenades were good. The grenades changed everything. Even if he couldn't beat the mouse in combat, Leptin was pretty sure that with this many grenades he could blow them both to bits. As long as he could do it without upsetting the tomb, it would be worth it.

He had never wanted to die so far from home, but had always expected it.

He took a few deep breaths. Gherin had been wrong. This would be fun, in its way. When you have nothing left to live for, death and violence are the last great adventure. Leptin hoped Gherin would never understand.

He fingered a grenade. The kid was odd, but he'd be all right.

He stood up and ran down the path into the lit area by the tomb below. Guards shouted as he passed, but moved too slow to stop him. Guns were drawn. Leptin leaped into the air and grabbed a human man by his neck, forcing him to the ground. He stood in front of the sarcophagus, his claws at the human's throat, using him as a shield.

"Pounce!" he shouted. "Pounce! Want talk! Tell soldiers put guns down, will let soldier go!"

From around him, soldiers shouted. "I've got a clear shot!"

Leptin changed position, and the soldiers scrambled.

"I've got a clear shot!"

"I've got a clear shot!"

"Want talk mouse! Put guns down let soldier go!"

"I've got a clear shot!"

"Hold!" The mouse's voice was high and strong.

Everything stopped.

"Sheath your weapons," Pounce said, jumping up on the sarcophagus from behind it.

"Sir . . . ," said a woman with short cropped hair and piercings through the back of her neck, "I have a shot."

Pounce shook his head. "Mercy is a quality much strained in the world of goblins and mice, but I will not abandon it entirely upon the cavern floor. Put your weapons in their holsters and give him a chance to prove he is an honest man."

Three of the ten did.

"That's an order!" Pounce shouted, and the rest leaped to attention and holstered their weapons.

Leptin nodded. "Good. Yah. Good." He raised his hands and let the soldier fall to the floor. He stepped back. The man scrambled to his feet and ran over to his comrades, where he stood at attention.

Pounce nodded. "Very good. Each time an enemy honors his word, I believe the world grows stronger. So, brave goblin, are you a companion of . . . ," he stopped.

He walked to the edge of the sarcophagus. He peered closely at Leptin. "Have we met before?"

Leptin nodded. "Yah. Blood Oasis war."

"Ah. Ah! You were with the goblin regiments who joined the struggle against the obsidian giants."

"Yah."

Pounce nodded. "That was a dirty business."

"Yah."

"I am sorry for your comrades who fell. They brought glory to your army, and you honored their sacrifice in victory."

"Thanks. Mouse fight good too."

Pounce bowed from the waist. "I recall you being a soldier's soldier, willing to sacrifice your men for victory—but absolutely no more than required."

"Sure."

"It is a quality I admire. Forgive me soldier, I have forgotten your name."

"Leptin."

"Yes! Of course. A name I also recall from conversations around tables of veterans and minstrels. If you will excuse me a moment?"

Leptin nodded slowly. "Um? Okay."

Pounce turned to his soldiers. "Men! The goblin Leptin, who will likely die this day by our hand, once fought at my side as a true soldier. Though fighting for causes I would not, he has distinguished himself in legendary battles. Let us salute him, as a brother comrades-in-arms!"

As one, the unit saluted.

Leptin stared. His jaw dropped. His breath caught.

Pounce put his hand down, and the squadron followed.

Leptin wiped his eye. "Ah . . . big thanks."

Pounce nodded. "Of course. Scars must be honored. Now, to the unpleasant matter at hand. May I assume you are a companion of the goblin Gherin, who also stalks the city in this time and place?"

Leptin sighed. "Hoping you not think bring that up."

Pounce's expression hardened. "And yet I have. He and I exchanged harsh words that resolved nothing. Have you come to continue that conversation?"

"Yah. Sorry 'bout Gherin. Him kid. First time big mission, lots not know. Get better."

"It is not the state of his conscience I worry about, but the lives he takes under the banner of that corrupt rabbit."

"Yah," Leptin sighed. "Yah. Not happy that. Him want live high culture, abandon home, bad bad, try talking, kid no listen . . . ."

"He should be allowed to make his own way in the world, Leptin, as we all must do."

Leptin scowled. "Well, complicated. See, goblins no got high culture."

"Neither do mice—and yet I crossed the world to learn the arts of combat and the songs of justice. I, too, was told my path was not possible. This is no matter. But even well-meaning novices must be held to account for terrible choices they make. Willie O'Shaughnessy is not a rabbit but a shark, and sharks have no culture—no matter what waters they swim in. Gherin shall learn nothing of culture from him but the taste it makes when you rip its flesh and swallow it."

Sitting on the ledge, Gherin listened, eyes wide.

Leptin sighed. "Yah, look, this not conversation me want have."

"No, I'm sure not. Yet all things connect on a delicate web of causality that—"

"YOU STANDING ON CRYPT ANCIENT SYMBOL TOO TERRIBLE WORDS!" Leptin shouted, pointing his claw. "Me want talk 'bout that!"

Pounce nodded his head ruefully. "Forgive me, I have a bad habit of lapsing into lectures. It's probably the consequence of a life spent giving rousing speeches."

Leptin threw up his hands. "What me got do, kidnap soldier every time want get back topic?"

Pounce pursed his lips. "Very well, Leptin of the goblins, friend of Gherin of San Francisco. Speak."

Leptin nodded and took a deep breath.

"You know what buried here. Ancient symbol, evil symbol, represents ancient truth everyone know, not face. Bad bad. Bad for humans. Bad for mouse. Bad for goblins. You think wake up thing shake hand goblins? Invite goblins drink tea? No. Kill goblins, just like humans. Kill all goblins if hungry, goblin tribes like field strawberries pick and eat. You say goblins evil? Fine. You say symbol evil? Fine, yah, sure. But not mean same thing.

So why goblins come, say not kill symbol? Symbol die, mean not eat goblins. Good for goblins, yah? Sure. But goblins part of world. World die, goblins got no place have sex. No fun. Bad for future. Goblins die like everything.

So am here. Telling great hero goblins know something hero not: bad things make world go. Bad things make world go. Not nice, but truth. Why goblin get up in morning? Hungry. Hunger make goblin go. Why man build cathedral? Yearning. Yearning make art go. Why man build homes with walls? Fear. Fear make man go. Goblins, ogres, high culture—bad things make them go, only difference is what do with. Goblins, ogres, animals, take bad things: feel them, live them, know them like lover. High culture take bad things, grinds them up to make cities and art and economies. Bad things push first - only difference what high culture do with.

Bad things make world go too. Evil symbols in crypts like fire, make spark: spark make world turn. Symbols gone, no spark. No spark, world no turn. See?"

His words echoed through the chamber, and came back again. "See?"

Leptin put his hands together and held them in front of his chest. "Must stop. Soldier telling soldier: war must stop."

All was quiet in the crypt.

Pounce's eyes blazed. "And there it is," he said. "The greatest evil of all, one far more deadly than what sleeps here. One branded onto the backs of every oppressed soul to burn the truth out of their minds. One sung, over and over again, like a hymn in the church of the powerful: that the world cannot be made better than it is. That the way things are is an immutable law that time or nature or history or self-serving logic have made sacrosanct. I tell you, soldier Leptin, that I do not know if your words are true. It seems to me that man and mouse and goblin alike are governed by love and curiosity and playfulness as much as evil and hunger and fear. But I am not a learned mouse, only a swordmouse who sings of justice, and your words may be true as the morning sun. But Leptin, who once stood at my side to fight giants, I tell you this truth: I am willing to take that chance. I am willing to break the wrongs of the world in order that they may be replaced with rights. I am willing to extinguish the fire of evil that turns the world, if this be so, in the knowledge that love too can burn, and that we are as heroic as we are afraid."

Pounce's words also echoed through the chamber: "we are as heroic as we are afraid."

All was quiet in the crypt.

"So sad," Leptin said mournfully. "So sad world not live up to mouse expectations."

"Enough," said Pounce. "This debate is finished. In honor of your sacrifices, I will give you your life if you leave us in peace."

Leptin's eyes narrowed. "Will let soldiers live if drop guns, leave fast."

Pounce looked over his troops. "His offer is on the table."

Two of the soldiers pulled out their guns and pointed them at Leptin. The rest followed.

"They rebuke you," said Pounce. "They are soldiers for a cause."

"Yep," said Leptin. He threw a grenade before the soldier it landed next to could pull a trigger.

The explosion scattered the soldiers on his right flank. Leptin pulled his pistols out and ran toward them as he shot toward his left. Pounce leaped off the sarcophagus to engage.

In the commotion no one noticed Gherin's first shot, which missed. His second shot hit the soldier next to the far detonator straight in the chest, and he dropped.

"Sniper above the east perimeter!" Pounce shouted. "Target and kill!"

Bullets stopped whizzing by Leptin and as the living soldiers turned toward Gherin and fired at his position. He shot again, hitting the soldier at the near set of explosives in the shoulder, and then cowered at the back of his perch for cover.

Pounce's sword was drawn as he circled Leptin. The goblin fired three rounds—Pounce seemed to pirouette around them without breaking stride. "Is this the fight in your heart, Leptin of goblins?" he asked.

"Nah," said Leptin, firing again. "But bullets kill mouse good."

Pounce dashed forward under the hail of bullets, and when the projectiles were behind him he leaped into the air, sword aimed straight at Leptin's heart. Leptin turned aside, his chest twisting just enough to let the mouse fly by, but as Pounce passed Leptin's right hand he somersaulted in mid-air and his sword dashed out, penetrating the knuckle on Leptin's trigger finger. Leptin's hand jerked and the gun, always a bad fit, went flying on top of the tomb.

"In Japan," said Pounce as he landed, "that maneuver is called the 'Breath of Heaven strike.' I studied with its last living master."

"Huh," said Leptin, aiming carefully with his left hand and shaking his right. "Killing you like fighting pub quiz." He fired.

"Touché," Pounce chuckled as he slipped out of the path of another bullet.

The mouse dashed forward, under a bullet, and sprung, sword first, at Leptin's knee. The goblin jumped in the air, and Pounce soared underneath him. Leptin landed and fired again. As soon as Pounce's feet touched the floor, he back flipped, reversing momentum, climbing high into the air, over the bullet. Leptin's free hand shot out, claws first. Pounce slipped between the claws and landed on Leptin's forearm. The sword struck, biting through skin. Leptin swung the gun around like a club to knock the mouse off, but Pounce jumped onto Leptin's shoulder. His sword struck there too.

Leptin ran up to the sarcophagus and jumped against it with one foot, flipping backwards. Pounce scrambled to stay on, but gravity got him first, and he fell to the ground. Leptin landed and kicked out with his talons, but Pounce scurried out of reach.

Good, Leptin thought. Good. The mouse was confident now that he could get through his defenses and strike any time. That meant a close-up fight, and that meant Pounce would put himself right next to the grenade belt and not see the trap coming. Good. As long as the explosion didn't open the sarcophagus, Leptin could complete the mission by taking them both out. Gherin could handle the remaining humans—and even if he couldn't, they'd never be fools enough to open the grave without the mouse.

This would work.

Gherin huddled back against a storm of bullets. His biggest advantage was that he could see in the dark and the humans couldn't. The bullets slowed as the soldiers organized, spreading out to get a better vantage point on his cover. He stood up and fired at one of the human's electric lanterns. It shattered in a small explosion of glass and the cavern got darker.

Leptin snarled as he and Pounce circled each other. What was Gherin doing? It was good strategy, actually—but fighting in the dark might make Pounce change his tactics, and Leptin couldn't have that. He needed to be sure, absolutely sure, that Pounce would be committed to coming in close when he blew himself up. Leptin's jaw tightened as he and Pounce traded swipes. It was now or never. Time to join his family. He hoped they were proud of him.

Another round of bullets flew at Gherin as he huddled back at the end of the ledge. Their aim was worse in the dark. In spite of his terror, Gherin was proud of himself for hitting the lantern. That was a good shot! He stood up again and fired at the closest of the three remaining lanterns.

He missed. Then there was a crack and a searing pain in his side. He was bleeding! Where . . . his left side. Oh . . .

He fired, fast as the rifle would allow, and one of his shots hit the next lantern. More bullets flew past. He collapsed back against the ridge. Not a bad wound. He didn't think it was lethal. Needed to stop the bleeding. If only the humans would stop shooting at him . . .

But the bullets kept flying from more directions. Too many soldiers were aiming badly now, and too many bullets were ricocheting off the cavern walls. As Gherin steeled himself to slip out into the darkness and change positions, a bullet aimed at shadows bounced off the cavern wall and into the pile of explosives at the close end of the sarcophagus.

The explosion roared through the room, the impact ripping the nearby soldiers apart and even sending Pounce and Leptin, at the other end of the cavern, flying through the air.

Leptin found himself on the cavern floor. What? He wondered. What? I didn't do that. I'm still . . . what was that explosion?

Then he realized. Oh no.

"No!" shouted Pounce. "We had a strategy to beat it! We're not in place!"

From out of the shattered sarcophagus, a white fog with many eyes began to fill the crypt.

Nothing its body of mist touched remained clear. Nothing it enveloped remained certain. Life was revealed to be the dream of a petulant child, or a burning sun with no days left, or a door always just out of reach. Only the eyes were true, and they saw you. You. The eyes saw you alone at night, and they saw you weeping for the death of your mother; the eyes saw you when a whole room was laughing at you for something you never should have said. They saw you realizing that there is nothing to save you.

The mist took the world away as the eyes saw everything you are, and then they shared a secret. That there was a way out. The first wounded soldier it enveloped stared into an eye, and wept, and then unzipped himself . . . undid himself, as though there were a string you could pull to take back everything you've ever been.

In the mist, there was. That is how it feeds.

The mist spread over the remaining wounded soldiers who lay on the ground open and in pieces, and they could not look into its eyes, and they reached out into the fog and pulled their strings and unraveled.

It hovered and expanded. It saw Gherin on the ledge, holding his wounded side. It spread toward him.

Gherin ran.

He leaped off the ledge and had a split second to make a choice—run through the exit toward the river and the surface world or run over to Leptin and Pounce.

He ran to Leptin, wincing with every step, and helped the older goblin up.

The ancient symbol did not pursue: instead it expanded to cover the way out, a wall of eyes and mist blocking their escape. And still it poured out of the broken sarcophagus. Infinite.

"Damn you!" hissed Pounce. "I would have woken and killed it, but now you have allowed it entrance to the world!"

Leptin snorted. "Goblin say no open crypt. How our fault?"

Gherin looked around. "See crack in wall," he said, pointing behind them. "Think turn into path. Maybe to river."

"Yah," said Leptin. "Yah." He saw Gherin's wound. "How bad?"

"Hold!" said Pounce. "We must fight it together!"

"Feh," said Gherin. Leptin looked closer at the wound.

"Between us we have guns and grenades, sword and claws!" said Pounce. "It will be difficult, but victory is possible. We must face it at the river!"

"Clean," Leptin said, with one eye on the wound and the other on the fog of eyes that filled the room and wafted toward them. "Clean good. If can run, better chance than fight."

Leptin held Gherin by the shoulder, and together they scurried up toward the crack in the cavern that Gherin had seen, climbing up the wall to reach it.

"Wait!" shouted Pounce. "Wait! We must coordinate!"

The mist slipped over toward him. A tendril reached out. "Hah!" he laughed, and leaped into the air and ran the nearest eyeball through with his sword.

There was a sound like a door closing on a weeping infant. The mist shuddered. The eyeball vanished.

Gherin looked behind him, in awe. "How do that?"

Leptin shrugged.

The crack was too small for a human to get through, but it was enough of a path for them. Leptin nodded. "Goes through." They squeezed in as quickly as they could.

Pounce dashed after them as the mist pressed forward, trying to envelop him. "You see!" he shouted. "It can be beaten!" He was not a natural climber like the goblins, he struggled up the wall in his little boots . . . but he made it, and scurried after.

The mist followed. It had no problem squeezing through tight spaces. Dozens of eyes stared at them from the opening.

Leptin could hear a sound like whispering. "*Come,*" it seemed to say. "*You were going to end yourself before. Die now.*"

"We can beat it!" Pounce cried, catching up. "We can beat it if we stand together."

"Mouse not listening," Leptin muttered. "Mouse never listen. Not want thing die. Asleep best. No got that, escape okay."

The tunnel ended at an opening above the mighty river. The goblins looked to see if they could reach the narrow stone bridge, but it was already covered in mist. Hundreds of eyes watched them from it. The creature began to float over the river toward them, even as the fog behind them advanced too.

The goblins scanned the walls around the river.

"There," Gherin pointed. "Other passage. Through ceiling." He pointed to a hole in the rock, and a small tunnel in the cavern's ceiling, closer to them than the bridge. "Goes up. Up good."

Leptin eyed him carefully. "Hard climb. Gherin wounded."

"Yah," said Gherin, wincing. "No good choice. Fight or climb."

"Fight!" said Pounce. "Fight for your lives, damn you! Fight for the lives of those who can't run!"

The goblins leaped onto the wall and began climbing up to the ceiling. This part was easy. Hanging from the ceiling to get to the opening, that would be hard for a goblin with a chest wound.

"Then we part ways here, faithless creatures," Pounce said.

He stuck the point of his sword in the ground and kneeled before it.

Gherin and Leptin reached the ceiling. The grip was hard for Leptin: the thumb Pounce had struck would not stay steady and his right hand kept slipping. The wounds Pounce's sword had made in his leg and his shoulder stung and opened again.

Gherin screamed as he hung from the rock and stepped forward, the hole in his body shifting, clotted blood ripping apart, muscles clenching in spasms. One hand in front of the other, screaming, one step, one step. Thirty paces to go.

The fog rolled toward Pounce from both sides, even as the ancient creature's many eyes watched the goblins, following their escape.

Twenty paces to go. Leptin called for Gherin to hang on, to think of the scar this would leave.

Fifteen paces to go.

"Oh creator of all things," Pounce intoned, "who has blessed me to rise above my station and given me the hands with which to offer comfort to the weak, hear now this prayer."

Leptin heard the almost voice: *Find the only true rest, be unmade, be at peace.* He clutched the rock more tightly. Did not look down. His right hand slipped again.

There are shapes in the water, Gherin told himself as he screamed. It was the only thing that kept him holding on through the pain. Those terrifying shapes in the river at the bottom of the world.

"Since the day grace first lifted my eyes from the field to see the rising sun, I have sought to bring this light to all who suffer in darkness."

Ten paces to go.

"No holy quest is grounds for sorrow, nor just cause a burden to bear, though the road be steep and the enemy wicked. "

Give up what you would have surrendered just moments before.

There were terrible shapes in the water.

"Still the righteous shall sing in noble chorus to the coming of the dawn, and be glad."

Leptin put one foot in front of the other. Only his left hand could keep a grip. Gherin screamed with each step.

"This I have witnessed—and am grateful."

Five paces to go.

The only truths in this world will break your heart.

"I offer you all I have: these hands, and the unworthy soul that wields them."

The pain in Gherin's chest grew white hot. His grip broke. He fell.

Leptin let go with his left hand and swung backwards, hanging on to the ceiling with just his feet. He grabbed Gherin's arm with his one good hand as the weight of his friend swung him back . . . and then forth . . . and he hurled Gherin into the passage above. "Reach!" he shouted.

"Grant me only this: that when I stand alone in this world I am not lonely. That I may find strength in those I serve. "

Gherin stretched out his legs and held himself steady inside the opening, panting and weeping. It was easier to push than it had been to hold on. He raised himself up into the passage as Leptin swung back, clamped his left hand into the ceiling and scurried the rest of the way. Pounce stood up as the mist approached him from each side. He removed his sword from the ground. And laughed.

Exhausted, panting, wincing, the goblins watched him take his stand.

Whisps of fog surrounded him. An eye floated forward. And another. And another. They looked into Pounce, and Pounce stared back over the blade of his sword.

Everything but the river was still.

The fog shuddered. Pounce struck. An eye vanished with the sound of a poet dying before meeting his muse.

Two more eyes rolled in as the mist grew thicker.

Pounce's gaze did not waver.

"Can win?" Gherin asked, incredulous and out of breath.

Leptin shook his head.

The mist had almost closed around the mouse now, obscuring him from view.

"Can win?" Gherin asked again.

"Nah," said Leptin. "And, if win, bad bad. World end."

Twenty eyes by the stone bridge turned toward the goblins, and a new wave of fog covered the bridge and sent the eyes floating toward their hiding place.

Pounce was gone, covered in fog.

"Can help mouse?" Gherin asked.

Leptin put his hand on Gherin's shoulder. "Maybe mouse can stare impossible truth, live. Fight. Maybe. Leptin no. Leptin can no fight this. To run is live."

He steadied himself for climbing. "And Gherin?" he asked. "Can Gherin stare many eyes terrible truth and fight? And win? Can Gherin help mouse? End world?"

Down below them, the fog still poured out of the crypt, filling the ancient cave. The eyes too numerous to count.

Gherin took a deep breath . . . and began to follow Leptin up the tunnel. The sound of the river was all they could hear.

They crawled through cracks and crevices, through branching tunnels and twisting paths, always looking for the way up, always listening for noise behind them, or the terrible sight of white fog.

When their best path came to an end, with them on their hands and knees, Leptin pointed to the ceiling.

"Dig," he said.

"Yah?"

Leptin nodded as he began to tear into the roof with his claws. "Weak rock. Dirt. Near surface. Near surface!"

Gherin, too, began to rend at the rock, wincing each time he encountered resistance. But Leptin was right: they were making their own path.

Five feet later they emerged into the moonlight. Trees were all around them.

"Where?" asked Leptin.

Gherin knew. Golden Gate Park. Near the tea garden.

They stood and looked at the hole they had made.

"Bad bad," Gherin said.

"Good!" Leptin said. "Symbol live, mouse stopped. Mission done. World save."

Gherin looked at his friend. That didn't seem right.

"Maybe mouse win."

"No."

"Maybe mouse live."

"No."

"How know?"

Leptin shook his head. "Too much. Too much."

"But—"
An eye on a cloud of mist rose up out of the hole.
It looked at them. They ran.

Chapter 40

They ran on instinct. They ran as fast as their wounds could allow. The ancient creature wafted after, as though carried by a slow breeze.

They looked for someplace to hide. Someplace it could not find them. On impulse, they ran to the only home they had here, up the big hills of the Sunset District, empty of people this late at night, to the apartment of James and Mari.

There was no fog in sight as they pried through the window and slipped onto the floor. They had made this entrance in perfect silence a dozen times before, but in their fear Leptin tripped over a tiffany lamp and Gherin gurgled as he leaned against the wall.

They froze, waiting for James to wake up on the futon and see them, waiting for the curse to appear.

But James was not on the futon.

Still they froze, waiting for the voice of Mari in the bedroom to call out and see what was wrong.

But Mari did not call out.

"Hide!" Leptin hissed. But Gherin crept forward, toward the closed bedroom door, wondering what was wrong.

"Hide!" Leptin hissed again.

"Meeeow!" screeched Caramel the cat. It was the only sound they heard in the apartment.

Gherin looked at the cat and shook his head. He reached his hand out and gently turned the knob. He looked inside her bedroom.

Mari was not there.

Gherin looked back, and Leptin shrugged. How could he know? And Caramel, a domesticated animal, could not tell them.

Without humans to hide from, Leptin crept back over to the window to look out carefully for signs of fog.

Gherin limped over. "Clear?"

"Not know," Leptin whispered. "See white?" he peered out the window at the streets several blocks beyond that were laced with what could be an ancient symbol from the beginning of time or could be ordinary San Francisco fog. You couldn't tell without seeing the eyes, and this high up the hill that was impossible.

They crouched down and waited. Watched. The mist slowly crept up the hill.

Leptin's face grew grim. "Creature," he said. "But . . . no good track. No good hunt. Just follow direction. Not know where hide."

Gherin nodded. "Hide here? Run?"

Leptin looked at the fog, perhaps four blocks away. "Not go in buildings now," he said. "But maybe soon. Run better. Run far far. City doomed."

Gherin's ears fell. "Like city."

"Sorry. But Gherin got goblin scar now. Can come home."

Gherin's face pulled in every direction at once.

"Run," Leptin said again. "Live."

Gherin nodded, stretched his aching and wounded muscles to climb out the window. Then . . .

He saw a late night bus drive two blocks down.

He saw it stop at the corner.

He saw Mari and James, in formal attire, get out.

The bus drove away.

James and Mari started walking up the hill, toward their apartment. A block and a half behind them, twenty eyes turned to look at their backs.

Gherin pointed. His mouth open.

Leptin shook his head. "No. No can help. Doomed."

James and Mari got closer to the apartment. The fog came closer to them.

"But . . . ," Gherin whispered. "Most beautiful girl in world!"

"Doomed!" said Leptin. "Can no fight fog! Can no save girl! Run! Live!"

Gherin's mouth set. "Can warn girl, and stupid singing boy."

"No!" Leptin hissed. "If warn, break treaty! Doom to Gherin!"

"Give chance," Gherin whispered, steeling himself. "Give chance!"

He leaped out the window and onto the sidewalk. Pain exploded in his chest with the impact. He stumbled down the hill toward the human couple. "Run!" he yelled. "Run! Run from fog! Run from eyes!"

Leptin cursed and watched from the window. They were all doomed now.

Gherin nearly tripped over his feet as he reached the human couple. "Run!" he croaked. "Run fog! Run eyes!"

They stared at him. Mari gasped. James raised his eyebrows.

"What ... what is that?" Mari asked.

James shook his head.

Leptin told himself to run. Told himself at least one of them should make it out alive. But he could not turn away.

"My God," Mari said, seeming more surprised than afraid. "It's not a ... but it's a ... who are you?" she asked.

Gherin's breath was gone. He could only point.

Now they turned. Now they saw. The ancient symbol was a wall of eyes behind them.

Now Mari screamed. James' face drained of blood.

"Run," croaked Gherin.

They stood ... and stared.

The fog billowed closer. James removed his arm from hers, put it inside his coat.

"I know what you're thinking," she whispered. "Don't be a hero. Please."

He smiled, just a little, and very sadly. "Do you really want to die together?"

She winced. "No ... but ..."

Gherin pulled himself forward. This was going badly. They were dawdling. He could only think of one way to save them now. He wobbled to his knees and embraced his certain doom. Because ... she was beautiful. Because she was good. Because most of all he didn't want to live in a world where such beauty and goodness could be sacrificed to a monster like this.

"Sorry," he said.

They turned to look at him.

He grabbed Mari's arm. She flinched, but he held tight. "Sorry sorry," he said again. He held out his other hand. He flexed his claws.

"Stop!" said James.

Gherin made a small incision in her arm, tiny but deep. Blood welled up.

He turned her arm over. A drop hit the ground.

The mist was like a wall before them.

Gherin collapsed. He'd done all he could. He imagined he could hear Leptin, hiding behind the window, hissing "Fool!"

The blood boiled on the concrete. It rolled around the ground, leaving a thick trail behind it, forming a circle within a circle, and then a half moon, and then a coded letter from a 12th century alchemical text, and then ... at the very center ... the signatures of ancient and powerful beings.

The wind stopped. The moonlight was heavy, as though it were holding everything in place. The fog halted its advance. Its many eyes started at the humans and goblin before it, but its gaze did not cross the blood sign.

The elements of the world, that just a moment ago the fog had turned to endless white, came together: the red of Mari's blood, the white of the moon, the green of a leaf, the sound of a distant bus, the shape of James' coat, the sharpness of Gherin's teeth ... somehow they connected, like pieces of a puzzle, to form a cliff over which the world could fall.

"The treaty has been broken," came a deathly recitation from the other side of the cliff. "The signatures of the One Hand, witnessed by the Four Faces of Matter, written upon the Suffering Child, decree its terms and descendants shall be defended."

Vertigo. As though the world nodded its consent. Thunder clapped. The translucent image of a man floated above the blood sign, colorless.

His beard was long, his fingers were nimble, his robe was brown and decorated with a purple shawl containing symbols that reflected silver against the moonlight. His breeches were thin and dirty, as though he had been traveling a long way. His fancy boots were worn. His glassy eyes stared at Gherin, and someplace dark and dangerous stared through him.

"Oooooooh," said Gherin. So that was what a terrible death looks like. Funny, he'd always expected it to have a giant scorpion's tail. But there was no mistaking it.

Up the street, Leptin looked through the window and trembled. Death he could deal with. He had been prepared to die tonight. But not a curse, not an eternity spent with regret.

"Low creature," the specter recited, his voice a recollection, an echo, of things a living man had once said, "you have been seen by the children of high culture, and drawn their blood. No power in the universe remains to save you from judgment."

Gherin got to his knees and put his hands together. "Yah," he said. "But turn 'round first. Please."

The translucent man did not listen. Small bursts of lightning arced from his fingers as he raised his hand.

"Wait!" shouted Mari, her voice painfully human.

The specter turned. Saw her. Saw her humanity. She pointed the same direction as Gherin.

Hesitantly, the image of John Dee turned and beheld the ancient symbol behind him.

His eyes, his terribly transparent eyes that looked from far away, seemed unable to process what they saw. Color crept into them, making them solid, the robin's egg blue eyes of a living man in a ghostly body. The living eyes widened. Then color and solidity spread through his face until it too was flesh and it blanched at what was before him. He took a deep breath, and his throat turned pink as the words rose up through it, while his human eyes, having done their work, faded into spectral translucence once again. There was the warmth of a human emotion coming through his snapping voice now, which sounded nearer.

"Oh bloody hell!" The specter of John Dee said. "Who let that out!"

He raised his hand and the blood sign beneath him glowed red in the moonlight. The world groaned.

"Embarrassing to have to be told it's there," he said, his lips and portions of his face becoming flesh again as he spoke, then fading away into transparency when the words were done. "It's the sort of thing you'd think I'd notice. I'm a very accomplished dead wizard, you know. Lots of practice."

"It … it happened to us, too," Mari said.

He focused his attention on the creature. "It seems so big when you look at it straight on." His voice was almost that of a living man. "But then, symbols always do."

Mari shook her head. "I don't … understand …"

But Dee ignored her now. He turned to face the wall of fog and eyes struggling to cross the blood sign on the ground. He stared into the eyes. They stared back at him. Everyone could hear the whisper: "*Let go. Let go. Put your burden down. Far better not to be, and at peace.*"

All Dee's color, all his life, drained away at the symbol's words. But the specter remained.

"Stay behind me," he warned the humans, his words ghostly echoes of thing spoken long before, in life, to others. "It will not cross the treaty's seal."

"We could run," Mari whispered to James.

"It's too late," James said, desperately sad. "It's far too late."

Gherin wasn't sure whether to look at them, or the wizard, or the ancient symbol. They didn't understand. He was doomed, the terms of the treaty were clear, but they were saved now.

Surely they were saved.

The specter of the wizard Dee held up his hand before the ancient symbol, and all its eyes were upon him. "Among the many advantages of death," he said, his nose and lips flesh again for a brief moment, "is that I am beyond the power of most symbolism to affect." He twisted his transparent fingers through the air and a large glass marble rolled along them, growing in size until he flicked his wrist and it fit comfortably in the center of his hand.

"See," he told the ancient symbol in his distant voice. "Look." Now the orb floated above his palm. "It is as you were promised, before the world was young."

One by one, the floating eyes turned to look at the glass sphere. It began to spin.

"See," the wizard said, and his lips and throat flashed back into flesh once more. "Truth lies within."

A great ocean appeared inside the orb as it turned, a great ocean in the shape of a tree, floating in space. Gherin, too, could not turn away, and saw islands in the water, each one round like a marble. Closer still, and within each marble were scenes from history. The invasion of Normandy. The burning of Joan of Arc. The discovery of America. The Blood Oasis War. An infinite number of marbles, of moments plucked from time, rolling in the vast ocean, along the branches of a tree … an endless parade of moments to see, to study, to live, to be lost in … all of time, all of history, to explore.

But the symbol saw them. Suddenly each of the marbles was an eyeball staring out. Time vanished in its gaze. The endless sea was a column of fog that covered them all, and there was no more world … only this sad and lonely life. Meaningless. Unbearable. The eyes saw you, struggling pitifully. Inadequate.

There was no sign of the wizard Dee. He had vanished with history. No victory was possible now. There was no reason to fight. No purpose to winning. Gherin felt himself reaching for a string that dangled from his soul, a way to have never suffered at all.

He saw Mari and James falling in the empty white world. Saw her collapse to her knees, weeping. The wizard had failed them too.

It doesn't matter. She will never love you anyway.

He found the string.

James raced through the foggy void to Mari. Somehow he could run in it, his feet seemed to leave prints as though it were snow. He grabbed Mari by the waist. Lifted her up. "Listen!" he shouted. "Listen!"

He sang. With all the strength and conviction he had held the night Gherin had been waiting outside to kill.

There was no musical accompaniment this time, no brass, no strings, no harmony, but centuries of high culture had gone into the making of that song and the passionate voice ignited them all. Reality flashed like lightning across an empty sky. The endless mist melted around James, dripping away to reveal patches of color behind it.

Gherin watched. Hesitating. Wondering.

You are alone in the world, with nothing. No people, no respect, no love.

It was true. All of it. But the song was still beautiful. And Mari was singing now, too, her voice a pleasant squeak next to James mighty tenor. Gherin didn't know how to sing like humans did, but he raised up his throat and imitated James, desperately trying to be part of it.

It wasn't quite right. In fact it was terrible. But the fog melted around them. The world began to return. Birds and bicycles and ice cream.

And whiskey. Gherin wept to remember whiskey. And bridges. And architecture. And all the music that was left to hear.

His hand drifted away from the string, and a moment later he couldn't find it.

The eyeballs were trapped inside the marbles that once contained history, and floated farther and farther off. The white fog was gone. They were standing in the middle of the street on a hill in San Francisco. The blood sign had grown enormous under their feet, and the wizard John Dee held the spinning orb in his hands. It was filled with white fog, and eyeballs, slowly falling asleep.

"Forgive me," the specter said, its voice cold and distant again, repeating words he had once told a colleague centuries before. "It is complex magic to bind such a creature. I had not meant for you to fall in." Then his voice turned warmer, and seemed to come from a closer place as his lips and eyes were momentarily solid. "Magic is often hard on bystanders. You did well."

Mari started to say something, but Dee's attention had already turned back to the orb. "Return to your tomb," he said, and once again it was a distant echo of something said long, long ago, repeated by the image of the man who had said it, "to sleep endlessly, and spin the world around."

He blew upon the orb, and its form wavered like a drop of water, and then it flew through the air back towards the ocean, and the river, and the crypt.

Across the block, a bird sang.

Floating above the ground, the image of the wizard John Dee turned around to face the three of them. "Now," he said, his voice a terrible echo, "there is an equally great matter to attend to. My treaty has been violated, and it must be made right."

Gherin cowered.

Chapter 41

"Great creature," the specter recited, his voice a recollection of things a living man had once said, "you have hidden among the children of high culture, a dagger at their throat. No power in the universe remains to save you from judgment."

Mari stepped forward.

"He didn't mean anything by it!" she shouted at the dead wizard. "He isn't hurting anyone! He just wants a new life!"

Gherin looked up, his eyes wide. How did she know?

The dead, translucent, eyes of the ancient wizard stared through her. Lightning crackled between his hands, and ran up and down the sleeves of his fine cloak like serpents. "This …" he said, very slowly, his voice like the cracking of ice and the rumbling of earth "…is not your concern."

She was fearless. "It's not yours either! Who are you to tell someone where they can live, if they're not hurting anyone?"

Gherin's heart leapt, then fell. She didn't know. She didn't realize … but the wizard surely did. He had hurt people. Not high culture humans, no, but, were they the only ones who mattered? The wizard might not accept this argument.

"The great powers of the world," the wizard said, and it was a statement as old as the carving of mountains, being repeated automatically by a dead thing, "do not require your consent to secure your future. That is the first lesson." Thunder clapped around him. The wind picked up, but the moonlight was heavy and kept every leaf and twig in place. Lightning danced across his fingers like the orb once had.

"Mari, get back!" shouted James, stepping forward, trying to move her away. But she would not let herself be protected. She tried to stare the wizard down, as though the dead had pity.

She was still going to die, Gherin realized. Despite his sacrifice she was still going to die. Gherin slowly climbed to his trembling feet. He was doomed. But they didn't have to be. "No hurt!" he shouted at the wizard. "Gherin surrender! Gherin surrender!"

James turned and stared.

The wizard's translucent dead eyes focused on Gherin, and once again they could not process what they saw. Living color slowly filled them in again, blue, piercing, and kind.

The wind began to die. The wizard's whole face began to fill in with solidity and life. The thunder quieted.

James stared down at the goblin. "Who the hell are you?" he asked in a voice stronger than Gherin remembered.

The wizard's neck and shoulder's were alive now, too, and the life spread further down to his arms, and then his shoulders, and even his hands.

Mari turned slowly, and blushed when she saw Gherin. "I'm ... I'm sorry," she said softly. Apologetically. "Did you think we were talking about you?"

Gherin's eyes widened as his heart fell. His face fluttered through several realizations at once: the nobility of the sacrifice he had tried to make for these humans, his uncertainty about what was really happening ... he had never been so embarrassed in his life.

And then, for the first time in 300 years, the wizard John Dee laughed. A full laugh, a living laugh, a belly laugh. Life spread down through his legs as his shoulders convulsed and he clutched his arms to his chest. When it reached his feet – when they were as solid and real as any man's – he could float no longer, and dropped to the ground, his worn boot scuffing against the asphalt.

"Oh," he said. "Oh, oh, oh that feels good. You don't ... really, you have no idea how little you laugh after death. That and drink mead. I miss them both so. In fact, do you have any ... while I'm still alive I mean ... oh, by the Virgin Queen I'm enough of a wizard to do this myself."

He held his hand up and spoke a word that made the world wince. Lightning flashed down from the sky and into his hand, and in the smoke it left behind there was a goblet overflowing with honey wine.

"A bit flashy," he admitted. "Unnecessarily dangerous. But I'm in a hurry. And really, what have I got to lose? I suppose if Francis were here he'd have at me for bad form, but ... who's the living dead one now, eh Francis? Hmmm?" He raised goblet and sighed. "To old friends left behind." He drank. Deeply.

Mari tapped her foot. "Well I'm glad you're having a moment. Because it's all about you."

Dee shook his head after swallowing half the glass. "You have no idea the sacrifices I've made for this world. All so that other men could enjoy honey wine. If you can't show some respect, can you at least not deny me a moment's pleasure?"

He cracked his knuckles. Then stared at his hand. "That's not as much fun as I remember it," he said, frowning. "Oh, I wish there were more time. I've heard so many good things about smart phones."

Mari watched the wizard closely. "I think," she said, "we could kill you now, while you're mostly living."

Dee finished the rest of his wine in one long gulp, and dropped the goblet to the ground, where it clanged against the concrete and rolled downhill onto the sidewalk. "No," he said sadly. "You very much couldn't. But ..." he glanced over at Gherin. "Unless you'd like to really indulge me by singing a madrigal while I still have the capacity to enjoy it, let us be compassionate in our habits and magnanimous in our judgments and tend to the least among us."

James nodded slowly, his fist tight.

"Okay," Mari said, eventually.

The wizard stepped over to Gherin. Went down on one knee to look him in the eye. "I'm sorry, you little beast, for frightening you. But we have no quarrel now."

Gherin started to speak, but the wizard held up a finger. "Yes, you violated the letter of the treaty, but once my eyes were living again I could see you did it to protect my people. That is the very spirit of the treaty as written upon the flesh of the Suffering Child – and the whole point of my being mostly dead, rather than entirely dead, is just so that I may accommodate the strange exceptions life always provides, rather than dispensing an eternity of justice that is dead to the needs of the living. It would be perverse to punish you for upholding the spirit of my treaty so conscientiously. I will not do so."

He smiled ruefully. "Samuel Johnson was the perverse one, if you must know."

He waited for someone to laugh. No one did.

"That would have been quite mirthful 200 years ago," he muttered. "Just so we're clear."

"So ..." Gherin shook his head. "Gherin free? Gherin okay?"

Dee took a deep breath. "No one is free. There is still a sword dangling over your head. You don't get a pass for good behavior, and ..." His eyes seemed to look through Gherin for a moment. "You did kill Mordecai."

Gherin hung his head.

"I believe you will spend the rest of your life dealing with the decisions you have made here. But I will not punish you for doing my cause a service. Which, whether by intention or accident, you did." His voice darkened. "If you stand in the shadow of high culture for much longer, I strongly suggest you make it intentional."

"Yah," said Gherin, light headed with relief. "Yah."

Suddenly Dee was floating again, two feet above the ground. He was translucent up to his knees.

"And there we are," he said. "There are so many good ways to describe the tragedy of what is happening here in Latin. I do so wish one of you spoke it. But ... tragedy always follows the end of laughter. It is the nature of things."

He stared down at James, and pointed a still living arm. "Make this easy on all of us, and be gone from here."

James crossed his arms. "I ... don't want to."

"I don't want to be mostly dead." Dee shrugged. "None of us are free."

James tried to scowl, to stare with the force of a killer. It didn't quite work with his features. He looked ... constipated. But his voice was steady. "I don't think you want this fight."

Dee let out an exasperated sigh. "It won't be a fight! I am ordained in this matter by the cowl that judges! I have dominion here! Your sight is blind here! Your touch is numb! Catch me in the Elysian Fields or the Marble Caverns and try your luck, but in the lands of high human culture mine is the only magic that counts!" He rubbed his temples with his hand. "You ... you were a signatory to the Treaty, for Jupiter's sake!" He pointed to the blood sign upon the ground. "Your signature is contained within the very sign you stand upon, upholding my justice in this matter!"

All was quiet in the world. James' face fell.

"You must want to stay very much," Dee said. "I can only imagine what troubles you. But there are no circumstances under which I can allow you to remain."

Mari pointed at Gherin. "He gets to stay."

Dee nodded as his torso began to lose its color and solidity. "Here, high culture is a sword hanging over his head." He pointed at James. "But he is a sword hanging over high culture's. It is not possible."

James nodded. "All right."

Mari turned. "No!"

James sighed. "This doesn't end any other way. There's ... there isn't a way out. It turns out I'm still trapped. And ... maybe it wasn't working anyway."

She put her hand on his cheek. "It was going to work. We were making it work."

"I don't know."

"Yes you do!"

"Okay." He looked away. "But ... there isn't another ending. I probably knew that. I'm sorry."

"Don't be." She leaned in, and kissed him tenderly. At least one of them was crying, but Gherin couldn't tell which.

James stepped back. "Cover your eyes," he said.

"Must I?"

"Please."

She softly put her coat over her head.

He turned to look at the wizard again. "John Dee, John Dee, Dr. John Dee. Should I ever see you again, far from this world of mud and stone ..."

He reached inside his coat, and pulled out a vast and flaming sword.

The flames roared like a bonfire. James stood tall, then taller. Dark armor appeared around him from the legends of history as human skin fell to the ground in cinders.

"Then you shall see my justice," said James, his voice like the roar of a river at the bottom of the world, **"and fall upon my mercy."**

"Excior," Gherin whispered, going pale. It had been true all along. "Stupid Dark General."

Excior, Dark General of Skaris Cragg, surveyed the world with his ancient eyes.

"Another advantage of being mostly dead," said the wizard Dee, only his head solid and alive, "is that such threats as yours mean little. I will allow you some time for farewells, if you swear you will do no harm and then be gone from here. Tell me that my work is finished."

From deep within the dark armor the terrible voice spoke. **"I shall honor your treaty."**

Dee nodded, and the final color drained from his body. A specter once more. "Then," he said, his own voice terribly far away, "I am satisfied that Excior is an honorable man."

He stepped forward across the threshold of the world and vanished. The cliff he had stepped across fell into component pieces again. The world was as it had been.

Save for the great and terrible gaze that looked upon Gherin.

"You, goblin, brought this upon me. I am offended."

Gherin's eyes widened. He had been wrong before. THIS was what a terrible death looked like. It didn't need a scorpion's tail.

"No! Stop! Hold!" Leptin leaped out the window, ran toward them. "Stop!" he shouted. "Stop!"

The Dark General turned his attention to the older goblin running toward him. A terrible, terrible laugh escaped his helmet. **"There are easier ways to die, little goblin. But none less glorious. If you . . . ."**

He stopped. He stared. He took off his helmet. His face was not human, or perhaps it was so terribly scarred that it was impossible to tell.

"You were at Goren Vaj," he said.

"J . . . James?" Mari called from underneath the coat. "Can I come out now?"

"Not yet, my love," Excior said, and the words were an unwilling battle cry. **"I want you to remember me as I was. Soon that memory will be all that is left of him. Do not stain it."**

"Okay. Who are you talking to now?"

"Yah," said Leptin. "At Goren Vaj. Saw you kill moon."

"Leptin," the Dark General said, remembering.

"Yah."

"Who?" asked Mari.

"An old acquaintance from a terrible time," said Excior. **"One of a small band who have sworn never to raise our hands against each other again."**

"Oh." She considered. "That sounds nice. You didn't have a lot of friends."

Excior looked over at Gherin again. **"He is your comrade?"**

Leptin reached down to Gherin, who lay trembling on the sidewalk. Turned him over. Showed Excior his bullet wound. "Yah. Got wound with Leptin."

"Very well." Excior leaned down and touched the bullet wound with his black spiked gauntlet. The wound sizzled, cauterized, and scarred over.

Excior put his helmet back on. **"You will go,"** he said. **"You will both go, and pray that you never trouble my happiness again, else I shall find you in the goblin lands with a vengeance far greater than a wizard can imagine."**

"Yah," said Leptin. "Okay."

"Go now, and leave me in peace to say goodbye to my love. You have met two great powers this night and come to no harm. Such things are rare and fortunate."

"Wait," said Gherin, getting to his knees. "Can't leave her!" He finally understood: the most beautiful woman in the world deserved a great general.

"Yes," said Mari sadly. "He can."

Excior closed his eyes. **"We make great and terrible sacrifices for love,"** he said. **"But I could only reduce to mortal form the once. To do so again . . . ,"** he shuddered. **"Even if the wizard permitted it in his realm, it is not possible. Our sad time together is done."**

"You'd never been human before," she said beneath his coat. "I warned you it would be harder than you thought."

"Your heart was always wiser than mine. But these are private moments."
He turned to the goblins, and a thousand battles flashed through his eyes.
"Begone!"
The goblins ran again, and this time they had no place to go.

Chapter 42

The young woman with the severely beaten face wore a hoodie to try and hide the damage. Every time someone caught a glimpse there were stares, gasps … sometimes questions, which were trouble. It was a reminder, as if she needed one, that she didn't belong to their world anymore.

It was already dark when she got on the cable car on Van Ness. The historic ride was full of tourists looking out at the sites; she kept her head down. She hopped off, without a word to the conductor, near the top of Nob Hill. She walked up to Grace Cathedral, where she'd never been before despite living here 12 years, and walked around its side. There, as promised, was a medieval labyrinth painted onto the stone, a precise copy of a labyrinth etched in stone on a faraway continent some 800 years ago. It was empty in the moonlight. A little ways off from the labyrinth was a door into the cathedral.

The door was unlocked, just as she'd been told. She looked around, showing her face to the world to get a better view and make sure she wasn't followed, and then walked in. She closed the door behind her.

She looked around at the high ceilings and the smooth stone floors, she stared at the altar and the frescos and the stained glass, and without thinking she bowed her head. When she realized what she'd done she pulled her sleeve away from her fist and flipped the altar off.

There, painted on the floor between her and the great hall and its empty pews, was the second labyrinth.

She sighed and looked down, shifting her weight back and forth on her feet. There was only one way to enter the labyrinth, and only one way to go: around and around until you reached the center. That was a mistake, in her experience. Always have a second way out.

But she walked up to the entrance to the labyrinth inside the empty cathedral, and gingerly put one foot in front of the other, walking around and around the only path. Hating every moment of it. Fidgeting too much to enter a meditative state; fidgeting because she didn't want to enter a meditative state.

There she was, suddenly, at the center, and despite herself she exhaled. She let her shoulders droop. She had no idea what came next.

"Ahem?" came a small voice, not so far away. She looked up, and saw a small mouse standing on top of the holy water basin. For a moment her heart leaped. But … no. Not even close.

"Can you … can you hear me?" the mouse asked.

"Yeah," she said. Still a little embarrassed by the fact. Still not entirely sure she wasn't crazy. But then, maybe that's what wild humans are. Maybe that's what it means to be wild in a civilized world.

"Oh good," said the mouse. "Can I help you?"

"I'm here for the meeting," she mumbled.

"Excuse me?"

"For the meeting," she said again.

"Oh good! If you'll follow me, I'll show you the way." He seemed excited to be helpful.

"Yeah," she said. "Okay." She tried to smile. It hurt.

He leaped to the floor and scampered into the main hall. She followed, stepping right over the lines in the labyrinth, but didn't move too quickly. They went through a door, and then a back office, and then into a storage room … and behind a statue of someone she didn't recognize was an opening in the floor, and flight of stairs going down.

"If you'll excuse me," said the mouse, "I have to go back to the front and help with lookout."

"Lookout," she smirked. "For what?"

He stood on his hind legs and stared up at her. "Don't you know there's a war?" he asked.

"I …" she looked away and scratched the back of her neck. "I'm sorry. I'd … forgotten."

"Uh huh." The mouse shook his head. "Awfully easy for you, isn't it. So big and so tall, with opposable thumbs."

"Hey," she said.

"It's not so scary when the spiders and the cats and the dogs come for you, is it? It's not such a big deal when my family dies because they're in the Mission at the wrong time, is it? Doesn't change a thing for you! World keeps right on turning!"

"Hey!" she said again. "I'm sorry, but ... I'm a soldier too. I was just ... asked ... to fight a ... different ... war. And ..." And I got hurt, she thought. I got hurt. But she couldn't say it.

"Maybe we can help you," she said instead. "Maybe we can talk about that."

The mouse smiled. "That ... would be nice. Thank you. You're very nice."

"Yeah," she said. "Yeah."

"Go on down," he said, and scampered off.

She sighed and walked into the dark.

There were 12 steps. Five men and four women stood at the bottom, pointing guns at her.

"What do you have to say for yourself?" her friend Bryan asked.

She realized that they didn't recognize her all covered up.

"I seek the third labyrinth," she said, as she pulled the hood of her sweatshirt back.

They heard the password. They saw her face. They winced, and put the guns down.

"Rachel," said Bryan, his big body still intimidating even when he meant to be comforting, "I'm sorry ... we didn't know ..."

"It's okay," she said, leaving the hood down. "I didn't ... feel like being around for a while."

"We've got to watch security," he said. "Now more than ever."

None of them realized Leptin was hugging a dark corner of the ceiling, holding very still as his claws kept him anchored against the walls.

"Security," she said. "Against who? Who are we fighting now?"

"We're discussing that," said Tessa, her hair shaved so close she was nearly bald, wearing a military jacket and black and white striped leggings. "What happened to you?"

Rachel took a deep breath. "After he stationed me on guard duty I ... I think I got beaten by a goblin with a tire iron. But it was kind of ... it all happened so fast."

Around the room they murmured and nodded.

"Is there ... is there any word?" she asked, the words just bursting out of her. "Any sign?"

Everyone looked away..

"We haven't found anything," said Bryan. "But we haven't found a body either."

"That ... thing ... didn't leave bodies behind," said Reg, standing in the back fingering a knife.

"So this is it? We're it?" Rachel asked. "We're the last of Pitter Patter Pounce's army?"

"We're the ones who have come to the meeting," Bryan said. "That's not the same thing."

She looked around at them. 10 people, herself included, and not one of them well dressed, or stylish, or even well kept. They were all wearing pieces-parts, cast-away clothes, mismatched socks. Some of them were kept up better than others ... Lisa still had a job, last time she heard ... but most of them were falling apart, piece by piece.

"No mouse," she said, "no army. Come on."

"Bullshit!" said Myala. "That thing's still in there. We can go back! We can take it!"

None of them heard Leptin hiss, and slowly put his hand on a grenade.

"No," said Tessa, "I don't think we can."

"She's right," said Bryan. "We don't ... I don't know how to kill things like that without him."

"If I don't ever see another one of those things, I'll be lucky," said Tessa.

Leptin's hand held its place, but didn't move.

"We finish what we started!" said Myala.

"Maybe ... maybe we find another target," said Reg. "Something we know how to kill."

"Who?" asked Rachel. "Who are we fighting now? I don't ... I don't understand who the enemies are. I just knew he was ... he was my hero."

Murmurs of agreement went around the room.

Bryan slumped down in a folding metal chair. "Yeah," he said. "Yeah. I don't want to fight just for the sake of ..." He sighed. "I got into this to do the right thing. I don't know how to do that alone."

"We're letting him down!" shouted Myla, tears dropping to the church floor. "When he found me I was nothing! He saved me so many times ..."

Reg walked over. Put his knife away. Touched her gently on the shoulder. She fell into his arms, weeping.

Leptin quietly put the grenade back in the belt.

"I don't think he's dead," said Bryan. His jaw tightened. "I don't think he died that way. I don't think he could die that way. The goblins didn't kill him, and that thing didn't kill him, and he's out there, somewhere, standing up for people like us. I don't know why he isn't here, but I know what he wants: he wants us to stand up for ourselves."

"Yeah," said Tessa.

"Yeah," said Reg.

"Right on," said Myla, her voice muffled.

"If he makes our lives better, he wins," said Bryan. "If we fall apart, then we've let him down."

"There's ..." Rachel cleared her throat. "There's some kind of war going on. Between the animals. In the city. It sounds like some of Pounce's friends need help. We could ... we could ask them. What we can do."

Silence in the room.

"Fuck yeah," said Reg.

"Bring it," said Myla. "His friends are our friends."

"Hoo-rah," said Tessa.

Rachel smiled. It hurt, but felt good.

Bryan passed paper cups around the room, and unscrewed a bottle of red wine. "I want to toast," he said. The wine was poured. "To Pitter Patter Pounce," he said. "Long may he live."

Not everyone could say the words, but they all drank together.

When they had left the cathedral, and the room was dark, Leptin dropped down from the ceiling. "Good," he muttered. "Yah, good." Let the wild humans fight against the venom makers' war. As long as they no longer disturbed the tomb, as long as they didn't let the thing out again, it was their business. They could stay alive.

"Stupid humans," he muttered, "always fight wrong war."

He turned to leave. Saw that there was a little wine left in the bottle.

"Wine," he said. "Feh."

But he didn't walk away. Instead, he held up the bottle and poured the remaining merlot into the goblet John Dee had conjured and let fall to the ground. Leptin held it carefully. Protectively. No other goblin had a trophy like that. From the hands of the treaty wizard himself. It would be a triumph to bring it home, to place it with the weapons and clothing and teeth of his fallen enemies. He would be honored by all: perhaps he might never have to go to war again. The first goblin in his family to grow old. He'd have to see if he liked it.

He raised the glass. "Mouse," he said simply. And drank.

His eyes widened. The red wine had turned to mead.

He hesitated, then spat it out. "Sneaky wizard," he hissed. "Sneaky dead wizard."

Chapter 43

Gherin sat on the Golden Gate Bridge, sometimes staring forward at the city's illumination, sometimes looking back at the shadows of mountains that reminded him of home.

He nursed a box of amazing chocolate covered caramels. A present from Willie O'Shaughnessy. The rabbit had been furious, especially when Leptin had refused to give the remaining grenades back.

"Who want try take grenade from goblin with grenade?" he'd asked, and no one volunteered.

Jake had taken the blame, and since then the most violent of the brothers had been seen moping everywhere: whatever Willie had taken from him, it had been severe. But then Willie had taken Gherin aside and whispered in his ear. "I know my brother. I know it was your idea. And I want you to know that if you ever need something special, you come to me." He'd grinned, and handed Gherin the caramels and a bottle of very fine whiskey. Gherin had taken them, relieved at his friend's forgiveness. Then a shot had rang out, and the bottle burst in Gherin's hand.

"I also want you to know," Willie said, "that if you ever cross me like this again I will have no choice but to make an example of you."

Gherin had looked around the trees for the shooter, but couldn't find him.

"You understand?" Willie asked.

"Yah." Gherin nodded. "You waste whole bullet, shoot good whiskey?"

Willie's face had been cold and hard. Not even his whiskers twitched in the wind. "That's what I'm telling you: I know how to make an example."

Gherin had nodded again, and had stood by the rabbit's side as he'd met with the duke of rats and the Snake Hierophant and arranged a new peace treaty, one that Willie had ensured had something in it for all the right mammals and birds. When the next election came, Bevan would win in a landslide.

Leptin had been right, Gherin knew. Willie was a venom maker. Like the worst of his own family, only so much worse. And Leptin had told him he could go home again . . . if he left with him now. It seemed like a very wise idea.

On the other hand . . . the caramels were amazing. Like drinking melted sugar. How long could he go without this taste? And if he left he'd probably never get to see a bridge this big again. Gherin found he liked bridges.

He looked at the city below, then back at the mountains, then popped another caramel in his mouth. He found they were best if he savored them slowly, but he wasn't very good at that.

A shadow crossed the moon. Gherin looked up and dropped the caramels. Excior stood above him, mounted on a floating steed with fire instead of hooves.

The caramels hit the water and were gone. Gherin looked around: the best way to flee was to slide down a bridge cable like it was a pole.

Excior raised his hands. "**Hold**," he said. "**I come without weapons.**"

Gherin hesitated. "Think not need weapons kill Gherin."

"**Well, yes.**"

"Think horse can kill Gherin."

"**Almost certainly.**"

"So . . . ."

"**I have no wish to harm you.**"

"Okay," Gherin nodded, his muscles still tense and primed for flight.

Excior leaped off the horse and floated in the air beside it. "**You seem troubled**," he said.

Gherin nodded. "Lost caramels," he said, looking down into the ocean.

"**Ah. I see.**" Every word he spoke could have been a declaration of war.

Gherin looked at him. He seemed too big and imposing for a human: what had once been fat on James was the mass of an unstoppable juggernaut on Excior. Perhaps magic could only make him so small. "Thought you go?" he said.

Excior nodded. "**Soon**," he said. "**Soon. My presence here will become dangerous if I linger too long. John Dee's experiment with human high culture is still too fragile to tolerate my presence.**"

"You like human culture?"

"**In this moment, I am two people, little goblin. I am become Excior again, and the heavens fear the approach of my chariot. But I retain the memories of James Beakman, an insignificant human speck who loved culture more than anything in this world.**"

Gherin nodded. "Sound good." Once again he was jealous of what the Dark General had.

"It will pass. Each memory I recall clearly is now seen through my true eyes, with my true mind. As I recall James Beakman, I annihilate him. When the process is complete, I do not think I will feel any mercy or compassion toward it. But I admired Dee, and I have always found his experiment to contain great beauty."

"Yah," said Gherin. "Yah, Yah."

Excior's face hardened. "James did not know you stalked him. James did not know you mocked him. James did not know how close you came to killing him. But I do."

Gherin leaped off the bridge and plunged down toward the ocean—any escape would do.

Excior's hand reached out and plucked him from the air and set him back on the bridge. "I told you I have no wish to do you harm. Though I suggest you do not try to escape again."

Gherin trembled. "Sorry! Sorry! Sorry sorry!"

"It made sense when I recalled your stupid cry that I could not leave Mari, as though such a union were possible in my true form. I realized, then, that you had approached my presence to warn us of the ancient one, in spite of your knowledge that to do so was to trigger Dee's curse."

Gherin nodded. "Yah! Yah! Warn! Try!"

Excior nodded. "You would not have risked a terrible death for me, but you risked it."

Gherin waited, fearfully, for Excior to finish this thought. The ancient symbol had scared him more, but at least he'd known what it was going to do.

Eventually Excior grew impatient. "It occurred to me that we had something in common."

Gherin nodded, then cocked his head. "What?"

The Dark General's eyes narrowed. "That I was once a man motivated to travel from one world to the next."

Very, very, hesitantly, Gherin shook his head. "Not follow."

The Dark General's mouth hung open. "That we might have similar motivations for seeking a place in this frail and fragile world."

"Like what?"

A snarl escaped Excior's lips. "You love my girlfriend, jackass!"

Seismologists would register a 3.2 earthquake in Marin.

"Oh!" said Gherin. "Oh!" He cringed. "So sorry, sorry sorry! Not know! Not know!"

Excior held out his hand. **"Gherin,"** he said. **"I would have killed for her too. I even killed myself, for a very long time."**

Gherin nodded very slowly.

"And now I believe you stand on the border of two worlds, both of which I know well, trying to decide which way toward home." His expression softened as much as it had in a long time. **"I thought you might want to ask me for some advice."**

"Ohhhhhhhh," Gherin thought about this. "That surprise nice."

"For me as well. I suspect it is James. I think he fights my memory, struggling to survive in small ways."

"Kill him!" Gherin snarled.

"I shall."

"Him make woman big sad! No deserve live!"

Excior shook his head. **"There I fear you might be wrong. Love is simpler in your homeland, where a goblin feels what he feels and feels it deeply. In high culture the sound of love's call is often translated into so many other sensations that one does not know what he feels at all. Worse, many other feelings will disguise as love."**

Gherin was quiet for a while. "No understand."

"I doubt you shall for a long time. For the moment, simply know this: if you choose to live here, you will find love difficult in ways you may never understand."

"Oh. That bad."

"James tried his best," Excior said. **"I remember . . . ,"** he shuddered, then his face changed, losing more of what little humanity it had. **"Yes, I would prefer not to recall that as he did. But I do not destroy him because he was a bad man: I destroy him because he is inconvenient."**

"That understand!"

"Yes, but James did not. And he understood high culture better than both of us."

"Oh."

"Indeed."

Gherin took a deep breath. "Why you come here, live stupid human, forget glory?"

Excior nodded. That was a question he had been expecting. **"Much in the way your people live outside the human's time stream, and hop from point to point in it, I exist outside of time as you understand it. For a time beyond your reckoning my name has been synonymous with war. It was an art, and a sublime joy. But I perfected it long ago, and still there were battles.**

A weariness descended upon me the likes of which you can never know: a tedium to last a thousand years. But there was no other way to live, until the Wizard Dee offered humanity a new path. Dee offered his life to ensure a treaty that no one thought valuable, but when it was signed and high culture was safe from the interference of kinds like yours . . . from the perspective of those of us far beyond your time the universe changed instantly. High culture brings choices to the universe that it has never had. Eventually, weary enough, I decided to take one."

"Not like me."

"No. You are young and eager for beauty."

"Worth it?"

"I do not yet know."

Gherin nodded, considering. "Tell me later?"

"If I meet you again, I shall not notice as my chariot grinds you beneath its wheel."

"Fair." Gherin considered his next question carefully. "How meet Mari?"

"She was a wild human, her family were thieves in the City of Mendicants, after the icon's fall. They were temple robbers, stealing the treasures priests offer up to gods. Her path crossed mine when her family sent her to the sacred city of Mazalon to steal the cloak of Dire-Fen, believed to be made from the pelt of one of Hela's children. She was in the process of removing it from its chamber when my legions occupied the city, and I found her cowering in the treasure room when I unlocked it with the virgin key to see if there were baubles that might appeal to me. She presented a curious case, as ownership of the pelt had changed during the commission of her crime. Did I consider her a criminal against the old regime, which was of no consequence, or a thief against my property? I resolved the issue by declaring that since she had been found in my treasure room she belonged to me, and sent her to join my court. One does not waste a good thief."

Gherin nodded. "Sound like Willie."

"Who is that?"

"Um, rabbit?" He waited for a response. "In city?" Still no answer. "Here?"

"James has no memory of him, and the affairs of rabbits are beneath me."

"Okay."

"She was fascinated by high culture, and begged leave to speak to me when she learned of my friendship with the Wizard Dee. It was granted, and in that conversation she became the only servant in all my legions to see that I was tired. This changed her position considerably. There is no greater skill in this world than to read the heart of a king."

Gherin considered that carefully. "Good know."

"Giving up personal power for new choices is the essence of high culture. Eventually, that became a shared dream, and we escaped here."

Gherin gripped the bridge tightly. "In all time and place universe, chose be here."

"Yes."

"Maybe good place be, then?"

"We all must end up somewhere. Some places, I think, attract more exiles than others."

Gherin nodded. "But not sure worth it."

"No."

Gherin nodded again. This was, he thought, helpful. "Good luck us find you."

"Luck?" Excior's face hardened, until it was almost severe as his helmet. **"Do you think it is luck that the two of you, in all the city, came to make your home in my unassuming apartment? Oh, I do not think so, little goblin."**

Gherin tried to make his face hard too. It would have frightened a rabbit. "Maybe?"

"Unlikely. It is possible there was a connection between your natures and mine, between veterans of Goren Vaj and out-of-place aspirants to high culture, and that this brought you instinctively to my doorstep. But I think it is more likely that some other force is at work, that you were led there by some agency I do not know, working in shadow."

Gherin's eyes were wide. "Who?"

"I said I don't know.

"Yah. Yah."

"It takes but little power to steer the likes of you off their course."

Excior tilted his head, as though hearing some call upon the wind. **"I believe our time here is coming to an end. The death of so many ancient symbols has raised an ill wind that must be met."**

"Wait, wait! Got question! Pounce dead?"

Excior's head turned. **"Pitter Patter Pounce? The swordmouse?"**

"Yah!"

"Was he here?"

"Yah. But maybe dead."

Excior closed his eyes and stood still, floating in the air above the ocean. **"I cannot find him,"** he said. **"Neither living nor corpse. But I am not a seer. There are many things that escape my notice."**

Gherin shook his head. "Okay."

"I hope this has been helpful, and thank you for your timely warning. But there is no debt between us, and no bond to be honored."

"Not like Leptin?"

"No. Not like Leptin, who fought at Goren Vaj."

"Should Gherin stay?" It just came out.

"I no longer care." He mounted his horse. "Fight for what you want to survive in this world."

"Wait!" shouted Gherin. "Got advice Dark General!"

Excior's head turned. So did the horse's. "Best not offend me, little thing."

The horse's breath was hot as a forge, and its teeth were sharp. It had been hunting for decades after its master disappeared, waiting for the battle cry.

Gherin trembled, but still spoke. "One thing Dark General not want forget. James sing opera. Sing beautiful. Dark General learn sing from James, sing more, be less tired. Gherin know."

Excior threw back his head and laughed. The war-horse reared up and shrieked. Thunder roared over the bay as Excior rode toward the shining corpse of the moon. The last sound Gherin heard, as Excior disappeared, was a monstrous bass voice singing a Mozart aria.

Chapter 44

Gherin stared at Leptin. Leptin stared at Gherin.

"So," said Leptin.

"Yah," said Gherin.

Leptin pointed at the bullet wound, ugly in Gherin's side. "Good scar."

"Yah."

There was a long silence.

"Sad sad," said Gherin.

Leptin nodded. "Big mistake."

"Sad sad," Gherin said again.

"What tell family?" Leptin asked.

Gherin thought about this a long time. "Tell fought mouse. Tell good scar."

"Okay. Yah. But not like."

"No," said Gherin. "Not like."

Gherin moved to embrace, but Leptin only offered him his hand. They gripped forearms, and then let go.

"What do now?" asked Gherin.

"Go home."

"Yah. Then?"

"Go home," said Leptin.

Gherin shook his head. "Okay."

"Okay."

Leptin turned and walked down the hill, finding a path out of this time and place and into the world he came from.

Gherin watched him go, saw him vanish, wiped his eyes.

He turned around and walked up the block of colorful houses split into apartments. As he passed a little garden he plucked a few flowers from it, and then, at the top of the street, walked over to a yellow building and climbed up to the second floor.

He rapped on the window.

"Yowl!" went the cat.

He rapped on it again.

It was late, and it took a while for Mari to come out, wrapped in a robe with pictures of San Francisco on it.

She opened the window.

Gherin offered her the flowers.

"Oh," she said. "Oh. You're . . . you were with Ja . . . with Excior's friend."

He nodded, still holding the flowers.

"Well . . . you can't just sit there in the window for someone to see you. Come in."

About the Author

Benjamin Wachs is frequently accused of being a fictional character.

After living in a Buddhist monastery in India, he was employed as a nightlife reporter for Playboy.com and the bar columnist for *SF Weekly*. He is now the Instructional Designer for Burning Man and a member of its Philosophical Center.

He is the author of the short story collection *A Guide to Bars and Nightlife in the Sacred City* (Cary Tennis Books) and the forthcoming *Lamenting Avalon: Fairy Tales for Adults* (private publication). He edited *The Book of the IS: Fail to Win* (Last Gasp Books). He lives in San Francisco, where he is the Chairman of the Board of the San Francisco Institute of Possibility, an arts production and education non-profit. His business cards say "Fascinating Stranger."

Keep up with him at www.FascinatingStranger.com,
and www.Patreon.com/BenjaminWachs